Finch Books by Author

Single Books
The Cinder City Embers: Singularity

A Cursed Crow
The Seven Year Crow
The Court of Less
The Song of Blood and Bones

A Cursed Crow

THE SONG OF BLOOD AND BONES

LANNE GARRETT

The Song of Blood and Bones
ISBN # 978-1-80250-555-9
©Copyright Lanne Garrett 2023
Cover Art by Erin Dameron-Hill ©Copyright August 2023
Interior text design by Claire Siemaszkiewicz
Finch Books

Published in 2023 by Finch Books, United Kingdom.

Finch Books is an imprint of Totally Entwined Group Limited.

THE SONG OF BLOOD AND BONES

Dedication

To Hannah and William.
I love you to the moon and back.

They stole little Bridget
For seven years long.
When she came down again
Her friends were all gone.
They took her lightly back,
Between the night and morrow,
They thought that she was fast asleep,
But she was dead with sorrow.
They have kept her ever since
Deep within the lake,
On a bed of flag-leaves,
Watching till she wake.

— excerpt from *The Faeries* by William Allingham.

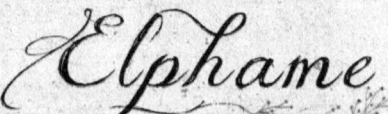

Elphame

~ ALFHEIM ~
THE GOLDEN COURT

SPRING COURT

SEELIE COURTS

SUMMER COURT

THE COURT
OF BLOOD
AND BONES

WILDELANDS · THE GATE

THE COURT OF
SHADOWS

THE COURT OF LESS

UNSEELIE COURTS

THE
HALLOWS

~ TYLWYTH ~
WINTER COURT

AUTUMN
COURT

Prologue

"Solas, she is a tool, nothing more. Do not grow attached to your pets," she scolded him. "She is useful until she is not. At that point, I don't care what you do with her."

"I need her, or this was all for nothing," Solas answered. "I won't just kill her."

"Need...such a relative term. You, Solas, need her. I do not."

From the hall, wrapped in the darkness of the shadows, I listened while another slice of my future melted away, as my life dangled along the edge of a knife. The faceless voice, who stood in the room with Solas, had come many times before. And each time she came, her distaste for me grew. Her voice was familiar, like a memory I couldn't place.

"You have allowed her to risk all we are. You have spent our fates between her thighs. The Gate needs..." Her voice was cut short by Solas' booming voice.

The walls shuddered as something large enough to crack the plaster hit the wall. "Perdi stays. She's under my protection."

I bolted from the hall to the safety of my bedroom. My hands trembled as I tried to lock my door. Fear poured from my eyes, and tears soaked my nightgown once again. I prayed to the Gods that Solas wouldn't come to my room, but the Gods stopped listening long ago. The thought of having to face him after spying yet again made my stomach curdle. Sensing my fear, the shadows crawled around me and blocked out the world I stood in.

"She has come," they whispered.

"Who is She?" I asked, tucked away from the eyes and ears of the Dark Court.

I rolled my memories around in my head and played them back and forth for myself and the shadows. I smelled and tasted each tear that had fallen when I'd died for Elphame. The Gate unwillingly gave me power the first time I came through. The second time, as it desperately tried and failed to kill me, I used that stolen power to close it. I left the mist and the Gate's failure with answers. But with those answers came more questions and a web of treachery and trickery I couldn't unravel on my own.

"You will try, and you will fail. She will not allow this."

"Who was She? And what does She have to do with the Gate?" I finally asked, unsure if I wanted to know or if I could allow myself the sweet mercy of ignorance.

"She is Blood and Bones," my shadows replied. "She sang the song that opened the Gate. The three Darkmore witches heard her call and helped create the path between worlds. She is the reason for this all. She is the one who picks the Crows for kings."

"She should never have picked me," I answered.

"She did not. She did not want you here. She is angry there are no more Crows. She will kill you if She can't use you."

"Elphame would be a better place without Her."

The shadows trembled against me. "Yes, before She finds a way to reopen the Gate."

"How do I stop Her?" I asked.

"The same way She will try to stop you."

"Kill Her," I answered.

"Kill Her," they echoed. "She will find a way to use you. She will use him to get to you."

I pondered for a moment, who he was, but I already knew…Solas.

"She needs to die," I finally said. The swirl of my shadows told me they agreed.

"We hope you saved your mask. You'll need it again."

"I never took it off," I replied.

Chapter One

I was born twice, once of hope and once of horror — once of the mortal world and once of Elphame. The second time, the pain was mine alone to bear, and I came out twisted and broken, like the other creatures haunting these lands. Like everything else worth having in Elphame, survival wasn't mine to keep. I had merely chosen to die on a different day. Each day between now and then, when the end finally came with my name, would be a struggle for the next. The day I put on these wings was the last day I didn't hurt. I'd known it wouldn't be easy, but I'd been foolish enough to think it wouldn't be this bloody hard. That was my fate, as it was for each Crow before me — to be Taken from my home and brought into this land to suffer, to crave a home that I was not sure even existed anymore, one where my heart was whole, my body loved and my soul left untarnished and unbroken.

I had been told to accept who I was, who I had become — a Crow, a Wildling, a Soul-Eater, told to face the horror of it all or I'd never heal from it. But I wasn't born in the pits of hell like the rest of this new world. I was dragged through it, and it was all too much to carry on a broken back and with a soggy soul. I couldn't put my pieces back together when I didn't understand how I had gotten so broken and why I had been fated with this life. It was in our nature—mortals—to question every intricacy of life, to wonder, to grieve over the baggage we carried. And the person I had grown to count on, Solas, had no answers for me. He hid more within his dark soul than I dared to understand. He was the only one yet to remove the mask he'd carefully constructed in the Golden Court. He still wore his every day, and I wondered if he had ever spent a day without it. Even in all of his secrets and lies, I envied his ability to choose his next step with such ease and not crumble under the weight of each decision. But I suppose one did not become a king or maintain that throne with an iron fist by worrying over the small stuff, like the condition of his soul or anyone else's.

Like a game of chess, I played back every move that brought me into my living nightmare. From the moment I had met Nix, then Faolan, to me now sitting in the forest on the edge of Solas' territory in the Dark Court, I relived each memory in hopes I had missed a clue to my freedom. Solas had said I was free—but I wasn't, not really. I wasn't free from Elphame, free to go back to Whitwick. No matter what he said or what I tried to convince myself of, I was no freer with Solas than I had been before him. I merely sat in a different cage with enough windows to almost believe I was still wild. Deep inside, beyond the prison with no bars, my Malice, my magick, threw itself against my ribs like a feral, caged animal. She craved release, but I couldn't risk it. I knew, with one misstep, the windows on my cage would be shuttered. I could see it in Solas' eyes when I would allow myself the courage to look. He, like me, sat on the edge of one wrong move, one bad decision, one shove over the edge. I had walked through hell, but my soul knew I was still there, and nothing I could do could change it.

Zephyr's shadows slinked around my ankles and darted between the grass and the woods. They slid along the earth as if no one owned them. It didn't matter how far they ventured. I could hear them in the back of my mind, like a soft melody playing in the background from miles away. We whispered our secrets and dissected our memories, always coming full circle to death. Everything in Elphame was solved in death. Countless lives were exploited until they couldn't beat their own hearts. For everything beautiful, there were hundreds of horrors. Every smile hid an ocean of tears. Every laugh had covered screams by the dozens. This place, Elphame, was a beautiful forest in the middle of hell. And the Dark Courts were just a roomier prison than my last. And like my previous one, I'd wreak havoc until I was let out.

I inched through the trees and motioned to the shadows, to the small wood and moss-built hut tucked into the thick underbrush, not twenty feet in front of me. "Ready?"

"We are, but are *you*?" the shadows replied.

I pulled my dagger from my pants and nodded. "He is the last in the Dark Courts to answer for what they did in Whitwick."

"Solas has asked you to stop hunting his people, that he would deal with it. He will not be happy."

"Does it look like I care what he has to say? He said he'd deal with it but hasn't. So, I will — and will do it in whatever manner I see fit," I answered. "They came to my home and killed my people."

"Garon did not *kill* your people."

"Yes, he did. He pushed a child in front of a horse to be trampled on the day of my Taking. He may not have wrung the child's life from his body, but he killed the boy, just the same." I groaned and paused against the tree. "Listen… If you don't want to help me, go home."

"We said we would, so we will. We just do not understand your need for vengeance. It consumes your humanity, which is the only thing that keeps you separate from the rest of Elphame."

"You don't get it. None of you do. Fae hunted us, and someone has to pay for it. It can't always be me who pays for what Fae did. Nix and I have spent weeks hunting them all down. If I have to suffer in Elphame, they can damn well suffer, too." I steadied myself once again. "Those who had no choice but to come, I left them with a pulse. I understand what it's like to be forced or have no choice. But those who came for no other reason than to revel in the death of children don't get to walk away without paying for it. Nothing is free, and this is their payment."

"We are glad this is the last. It is uncomfortable to watch," the shadows finally replied.

They didn't understand my need to punish those who tormented my people, who freely killed without penalty. We would always be lowly mortals if no one showed them any different. And I didn't care what Solas said. His people did not get to kill children and not suffer for it.

"Go grab him." I pointed my knife toward Garon's house. Garon was no bigger than I was and much less powerful. I had stalked him for days for this very moment. He knew I was there, and I knew he was terrified, just like the others had been. None of them liked the tables being turned, of finding themselves on the receiving end, hunted like animals.

With a blast of shadow, they were gone and ate up the ground like splashed ink, between Garon's hut and where I stood, waiting. I knew Solas wouldn't be pleased. But I didn't care, not as much as I should have. Zephyr wouldn't say a single thing about it because he knew it would be pointless to argue with me. When I first started hunting my enemies, Zephyr warned me that it wouldn't help extinguish the fire that burned in my soul, but he understood my need to snuff out what haunted my dreams. His understanding was the only reason the shadows had been allowed to help me. If Zephyr had disagreed, he'd have called them home, and I'd be out here alone. But I'd still be out here, and I'd still do what I needed to do. The shadows saved time, not lives.

Garon was spat onto the ground, half-dressed. He was a troll of a man, younger than most other trolls I had seen. His skin held a tint of green, like his hair, and not a single scar marred his body like they did mine. He jumped to his feet and spun in a circle, his green eyes widening when they landed on me. He took one step back, but the shadows were a black wall that gave him no space. He darted his eyes around as the wheels in his mind probably looked for a way out.

"Hello, Garon." I smiled. "I wouldn't run if I were you. You won't like what will happen if you force me to chase you down."

"Perdita," he replied. His voice was softer than I thought it would be. In my dreams, he had sounded monstrous, deep, rumbling. "What is the meaning of this?"

"I appreciate a man who gets straight to the point. I remember you, the day of my Taking," I answered, and his eyes grew wider. "The Dark Courts were forbidden to cross into Whitwick. They are not allowed to partake in the Taking of a Crow. Why, oh why, were you in the mortal realm, wreaking havoc?"

"Many of us went."

I nodded. "This is true, but those who went were forced. You went because you wanted to go."

"To refuse the call is to forfeit your life."

I rolled his words over in my mind. "I'll tell you what, Garon. I'll give you the same chance I gave everyone else I hunted down. You answer my questions, and I won't make you suffer."

He lifted his hands as if I would care he was unarmed. "I request a trial. You cannot kill me simply because I crossed the Gate. That decision is for the throne to make, not you."

"I'm not going to kill you for breaking Dark Court law," I answered. "But I'm going to make you suffer for taking the lives of my people. Whether you broke your laws to do it or not has nothing to do with me."

"I am Fae. My laws protect me. I request a trial."

"Alas, I am mortal, and my laws don't give a shit about you." I cleared the space between us and held my blade over his stomach. "You can choose your fate, unlike the choice given to me or my people. Answer my questions or suffer. Trust me when I tell you, your suffering will help me sleep better tonight."

He met my eyes and saw the truth. "What questions do you have of me?"

"You said that to refuse the call is to forfeit your life. Who made you go and why?"

He shook his head. "We're not allowed to talk about *Her*."

"She is blood and bones," I whispered, and he nodded. "Very well, if you can't talk about Her, I guess I've no more questions for you."

"Wait, wait…" His voice raised in panic. "I have other information you may like."

"Such as?"

"You must give me your oath that you won't kill me," he replied.

"I give you my oath. I won't kill you," I replied.

"You coming here wasn't a mistake."

"This isn't news to me, little troll."

"It should be. Haven't you ever wondered why only Wildlings have been called into Elphame? For decades, only Wilds have become Crows." His question piqued my curiosity. "The Caller of Crows has been looking for another Soul-Eater. With only one Soul-Eater in Elphame who is unbendable to her will, She calls on Wildlings in hopes of finding another."

"Why?"

He shrugged. "I don't know. Whenever we went to Whitwick, we were never allowed to harm a Wildling. We were told if we felt another Soul-Eater in Whitwick, we were to steal them back into Elphame, no matter the cost."

"And bring them to Her?" I asked, and he nodded. "Have you ever felt one there?"

"There is only one left, and he is already here. We've never felt another like him outside of Elphame," he answered. "Of all the Crows to come, you are who She hates the most."

I smiled. My secret was still safe. "Why does She hate me?"

His eyes grew wide as if I should have already known. "Because, Perdita, Solas stood against Her for you. You closed the Gate, and he let you live."

"Why should he kill me for that?"

He swallowed hard. "Wouldn't you wish to kill that which controls Solas?"

"I'm currently in that same boat, controlled by another," I replied. "That was worth your life, Garon."

My Malice flowed from me in a hot jerk and coated his body with my hate. I ate his energy in massive pulls and rolled his mind in my hands like a pearl. I pulled every drop of his magick from his soul and fought not to let him fall to the ground, a shriveled husk.

"But you gave me your oath." He groaned.

"I said I wouldn't take your life. I won't be the one to kill you. You've earned your life if you can make it back from the Sluagh. But remember this day, little troll, because it was the day I gave you a chance when you gave my people none. The next time I come, it will be for your life, and I won't give you the break I'm giving you now."

I motioned for the shadows, who picked his limp body up off the ground. They'd dump him in the caves of the Sluagh. If he made it out of there in one piece, without his magick, he'd have earned another day in a land that made us work for each and every one of them. And if he died, I'd feel nothing for his passing. He got the same chance I had been given when I came here — make it or die trying.

At that moment, I should have felt something more than satisfaction. It should have bothered me to punish the troll, but it didn't. It felt like crossing the last thing off a list. Like the others, Garon had come for my people and didn't expect me to come knocking. But now they'd know nothing was free, no matter what side of the Gate you stood on. I didn't kill any of them, but they certainly thought they'd die at my hands, just as my people thought they'd die at theirs. In my mind, we were almost even. *Almost.*

Garon, and those before him, were what it took for me to feel I wouldn't be hunted by the fog in my dreams. Those I could hunt down, I did, and I felt the balance restored as I exacted my revenge. I walked away and carried on as if I hadn't just terrorized a man, and it reminded me of how Solas and Zephyr could hold a conversation while in the middle of battle. To be honest, Garon, dead or alive, wasn't worth the mourning or guilt. The day he killed a child was the day he'd forfeited his own. So, I strolled through the forest and left whatever would become of him behind me, where it belonged. When the shadows returned, we didn't speak another word of what I had done. It was over. And I felt a little less broken because of it.

"Do you know why She is looking for another Finis?" I asked the shadows.

"Perhaps, if She were to get one at a young age, She could groom them into a shadow of herself. But outside of controlling Elphame with one, there is no other reason to risk trying to control a Soul-Eater," they replied. "She would be a fool to even try. Your kind is not easily controlled."

"Curious how Solas ended up with two of us," I answered and left it in the back of my mind to pick at later.

"He's not foolish enough to believe he could control either you or Zephyr."

"Yet, he tries."

"He'll die before that happens," they replied.

I rolled a shadow over my knuckles and released it back into its murky brethren, only to replace it with a new one. I practiced daily how to use my Finis' abilities without leaving a trail of soulless bodies behind me.

Calling a soul without eating it or wanting to eat it would take decades to learn, if ever. The desire to keep pulling would never go away, or so Zephyr, the only other Soul-Eater alive, had informed me. With Garon, I felt that hunger to keep going. For now, I'd use souls already trapped, shadows, practice or I'd risk eating half of Elphame. Eating this world was much more appealing than leaving it whole. If all were gone, nothing but a whisper left in the shadows, I'd finally have peace. The want to end it all edged on a demand from my soul. What a sweet ending that would be.

Nix's voice drew me out of my twisted thoughts — a dark place my mind always went to when I was alone and there was no one to keep it at bay. I spent my days wandering, looking for a way back home, and when I couldn't find it, I looked for anything untainted to take my thoughts away from where I was. But the darkness was always there and always willing to hold my mind with ease. It was a sad life when the only peace was found in the dark, when the only ending in sight carried with it the destruction of all.

"I see you've paid a visit to Garon," Nix piped up from my side. "You smell like troll turd."

"Indeed. It was short and sweet. Unlike the others, I didn't have to chase the troll across half of Elphame. He was dumped in Sluagh territory, and I think he'll fare a little better than the last one I dumped there," I answered.

"My money is on the Sluagh."

I shouldn't have laughed, but I did. A broken heart made some things funnier than they should be. "He had a few interesting things to say, but nothing different than what the others already said."

"I've asked around, but no one knows why another Soul-Eater is needed. Some are speculating that it is to repopulate the Finis line."

I cringed. "Zephyr is family. That's just—"

"Gross," Nix finished my sentence. "No one wants to talk about it, given that mentioning Zephyr's name terrifies everyone. Your guess is as good as mine as to the why of it. Maybe it's for power or control—of what or why, I don't know. But no one in Elphame gets out of bed for less than that."

"I don't blame others for not wanting to talk about Zephyr. I wouldn't want to," I replied. "Did you hear anything else? Any news on the horn I've heard? That blasted thing hasn't shut up in weeks."

Just weeks after I had closed the Gate, the world popped like a bubble in my mind, and I woke to the blaring sound of a horn. Everything had slowed, and the wind screeched in my ears, but only for a moment. It was a long enough stretch of time for me to feel the edge of warning on the whine still hanging in the air. Of what I was being warned, I was yet to know. Sounds became sharp as a knife, yet dull and lifeless, as if the sound ate the energy around it and spit out something made of broken glass. Birds and insects fell silent, leaving only the sound of a horn in the distance. The world shimmered in my view, like looking out from inside the Gate. Since then, everything felt not quite right, off in some way, tilted slightly, just enough for me to notice. Each breath was like eating soupy air, thick and full, and burned my throat. The alarm had clawed at the back of my brain until I had told Nix. And still, the unease wouldn't leave entirely. It stained the air like rotting fruit. Every sound, every word, echoed with a whisper of a horn.

"I've heard nothing," he answered. "People always forget to look down, so I hear things not meant for my ears, but no one has mentioned it. Wouldn't it be easier for you to find out?"

"Since the war, no one speaks openly with me anymore, if at all. I don't think it would matter. It doesn't look like anyone else is hearing it. No one else responds to it." I rubbed the center of my chest. I released a long breath, trying to will the dread to leave. "It feels like fate is following me around, deciding when to brain me with a rock. Something is coming, and we better find it before it finds us."

"I've poked around, listened in, but there's no mention of any horn or a feeling of unease aside from the usual anxiety all of us feel in Elphame."

"Keep your ears open. Others may be holding their cards close to their chest, scared of what may happen if they were to show them."

"This is why I left this place, willingly. The games we play are tiresome. More of us would live if we weren't so ready to die in secret."

"It wouldn't be Elphame if we worked together," I replied dryly. But I couldn't blame anyone for wanting to save themselves over others. I had been there before, choosing between my life and that of others — and had chosen myself.

We walked through my favorite part of the forest, a place where small white flowers bloomed. They reminded me of snowdrops back home that burst through the frost to become the first beauty of the spring season. They reminded me that it didn't matter how harsh the conditions were. Beauty could still be found if I looked hard enough for it. Some days, I really had to dig for it. On other days, I stomped them out and cursed their beauty.

"Do you trust me, Perdi?" Nix asked.

"Of course." I smiled and felt that truth all the way to my soul. "I trust no one more than you."

"I feel the same." He looked up with a hearty smile. He was not my blood, but he was the only family I had brought from Whitwick Gates, my home. "Perdi, I need you to come with me and ask no questions. Today, I need your trust more than ever."

"Whenever anyone asks for blind trust, it's either going to hurt or it's going to make me mad. Which one will it be?"

"Both. Yeah, probably both." His smile vanished.

Both it would be.

I frowned for a moment but followed him anyway. I was curious, not fearful. Of all the things that Nix was, the reason for my death would not be one of them.

Chapter Two

Nix scurried through the trees with me close behind him. He stopped every few minutes for me to catch up. But each time he stopped, I saw him looking beyond me, looking to see if we were being followed. Although my power had grown and I could hide myself, I could never truly hide from Solas and especially not from Zephyr, who knew every movement of his shadows. It is one of the reasons the shadows never stayed in one place too long, unless they were with me, in my bedroom. They, knowing I liked privacy, would stream through the trees away from me, drawing the attention elsewhere. Sometimes, just the illusion that I was free was enough.

"Nix?" I asked as we came to the edge of the last trees before Solas' territory ended and the Winter Court began. I felt the invisible line in the earth like tiny ants dancing on my skin. I knew I couldn't cross it, not without risking retaliation from the other side. Not to mention, Solas would feel me cross and would send his army. Enough people had died for me already. I didn't want a casual stroll to be another reason for blood to soak the land in my name.

"I can't follow you into Winter Court," I called out to Nix, who stopped a few feet from the border.

"Perdi." Faolan stepped from the trees.

Aside from my pounding heart, my body froze. In an instant, the fear was replaced with boiling rage that burned my gut. If I could have grown claws, they'd be out and ready to peel the flesh from his bones. It felt like all the time in the world had crawled by before I could blink or swallow. In between those moments, I had a choice to make. Did I stand as war, or did I give peace a chance? I had made so many horrible choices already, as war. But peace, with him of all people, would be a tough swallow. I'd prefer chewing on glass over peace with Faolan.

"How are you here without Solas knowing?" I asked. Of all the questions I had, that was what came out.

"I have my abilities, as you have yours. He'll know if I come any closer, if I stepped onto his lands. But the borders are no man's land—a large enough space for an army to stand," Faolan answered. "But, the longer I stay here, the likelier it is I'll be felt and found. But that is the crux of power. Everyone sees you eventually, no matter how hard you may try to hide who you are. You should know this better than anyone else."

I swallowed the rock in my throat. The look on his face said he knew more than he was willing to say out loud. But secrets didn't have power unless you were ready to keep your mouth shut for the payment. I wondered what he'd want for silence and if it was worth paying him over killing him, to keep those truths where they should stay...untold. *Leave no one alive,* echoed through my mind. This was the very reason

Soul-Eaters killed everyone, to keep their truths off the tongues of others.

"And do you have that army with you?" I asked as I scanned the forest. I'd wait for him to ask about my secrets rather than offering payment willingly.

"I am alone, Perdi." My name on his lips came out as a sigh, and I shivered.

I breathed past the memory of Faolan's voice and blinked away who I remembered him to be. But I did remember him to be smarter than this and doubted very much that he'd be stupid enough to come alone and would have his army close by. I didn't bother pointing it out. Not every thought needed to be spoken out loud for them to be mutually understood.

"Play stupid games," I muttered.

"Win stupid prizes," Faolan finished my sentence. "I assure you, I'm not here to play games."

"Everyone in Elphame is playing one game or another. Some are just smart enough to realize they're unwillingly part of someone else's game," I replied. "What stupid prizes have you come to the Dark Courts to win?"

"I came to talk to you. That is all," he answered. "That was my only request to Nix…just to talk."

I looked down at Nix and scowled. "What the hell is this?"

"Just hear him out," he replied with his hands out, trying to ease my temper. "I swear I'd never bring you to him unless I felt you needed to hear what he had to say."

"I don't care what he has to say," I snapped at him. "Bloody hell. Why on earth would you think I'd want to see *him*, of all people?"

"Just give him five minutes, then you won't ever have to see him again, and I'll never mention it," Nix answered.

"I don't want to see him now, let alone again. What were you thinking?" My words came out in a snarl. I tried to force myself to calm down, to remind myself Nix wouldn't have done this without a good reason, but I couldn't see beyond my anger and disappointment. My grief was greedy with my understanding. It hogged it all and left very little for my friends. "There's nothing he could possibly say that I'd want to hear."

"And I'd never bring you to him if I didn't think you needed to hear what he had to say," he countered. "I'd never lead you to him if I didn't think it was the right thing to do. Give me more credit than that."

Faolan drew his sword, and I stepped back, ready to run. I told myself I should already be screaming and questioned my sanity for still standing there. Instead of holding the blade up and slicing me in half, he tossed it at my feet. "Now, you're the only one armed. You can kill me if you want."

I smiled for a moment and thought of how utterly foolish he was to believe that I, even without a sword of my own, was unarmed. If he did know I was Finis, he didn't fear me like he should have. Between being able to eat his soul, Zephyr and his shadows were a call away. For a split second, I wondered why I hadn't included Solas in that mix of rescuers. Had we grown that far apart in the last months that I didn't count him as someone who would save me? I filed that thought away for another time. With my traitor just steps away from me, I had bigger things to worry about.

"Thanks for that." I didn't hide my intent. I picked up the sword, stepped forward, and pushed it against his throat. He backed into a tree but made no movement to stop me as I pressed it against his fresh. His flesh sizzled from the iron. The smell made me gag just enough for him to notice.

"Thank God, it's not too late." Faolan's shoulders sagged.

"Too late for what?" I asked, not moving the blade away from his cooking skin. Hearing it burn gave me the satisfaction I didn't know I needed, the tiniest bit of his pain for my own scars that would never go away. My mind and flesh bore his treason.

"You're still human enough that iron doesn't bother you," he answered.

"You came looking for your death to see how human I still am?" I asked. "You're stupider than I thought."

"I wish I had the time to be gentle about this, but we've run out of time. Perdi, the Gate isn't closed." Faolan blurted out. "You can go home still. You don't have to stay here. You're not trapped."

"Sorry, Faolan. I was there and closed the Gate myself. Even if I could, I'd be an oath breaker, and this crap would start all over again. I didn't do all this for nothing." I countered. "Nice try, though."

He reached out to grab my arm, and I stepped back, pulling the blade with me. "No, it's not closed. You damaged the Gate and it shut, but it's not closed for good. It's hurt but no longer closed. Ask Nix. Go ahead, ask him. He'll tell you."

I looked at Nix, and he nodded. "Why didn't you tell me?"

"I didn't know until Faolan told me, not but an hour before I came to you. It's why I wasn't there to torment the troll with you. I went and looked. I can cross back and forth. It feels different, like running your hand over a broken plate that's been poorly glued back together, but I can pass. I don't think anyone bigger than me could go into Whitwick Gates right now, but with enough force or time, perhaps that will change."

"What?" I whispered, more in surprise than anything else.

"If Nix can go through, you can probably go through as well." Faolan pointed out. "Mortals have always been able to cross with more ease than Fae. You're still mortal enough that you could go."

My mouth dropped open. If Nix knew, Solas knew. The Gate stood in his territory. Nothing like this could possibly happen without him knowing. How come he didn't tell me? Why did he keep that from me? Why wouldn't he have come to me right away? I could go home, and he said nothing. When I had woken from nightmare after nightmare, he said nothing. When I cried because I could never go home again, he said nothing. There was a way out of Elphame, and he kept it to himself. More importantly, he held back the fate of the mortal world from the one person who had died to protect them. If the Gate opened again, the Taking would begin all over. When my time as a Crow was up, another would be Taken.

"Solas has been going there every night and pushing power into it," Faolan explained. "Weeks ago, I felt the power of the Gate return to Elphame. I have had my scouts keeping an eye on the Gate, and they reported Solas' actions to me. I went and waited for him, to see for myself. I thought there must be some mistake, that perhaps you were working your magick to do something more permanent. But there was no mistake. We have watched him every night. I have seen him with my own eyes."

"Was he trying to close it?" I asked, more hopeful than a question to anyone in particular. I didn't know what was worse. Him trying to close it again, alone, or keep it open, and this nightmare happening to another child from Whitwick. Weeks ago, when I had heard the horn, Faolan had felt the Gate open. Was it the Gate I heard calling out to me? Or something else?

Faolan shook his head. "No. I believe he is undoing what you did when you closed it. After you closed it, Solas returned. At first, we thought he was making sure it was closed. The Dark Court always circles back to make sure there are no survivors. But he has been seen pushing energy into the Gate each time he has gone back to it."

"I don't believe you. Why would he do that?" I asked, more to myself than him. "Solas wouldn't do that."

"The amount of energy he is pushing into the Gate will eventually bring it down. Once it is broken, it will be wide open, and the mortal realm will be taken. There will be no Gate left to hold back all of Elphame," he answered. "You must understand... Once that Gate is gone, it can never come back. There are not enough Darkmore witches or power in Elphame to spell a new one."

"But the oath can stop them," I countered.

"The oath binds us first to the Gate. Without it standing, there is no oath."

"Like you care about the mortal realm?" I replied with a huff of a laugh. The lives of my people weren't funny, but his sudden care certainly was. "As if you care about anyone other than yourself."

"Whether you believe me or not, I'm here telling you the truth, at great risk and cost to myself and my people. I should not be here," he answered, and for the first time, in a long time, I believed him. To step this close to the Dark Court was flat-out suicide. "I have tried to protect both of our people, to protect the Gate, from what is happening right this moment. I am here and will pay for every minute I stand here, but I came to warn you. I have done many things for you to hate me, but, Perdi, you need to open your eyes and see what is happening. You need to pay closer attention to what's really going on around you. You're not safe. You're a Darkmore witch. You've never been safe here. Who you are, who you *really* are, puts you at greater risk than you think. I tried to warn you before. I tried to tell you what was coming. You didn't listen then, but you need to listen now."

I stared at him for a long moment and turned his words over in my mind.

"Listen and really hear what I'm saying. I cannot stop this from happening. It is beyond my control. It's beyond the control of us all. I have done all I can do. The rest is up to you. I cannot protect your people. None of us can. What Solas is doing right now will end with the Gate falling. Your people will be Taken or killed, all of them. There will be no end to the suffering, and there is nothing I can do to stop it from happening. Every single mortal with Fae blood will be Taken, along with their families. And everyone else will either be killed or enslaved. If this doesn't end now, there will never be an end to it."

"You betrayed me for reasons that had nothing to do with saving my people or me." I shook my head. "I didn't believe you then, and I don't believe you now. Solas wouldn't do this."

"Damn it, Perdi! Listen to me!" Faolan raised his voice.

I didn't want to listen to him. That was the problem. It wasn't what was being said. It was who delivered the message. I clutched his sword and wondered what the cost would be for killing a second king of Elphame. I stared at him and watched how the sun broke through the trees above and danced on his hair and face like little daytime stars. It was almost beautiful, if it wasn't Faolan. But even as the sun danced, I knew there were always horrors hidden beneath the beauty. Nothing here was free, not even beauty.

"Listen to you? Of all the people in this bloody realm, why the hell would I listen to you? You are my very nightmare, Faolan. You haunt my very existence. There isn't a day that goes by where I don't curse your name."

"Then we all die, not just your people. Those of us who don't relish in the demise of mortals will die." Frustration rolled over his face and pinched his brow. "I'm not who you think I am. I'm not the monster you've made me into in your mind. I am many things, but your enemy is not one of them. But if you believe I am, if you are measuring enemies by who is standing before you, you're in more danger than you thought. You have bigger enemies than me. You just don't realize it. Start paying attention."

"Oh, do I? I don't see any of them lurking around…only you."

"Then you're willingly blind and see nothing. At the end of this all, do not say I stood by and watched and didn't try to help you. You will not put this on me. I will not be blamed for this. I've stood by once, and I won't be responsible for it again."

"I'm not as blind as I once was. You didn't warn me then. Why should I believe your warnings now?"

"Because I didn't warn you *then*," he answered, then shook his head. A frustrated groan bubbled from his throat. "You were coming here, Perdi. Nothing I could possibly do would have stopped that. One way or another, you were going to step onto Elphame soil. Hell, even your own Guardians sold you out to the Fae. You sat at a dinner table with the Captain. I won't take responsibility for what he did. I will not be responsible for the fate passed down to you by your very bloodline. The deck was stacked against you from the start." Faolan pleaded with me to listen. The pitch of his voice rose with panic, and he began to fidget with his hair. He wasn't just nervous. He was scared. "Up until the point you were Taken, it is true. I marked you, so no one would Take you. It was the only thing I could think of. I thought if I marked you for myself, you'd be safe from the others. And it worked until I had no choice but to act. I planned to bring you to my lands and keep you safe. I planned on telling you everything, but I ran out of time. I had hoped I'd find a way to send you back home at the end of seven years, whether you hated me for it or not. But then Solas was sent to collect you, and King Aelfdene followed. But I tried, Perdi, to keep you safe, even if you didn't see it."

"No, you protected yourself." I shook my head. "You smell of lies and desperation. I've seen how you keep people safe. I've heard how you protect those in your care."

"I know what you've heard about me. And you've heard the stories I've willed into creation. But they're no truer than the lies Solas has built up around his own court." Faolan didn't just smell of desperation. He held it in his eyes like an endless pool. "To protect my people, I didn't care what the other courts thought of me. But I know what you've been told. I swear on my life I would never become that man. I swear I did not do what others claim I've done."

"Oh? Are you going to tell me that you didn't hurt Elswyth?" I asked. I tilted my head, trying to read him.

But I didn't know him as I had thought. I couldn't tell if he was lying or not.

"Okay, wait. I did hurt her. But not like that. I kicked her out, quite literally. I kicked her in her ass and told her she had until dark to be out of my territory. But I didn't touch her. She was never *my* prisoner. I will take whatever oath you want."

"So, she was not *your* prisoner. She was a prisoner in your lands. Whether you held her or not, you're still responsible. Everything ever done to her in your court is your fault. What happened after you kicked her out is on you as well. It matters very little to me if it was you doing the torture," I countered.

"No, I won't be responsible for what was done to her. Never that." As brief as a breeze, anger flowed across his face and was gone before I could focus on it. Throughout all my days of knowing him, he didn't hold on to anger for very long. "She was not *my* prisoner, ever—not mine, not of my control, not of my will. She was held in the Winter Court for a very long time indeed, and what happened to her there was not my fault. Did I know? Yes. I was there for it all. I watched, whether I wanted to or not. Could I stop it? No. There wasn't a way I could. I was not the king. I was a boy trying to survive a bloody nightmare. I did as the king commanded, as any young child would do. But once I was responsible and had control of what happened in my land, she was released. Did I release her in a way that was respectable? Not even a little. My rage had me in a grip, and I dismantled the court in a fury. I am responsible for *that*, but not what led me down that path." He released a long, shaking and heated breath, as if the memories had surfaced and plagued him with the pain of them all over again.

"There isn't a single day that goes by where I don't feel responsible, though," he finally said, swallowing whatever haunted his past. "You must understand. I was a child in a place much worse than any other court you've experienced. I lived in constant fear of my father. Weakness was punished, unlike anything you could possibly imagine. To speak against him wasn't an option, because it wasn't my life he'd take. He'd kill those I cared about — my friends, my people. They were the ones who would suffer in my place. Even if I wanted to do what was right, others would die for it, and that is the God's honest truth. I've built up so many lies that it doesn't surprise me to hear of these rumors, just as Solas has built his own dark machinations to protect his lands and everyone within them."

If what he said were true, I wouldn't blame a child for what horrors unfolded around them. I hated him, but not enough for that. "Why did you kill her parents?"

"I didn't. People die here all the time — some for war or love, some simply because they were at the wrong place at the wrong time. But I assure you, it was not me or by my orders. To be honest, I didn't know about it until now. Even if I had, I likely wouldn't have looked into it. It isn't healthy for any of us to poke too far into business not of our own making," he answered, and I actually believed him. I had no reason to trust him, but his words landed on my gut in a way that didn't make me take another step back. "I have been told that Solas married her off, to pay off a debt to get you here. When you brought the Golden Court down, Solas had made sure you'd get out, then had to pay that debt. He chose Elswyth as payment."

I looked at Nix, and he shrugged. "Is he telling the truth?" I asked but didn't really want the answer. Not truly. My heart couldn't take any more deception. The thought that this is what Solas was up to made my stomach knot.

"I don't know. His stress level is so bloody high, I don't know. His words feel true, but he's also holding a lot back. If you're asking for a certain yes or no, I won't bet on it. But I'm not the trusting type. As for Elswyth, I only have her word. I wasn't there."

"What about her marriage?" I asked.

Nix frowned. "She didn't seem upset. But she's lived a life of slavery. It wouldn't have been new for her. When the war started, I came back to help you. I haven't heard from her since the day she came to see Faolan in his prison. She left right after. I just assumed she was newly married, caught up in the celebration of it and the desire to forget about all of this. I couldn't really blame her. I'd give my left leg to be free of these games. I had no reason to think she was trapped or sold off. I would have told you, if I had thought she was at risk."

"She's dead, Perdi," Faolan's voice came out strangled. His control was so fragile. I could feel it. "They killed her after three days. Her husband, he... I'm sorry, but he killed her when she refused his commands. She requested aid from the Dark Courts, and Solas denied her any help. She was no longer of his court or under his protection. The words were heard from Solas' lips. I didn't see it or hear it from his mouth, but that is what Solas has said to many in his court. Courts talk, and it has come back to my ears."

"What?" I shook my head. "No. No, that's not true. I've heard nothing of this, not even a whisper."

"It is. Ask Solas for her. Ask him to go see her, and you'll see I'm telling the truth. If he says it's too dangerous, ask for her to be brought to his court, where it is safe. If it is safe enough for you, his most prized, it would be safe enough for her. If he still refuses, you'll know why. Not to discount the importance of your friend, but if it's not safe enough for her, why would it be safe enough for you? If Solas, and all he is, can't protect her, who the hell is protecting you? If he can't save someone who meant the world to you, how is he going to save someone who is supposed to mean the world to him?" he asked. "Perdi, everything I have said to this very instance is true. I will take any oath you'd like. I am telling you the truth. You are not safe where you are."

I looked at Nix, who was now as worried as I was. But something in his eyes, the agony and guilt he felt for not going with Elswyth, made it all the more painful. I glanced back to Faolan. "Why should we believe you now, after all you've done to us? Whether what happened to Els was your fault or not, you are not free from guilt. You stand before the woman you sold out and before Nix, whose people you killed when he was in Whitwick, to punish him. You hand delivered us the fate both he and I now live. And now you expect us to believe you?"

Faolan scrunched his face. "What are you talking about? I killed his people?"

"You killed his people. It's been said that you are responsible," I repeated. "His family, his people? They are dead because of you."

Faolan looked at Nix. "Nix, I would never harm your family. I swear it. Tell her I never once mistreated you, ever. When I found you in her garden, I thought you were an intruder and tried to chase you away. You can't blame me for that. I thought I was protecting Perdi. Once I knew you were invited and a friend, I never said an unkind word to you. I always treated you with respect and kindness."

"This is true. He has never directly harmed me," Nix confirmed.

Faolan turned back to me and released a strangled groan. "Damn it, Perdi. I'm trying to help you."

"I didn't see you helping me in the Golden Court," I continued. He may have been telling the truth about some things, but it didn't clear up everything. And since he was standing a dozen feet away, now was the perfect time to ask the questions that gnawed on my bones. "You tormented me. You came into my cell and taunted me. Then, once I escaped, you tried to kidnap me and threatened to hurt us if we didn't come. You were going to force me to marry you. You've done nothing to earn my trust."

"No, you only remember the worst of it all, and I'm not blaming you for that. I've been in the position of only remembering the worst of a man, and nothing anyone will ever say will show me anything more than what my soul remembers. I know how utterly horrible love can feel when the other person doesn't love you as you feel they should." He cringed at memories he didn't look happy to have. "But I did try to help you. I tried to get you to leave with me. I tried everything to get you to leave, but you wouldn't listen to me. I got angry when you wouldn't listen, so bloody frustrated. I tried so hard, but nothing I did or said would change your mind. Even as I watched you weave your Malice over King Aelfdene, I never once told him. Hell, I said nothing about you wielding that type of magick to anyone. When you were freeing his prisoners, who the hell do you think helped them get home? It wasn't Solas. It wasn't his people. It was me and mine. And when you finally broke free, I tried to get you to come, even then. But I was out of options, and I knew what they would do to you if you were caught. When I found you, I tried to be kind. I tried to get you to come. I gave you my word, and you still didn't believe me." Faolan stopped pacing and looked me in the eyes. "When you were on the run, I knew the Sluagh were coming. At the time, in my defense, I didn't know Solas planned to offer you sanctuary. When I found you, it was knock you out and explain later or all of us being attacked by the Sluagh."

"Why would you want me in your court?" I asked. "If what you say is true and you wanted to help me, why the force and threats?"

"I know it sounds stupid, but I thought if I brought you here, no one could take you away, and I'd have time to explain, time to show you the truth, and you'd see that everything I did was to get you back home, not locked away here. I spent all my options and had nothing left to convince you that my lands were the safest you'd ever be here in Elphame. I'm sorry. I just wanted to get you home. I've never been in a position with no options. I didn't handle it well," he replied. "The prospect of you being forced into the life you fought so hard to escape had dominated my every thought. Then I convinced Elphame to let you go home, but you still refused to leave."

"Because I didn't want another Crow to take my place."

"I know the reason, but I didn't have the ability to protect you and every other mortal. You were here, so you were my priority. I couldn't think of all the tomorrows, not when you were here today. Don't you think I'd have stopped the Taking of Crows if I could? None of us can stop it. None of us."

"I did."

He shook his head. "No. You've merely delayed it. And now we're left dealing with the fallout, and none of us have the power to stop what's left to come."

I understood what it meant to have very few options, and the only ones available were horrible. Even if I could forgive him, there were some things I couldn't let go of. There were some options, how very few he had, that were unforgivable. I knew those I had killed, and their families wouldn't forgive me, even if I told them my sob story. I deserved that hate because I took something from their families, and they hadn't done anything to me to earn that pain. And Faolan deserved my hate.

"What about my father, Faolan?" The anger within me finally bubbled up. "Even if I could leave, I don't have a home to return to."

He stared at me, confused. "He was alive when I left. I swear, he was alive. Once the Taking was complete, Fae left as they always have. The Guardians had surrounded your father. They were all very much alive. Whatever you've been told was either said to scare you into compliance or to torment you, as Fae do."

"Nix, is my father still alive?" I asked.

"He's dead?" Nix answered. "You never told me that."

"I thought I did. You came back just before the war. You had been away with Elswyth." I thought about it for a moment. How could I not have said something to him?

"No, Perdi, I think I'd remember that," he countered. "Who told you he was dead?"

"Elda… She said he was dead," I whispered, then I staggered. And replayed the entire conversation I had with her. "No, she didn't. She said she couldn't see him."

"Perdi, when you killed King Aelfdene, who do you think made sure his son, Theofanis, took the throne? The only son he has that isn't already crazy. It was me. I helped put him there. That favor helped buy you a ticket out of here."

I sarcastically clapped. "Well done. Because that served Elphame well. He cut off the heads of half the Seelie Royals."

"Theofanis is the least unhinged of them all, which says little about the rest of the family. Though, any Royals he killed were in line with his father. And I don't miss a single one of them. They deserved what the fates decided for them."

I shook my head, confused. "When you were taken prisoner, you admitted… Faolan, you told them…the new Golden King, Theofanis, planned to rule all. You said he decreed I had broken the oaths and the mortal realm would be invaded. You said that to Solas."

"No, that is what you all perceived. You saw me as an enemy, so my words were from an enemy. I told him what Theofanis was doing, taking the lives of the Royals. I even told him why. Do you really think Theofanis would still be alive if he had moved in on other courts? But we all, not just Solas, suspected the potential in his actions. But not even Solas would have stood by while one court ate up the rest. The imbalance of power would be too great. There would have been a war to stop it," he explained, and it oddly made sense. "And truth be told, you *did* break an oath. You *did* kill the king who held you. That was not news to anyone, nor was it a secret. I said the mortal world would be invaded if you left without the other courts agreeing that Fae would seek out a new Crow. This is not a secret to you. However my words were twisted are no fault of mine."

"Yet, you tell me I can go home now?" I asked. "I think you should run along, Faolan. Your minutes are up."

"Think, Perdi, please. I didn't risk my life for nothing. I am not your enemy. I truly gave everything I could to protect you. But I wasn't in the position that allowed me to become your savior. My people would have died. Solas could have saved you at any minute, and I blame him for not doing more. He was the only one there who had the power to stop it all. But he didn't, and not a day goes by that I haven't cursed his name for it. He could have called on the Sluagh, but he didn't. He could have called on the Aos Si, and they would have come. They would have helped you. But he didn't. He could have leveled the Golden Courts, but he watched you suffer. Each time I went to him and confronted him, he brushed me off, told me not to meddle."

I raised my eyebrows at his answer. I knew the Aos Si could not invade. They had been ordered by Zephyr not to. That Faolan had thought Solas commanded them was nothing more than lies over lies to protect the Dark Courts. "Knowing what I know now and the why of it all, he was right to tell you not to meddle."

"I will take your word on it, but know this. I will always share my blame with him. I will never look at him without seeing your face as you were…harmed." Faolan shuddered and couldn't finish his sentence. It was as if he fought to swallow it down. "By the time you left the Golden Court, your hate for me was so twisted and rooted you wouldn't believe anything I said and wouldn't listen to my warnings. Go to the Gate and wait. If I'm right, you know where to find me. If I'm wrong, you can send your darkness to kill me. I will give my life freely, without war. I'm not lying, but I really wish I was."

"And if you're telling the truth?" I asked.

"If you trust anything, trust that you are being watched. I warned you, Perdi, what hell you'd unleash if you closed the Gate."

"If I'm being watched by hell, why would you risk coming here?" I asked, wanting to catch him in a lie. I think I hoped he was lying because the truth would hurt much more.

"Because I know what She feels like, and She's not here today," he replied. "Be careful, Perdi. She will know we spoke, and I can't do anything to keep Her from you. Save yourself. You're the only one here that can save you now. I do not have the power to save you anymore — not from what's coming."

I tossed his sword to his feet. "I hope I never have to see you again."

"The ball is already in motion, and none of us can stop it. Whether you want to or not, our paths will cross again. You know where to find me should you need help." Faolan walked away from me.

I stood blinking for several minutes. I grabbed the tree beside me to keep myself standing. I didn't know where the lies ended and the truth began. Such was the way with Fae. I tried several times to speak, but I didn't know what to say. Even if there had been a kernel of truth in all his lies, it would be enough to end my life. None of it made sense, which made even more sense. Lies were perfect and lined up in a nice row. The truth, on the other hand, was like watching a stone skip across water. It was messy and unpredictable.

"Nix, was he telling the truth?" I finally got the words out. "Would Solas...? Why would he?"

"I don't know. I want to say no, but Elphame is full of nasty surprises. All I can say is that there's only one way to find out," he answered.

"The Gate," I said, and he nodded.

We turned our backs on the Unseelie territory. I didn't fear a knife in my back. Faolan could have killed me in a dozen different ways long before I would know my heart was gone. Sure, I'd eat his soul on my way out, but I'd still be just as dead.

"If he's lying, where would I find him?" I asked.

Nix looked up, perplexed. "What do you mean, where would you find him? At his court. We literally just stood between his border and Solas'."

"I thought Solas took that from him?"

"You can't just take a court from someone, Perdi. It belongs to Faolan. He is a blooded king. Solas would need to wage war, forcibly remove the king and take the lands as his own. They would then become part of the Court of Shadows. But no one has ever invaded Faolan's court and walked away. There is only one court that has never once been invaded. That's Faolan's."

"Solas has been invaded?" I asked.

"Not successfully, but yes," Nix answered. "Perdi, you were there during one invasion. They got pretty damn close. Wouldn't you agree?"

"That was a pitiful invasion," I replied. "It feels like I know nothing about this place."

"Solas doesn't share much, does he?" Nix asked.

"No, whenever I ask about something now, he changes the subject and tells me not to worry, that I've been through enough and to just enjoy my freedom. I've earned it. The same story, over and over. But you'd think he'd have shared that little tidbit about Faolan being free and wandering about," I answered. "Would

Solas know, even if he wasn't involved, that the Gate is damaged and open?"

"These are his lands, so I think he would, but I don't know. The Gate is an odd power. I'd imagine that having it on his land, he would feel it the same way he feels when someone powerful is in his lands," he answered. "Since we last passed through the Gate, it doesn't have the same ring to it as it once did. Have you felt anything from the Gate?"

"I don't go there at all, so no. After the war, I can't stand to go near that field." I trembled at the memories of the dead. I pushed it from my mind, now consumed with how much Solas could feel. Was my freedom much more of an illusion than I thought it was? "Do you think Solas can feel me wherever I go on his land?"

Nix shrugged. "You're powerful, Perdi. Even I feel it when I'm near you. But Zephyr and his shadows make it hard to feel you most times. It's like swimming in the ocean. You can't see the monsters beneath you, but you know they're there."

"That's news to me."

"When the shadows are close, I feel nothing but static. It's like my soul knows you're there, but it is blind. I know it makes Solas angry when you blip in and out—and angrier that Zephyr doesn't say where you are."

"Why does he keep that from Solas?" I asked.

"Zephyr says he doesn't know where you are. He knows what it's like to be in prison and understands your need to be free. So, he keeps the little things about you from Solas."

I grinned for a moment, picturing Solas frustrated and Zephyr doing nothing about it. They each toyed with the other, and every so many days, they'd slug it out.

"What the hell do we do if what Faolan says is true?" I finally asked.

"I don't know," he answered.

I thought for a few minutes, mulling Faolan's words over and twisting them to make sense. "Who is She? The one who is watching me? It's not the first time She has been mentioned, and each time, everyone is terrified of talking about Her. Faolan is the first one to talk at any length about Her."

Nix shrugged. "It could just be one of Solas' people. It would make sense to be guarded. Solas is, so why not you? But I'd put my money on something much more nefarious. It is the way of Elphame."

"Why would I need to be protected from Her?" I asked and only got a shrug back from Nix.

"Until we know what's going on, I'd suggest being careful in what you say out loud or do," he finally answered. "These bloody court games are damn tiring."

After thirty minutes of walking in and out of the shadows, spelled to hide us, we made it to the Gate. I couldn't see it, not as I saw trees or grass. It lived in the back of my mind. If I focused hard enough, I could see it through the shimmering air. The problem was that I shouldn't be able to see it this clearly. It should be closed and only a faint echo of what it once was. It should be nothing more than a hint of memory, a familiar place that you can't quite remember fully. Instead, the power of it rolled around me, slithered in and out of my mind. But something about it was off. As Nix had said, it didn't have the same ring to it.

We tucked ourselves out of sight, covered by branches and long willow grass. We whispered about Faolan, the story he told and how it could be false. There were so many reasons not to trust him and not solely because he was my traitor, but because trusting Fae usually ended in death. When the night fell, and my body shivered, I gave up. I kicked myself for ever thinking Faolan could be right. I wondered why he'd even bothered. Was it to cause problems, or was it simply because the Fae knew no other way of life outside of war games.

"I had to be certain," I whispered to Nix, who shook his head. I followed his eyes to the edge of the trees.

Solas stepped out of the shadows, and my heart sank. We watched him walk to the edge of the field where grass no longer grew. I watched as steam rose from him and mixed with the cool breeze. His scent filled my lungs. I had to cover my mouth to keep myself from screaming. Solas lifted his hands, and the ground trembled as he drew power into his palms. He threw raw power at a wall hidden from sight. His power passed through the wall and slammed into the Gate.

Still connected to the Gate, I felt each strike hit, like being punched in the ribs, again and again, until I couldn't breathe. I chewed the inside of my check until it bled, but I didn't scream. Even if I had wanted to, I had no air to form one. I clutched my stomach as the power rolled through me. When the world tilted, bile climbed up my throat, both from betrayal and energy. My ears rang from a small but sullen warning that crawled over the ground. I covered my ears until it slinked its way by.

We watched, in horror, as Faolan's words came to life in front of us, and there was nothing I could do to stop it. On my knees, we waited for Solas to finish and leave before we moved a muscle. It felt like hours had passed, even though mere minutes had. In those seemingly long moments, my trust for Solas burned away.

"What the hell was that?" I asked. My ears still rang.

"Faolan was right."

I shook my head. "No, that high-pitched sound? Was that the Gate?"

"I didn't hear anything. But I'm not linked to the Gate. You are."

I nodded. His guess was as good as mine. I had never pushed power into the cursed thing, only taken from it. "What the hell do we do now? How much of what Faolan said is right? Did we never even leave enemy hands, or were we just passed from one to the next?"

"Unfortunately, it doesn't matter where we are in Elphame. It is all enemy territory if you're weaker than everyone else," Nix answered. "I don't think Faolan's court would be any safer than here, no matter what he says."

Chapter Three

I sat across from Solas, as I did every night. Wherever he was in the courts, he had always returned to have supper with me. Even though each one always felt like the last supper, as we sat in uncomfortable silence, he still stayed until I was the one to call the night an end or someone came to call him away. No matter how hard I sought the man I had fallen in love with, no matter how much I asked for his return, I hadn't found him behind the wall he had slammed down between us. I could feel it press against me whenever I got too close. I didn't know if the wall was there to protect him or me. It didn't matter, not when it felt this awful. I needed to talk to him, but there was no room for any of my questions. There never was anymore. When I closed the Gate, he shut a door between us.

Sitting across from him — a king, a warrior, one of the most fearsome of Elphame — made me feel like I wasn't born for great things like he had been. I didn't think I'd ever find my place among his people, not when I held on to a ledge, pushed to the very outside of this world. But even as I tore myself to pieces to become who he needed me to be, I stared across the table with concern—not for myself, not for his people...for him. Before this, before he shut me out without warning, without an event, I could look back on and know why. There was always hope. At times, it was nothing more than a flicker against the storm outside, but each time I reached for it, Solas was there, flaring it back to life. The last time it had flickered, Solas had a choice between kindness and cruelty. It took no time for him to decide, shut me out and I watched that dying ember crushed under the wind of his cold darkness. How could he so willingly choose my suffering and do nothing about it? How could his only actions make it worse and never better?

"Why all the potatoes?" I asked. After an hour, it had been the first words I had spoken to him today. And although we sat in the room, utterly alone, it felt stuffy. "Every meal, there's always an assortment of potatoes. At first, I thought they were your favorite dish, but I have never seen you eat them."

"You're Irish," he answered, as if that meant something.

"And?"

"And don't all Irish people like potatoes?" he asked, a small smile on his face. He tried to look friendly, but he was out of practice, and it came across the table as arrogant.

"Seriously? You're Dark Fae, but I don't see you serving up a variety of villagers to eat," I replied. "Or do all Dark Fae, not like the souls of small children?"

"Point taken. Aoife liked them. I thought you—"

"Don't." I dropped my fork on my plate. Its clang silenced him. I glared across the table. "Don't speak her name."

"As you wish, Perdi." He went back to drinking his wine and reading the same stack of papers he always brought to the table. Court news, he had once told me. Everything is court news when you live in a court, I had rebutted. And yet, the papers still came, the reasons never changed and the silence only grew thicker.

"Did you enjoy hunting Garon down?" he asked, without looking up.

"Yes. I did. No one can outrun fate."

"Isn't that the truth," he replied. "I expect your hunt has ended? Is every name crossed off your list? Or is Nix now digging his way through another court?"

"The hunt has ended, for now. But the day is still young," I answered.

"That it is." He sighed his words.

He read while I sat in the pit that had become my world, decorated with my tears and nail marks on walls I couldn't see or scale, across from a man who couldn't even look me in the eyes without flinching. I felt myself pull back. I didn't even want to try again, to reach over, to break down the walls. Because each time I attempted to throw him a lifeline, he let it hit the floor, and it broke my heart even more, to know he was fine right where he was. In the darkness, with the very beast of nightmares, I sat and waited for it to eat me and everything we could have been.

I struggled to let go of the anger, to choose to give him the benefit of the doubt. Solas did nothing without a reason and having planned it expertly. It is why he was rarely surprised and never walked away without a win. He would have a motive that I would probably understand if he would just tell me. But how many chances would I give him before I died for those chances?

"Do you know what I love most about you?" I finally spoke up.

"What's that?" he asked.

"That you do nothing without purpose. Every single thing you do, don't do, say or don't say is done with a purpose. You don't waste words. You don't do a single thing without weighing every option and outcome. Even in times when I question your choices, I know that there is always a good reason for them."

"As a general rule, this is true of me."

I nodded. "What is your reason for this?"

"You'll need to be more specific. I juggle many balls."

"The second thing I love about you is that you're not a fool," I replied. "You know damn well what I'm talking about. If I wanted to keep playing games for the rest of my life, I'd have stayed in the Golden Court."

"If you don't want to play games, stop playing them and spit the words out already."

"I'd like to know the reason you've left me alone," I said, the dread of the conversation we were about to have flexed claws along my heart.

"You're not alone. I'm right here."

"Your body is here, but you're not. You left long ago. I can't even pinpoint when or why. And I'm not even angry at it, not really—more confused than anything else."

"As I said, you're not alone. You're never alone, not here," he replied.

"So, I've heard," I whispered but knew he heard me. "From a young age, I learned how to walk alone on a path that would end here in Elphame. I learned how to only depend on myself because one day, I could be selected as Crow and would end up here, and I would be the only one I had. I once thought it was a strength, knowing how to be utterly independent, just as I'm sure you think the same about yourself. But my body and mind crave closeness, touch, warmth and reassurance. I desire the partner I had when I came here to your court. Without it, I'm alone again, in this limbo of unknowns, and it scares me. I've been shoved to the side, and I'm watching life go by and have no power to live it. To have learned to depend on someone, to give that trust, only for it to be abused, is worse than being a Crow."

"Alone and lonely are two very different things," he replied with a voice void of the man I had grown to love. "One is self-imposed, and one is beyond your control."

"Which one is this, then?"

"Beyond your control…or mine," he answered.

"What the hell does that even mean?" My voice rose.

"Accept your solitude with grace and poise. Right now, it is where you are safest. Breathe deeply and walk through it—or scream and be dragged. But don't complain about something that could be a lot worse. We both know how awful this world can be."

"No," I answered, short and sweet. I knew he would appreciate the bluntness. "I scrubbed off my grace when I died for Elphame. This is brutal, Solas. I don't know what I've done."

"You've done nothing. This is what it is, at no fault of your own."

I nodded slowly, confused and frustrated. It made no sense. "If it isn't my fault, it is yours, which makes even less sense."

"If it helps you sleep at night, I'll take whatever blame you'd like."

I sighed, a hot and irritated breath. My mind was a scatter of thoughts, pieces of a puzzle I couldn't put together. And he did nothing to help it. Each time he opened his mouth, I understood even less. Perhaps Faolan was right, and I just didn't want to see it or admit what I saw in Solas. Could a man I trusted less than King Aelfdene, who I'd killed, be more truthful than the man I love? Faolan couldn't be the bringer of truth, could he?

"I'd like to go see Elswyth." I couldn't keep the nervousness from my voice. I chewed the inside of my cheek, which was already a meaty mess. Anxiety threatening to bite a chunk out of it. My stomach was a twist of knots that I had almost grown used to, but tonight, I only added to them.

"No. It isn't safe." He looked up from his meal. His face was neutral, but the fine lines around his eyes said he was curious about why I'd bring her up out of the blue.

I pushed my dinner away and leaned back in my chair. Solas' stare, which once made me writhe in pleasure, did nothing more than infuriate me now. After seeing him at the Gate and his lack of care for me, nothing about him made me squirm, in a good way or a bad one. All his goodness was just gone like it had never been there to begin with. Once, he was the kind of beautiful that got into my bones and glided across my flesh like a warm breeze. It spoke to me, unlike anything I had felt before. His voice settled the awfulness inside my soul. His very presence calmed me without him needing to say a word. But not now. It had chipped away at his perfectness. How could I love a man who hid the very parts of himself that I loved the most? To what end was this madness?

Last night, I had come home from the Gate and had locked myself in my bedroom. I couldn't shake my anger, the feeling of absolute betrayal that squeezed the life out of my tattered soul. I didn't know why I had been surprised, given that I was in the very land of lies and deceit. He had tricked me, and the fact that I was angry about it was almost laugh-worthy. Why did I think he wouldn't deceive me? He is Fae. It is who he is, just as I am a Crow. My father had warned me, and I hadn't listened. It landed me in Elphame. Then I did it all over again. But this time, it would burn me alive. I didn't have to see the flames to feel the heat. The fire sat but ten feet across the table from me.

"Then have Els brought here, where it *is* safe. If it is safe enough for me, it should be safe enough for her, no?" I countered. My arms were now folded. I had gone over this conversation a thousand times and had a retort for every possible answer he'd give me. And he always had many excuses he could draw on.

Solas set his wine down and frowned. "Yes, it is safe for you here at the moment. And no, I won't bring her here. She has been through enough. She has earned her freedom. She's earned her right not to be dragged around and ordered to obey the whim of others."

"I'm not suggesting you order her about. I'm asking you to *ask* her to come. If she says no, I will accept it. I would never force her."

"She deserved to forget her past, her part in all of this. However painful it may be for us to let her go, we must." Solas' eyes betrayed the pitiful look he attempted. The eyes said it all, and his were as cold as ice. "You may disagree, and you may not like it, but Elswyth is gone, and I can't bring her back just because you're feeling lonely. She deserved this."

"*Deserves*, not deserved." I couldn't hide my anger. Solas spoke of her in the past tense, like a fading memory of her. I knew, as I looked him in the eyes, he had told the truth, in a way. She was gone, truly and utterly gone. She was, as he said, free. I didn't doubt that death would be the only way he'd allow me my own freedom.

Solas smiled softly, but it wasn't as friendly as he was aiming for. He looked like he was irritated with my questions. "If you'd like to write to her, I'll ensure she receives the letter."

"The dead don't read," I mumbled.

"Pardon me?" Solas leaned forward. His stare fell on me like a sharp knife in my chest. My heart skipped a beat before I regained my composure.

"Nothing." I fought to not roll my eyes and call him a liar. I changed the subject. I didn't trust myself to keep talking about her. I'd play his games until I figured out how to win. It was, after all, the only way things were done in Elphame. "How is the rebuilding going in the villages and court?"

"It's going well. It's not something you need to worry about. You've been through enough. You deserve peace and quiet enjoyment of your new life." The mouth I had kissed a thousand times was pulled into a tight purse. I watched the muscles in his arms dance as he held on to control. He was so very close to ordering me to silence and obedience, the way I had watched him demand so many others. What I once thought was stress was really just the man he was on the inside, fighting to come to the surface.

"But I do worry. They gave their lives for mine. How could I not want to help them?" I couldn't hold back my curiosity. What excuses he'd give tonight. What reasons for keeping me from his world. It was dangerous, yes, but there wasn't a place between his world and mine that wasn't more perilous than the last. A Crow was safe nowhere.

He closed his eyes and exhaled a long and shaking breath. "Not right now. We have people who are out there helping, rebuilding and ensuring our people are cared for. Right now, I want you to focus on yourself, rebuilding yourself. You are as important, if not more than they are."

"And what am I supposed to do with my days? I can't very well take walks for the rest of my life here."

"You and Nix once had a garden. You have mentioned many times how much you loved it. Why don't you both start a garden?"

"You want me to start a garden?" I asked, surprised. A small laugh escaped me. "Are you fucking serious?"

He shrugged and lifted his hands in a shrug as if to say he didn't know. "I want you to be free to do as you please, but I also want you to be safe. We may have won the war, but we didn't extinguish the enemy — and you have many. If you go to the villages, you put my people at risk. What you're asking is for me to put my people in jeopardy for you to visit. I can't do that. I'm sorry."

"Freedom...that's funny. I seemed to have much more of this freedom you speak of when you wanted something from me. Hell, I had more freedom in the Golden Court, and I was an actual prisoner there."

"That's not true, and you know it. You're not jailed. But with freedom comes responsibilities. You're not free to risk my people. You're not free to do as you please. As much as I'd like to give you free rein, I must also consider the lives of my people. It's a responsibility I wish I didn't have, nor you. But this is what it means to rule...sacrifice."

"Don't talk to me about sacrifice. I've given my life and death to this place." I gripped the table and thought of all the things I wanted to say, but I closed my eyes and pushed my anger back down. He had a point, and I wasn't willing to lay out all my cards just yet. I couldn't risk him knowing what I knew. He was the man who would be the ruin of my people. I told myself that I couldn't risk his people, yet he had no problem jeopardizing mine.

"You're right. I'm sorry. I don't have any right to ask your people to risk their lives any more than you could ask me to risk my own people." I watched his eyes twitch at my statement. "It's just you're always gone now. I didn't even hear you come home last night."

"I was at the Court of Shadows last night. I had to deal with business." He answered as if that was enough information. He was king and didn't have to explain anything—or so that's how it now appeared. "The courts do not stop moving just because we want them to."

I nodded. I rolled his words over in my mind and picked them apart like carrion to a carcass. He spoke enough truth to keep me sated but offered nothing to settle the fear in my stomach. "You speak of risks and sacrifice. Why would my father risk his only child to Elphame? How did you know about my father's plan to get me here? Why would he sacrifice me to this place?"

"*This* place?" Solas looked up, insulted. "This place is now your home."

"For now," I answered without emotion and watched my words slide off him. I was used to it. Not much mattered to him anymore. I could needle him to anger, but I couldn't force him to care. The only way I would find the truth was to start at the beginning of the lies and slowly pull out the knots, one lie at a time until the web he weaved was nothing more than a ball of truth in my hand. "How did you know, though? You never told me."

"Your father knew of your fate. If I didn't intervene, you'd have gone to the Golden Courts alone. Your father, who worked his entire life to keep war from spilling out of Elphame, risked everything to end this. Aoif... Those who you'd wish me not to name, told me of your fate, as did Zephyr."

"Yes, you've said pretty much exactly that same thing before, word for word. But how did *you*, specifically, know of this?" I asked. "Did *you* talk to my father? How did this plan come to fruition?"

"I feel like you're accusing me of something. If you are, just say the words. Don't beat around the bush. I'm too tired to play any more games tonight." Solas' face drained of everything friendly and comforting, replaced with the glare of a tested and true warrior.

Behind him, I watched the shadows dance in the corner, warning me. I didn't need their whispers to know I was edging a line I didn't want to cross. Not yet, anyway. My creature, Orrian, tucked into my pocket, fidgeted. She could feel the pressure in the room build into something that made my ears pop. I pulled back from Solas' stare and calmed the storm that started in my gut. Solas was not the only warrior in the room. Like him, I could be a monster that rivaled what crawled in the darkest places of Elphame. And unlike him, I had absolutely nothing to lose. What could he possibly take from me that Elphame hadn't already? They had my life and my death, and soon, they'd have my people. There was nothing he could threaten me with that I hadn't already faced down.

"I wasn't accusing you of anything. Only the guilty suspect others of knowing their guilt. And I don't appreciate your reaction," I answered, my face just as unfriendly. "You said I was free. Does that come with the price of silence? For me to be free, does that mean I'm not allowed to ask questions or understand how I got here? How do you expect me to accept my fate when I don't understand why I've been given this burden? How do you expect me to heal when I don't know why I was chosen to be the one to hurt? When I try to do as you've asked, you posture. I can't even ask you a bloody question anymore without you puffing out your chest. What do you want from me? Tell me, and I'll do it. *You* stop beating around the bush and just say the damn words already."

Solas dismissed my questions with a shake of his head. "Why all the heavy questions?"

"You don't talk to me, which leaves me the only option of questioning you. I'm trying to put my life back together. Both you and Zephyr have told me to face it, yet when I do, I get this bravado." Sure, the truth would be healing in some way, but that's not why I picked at the scabs today.

"I thought your life *was* together? Here, with me?"

"Together? What pretty lies you tell." I swallowed my urge to laugh at his comment. "When was the last time we were together and not pushing food around on a plate? This—whatever it is we're doing—we're merely in the same room doing the same thing. We're not together. Surely you can see that. Or are you blind to that, as well as my suffering? We used to spend hours talking about the dark corners of the world, but now I sit in the dark corner, alone, waiting for monsters to come."

"I'm working to keep you alive, and trust me when I tell you, it gets harder and harder each day."

"Don't do me any favors," I muttered. The look on his face told me he heard each one crystal clear.

"I'll keep that in mind," he replied.

"Don't push me into a corner. You won't like the person you'll find once I have no options left. If you hate me today, imagine how much you'll hate me when I feel cornered."

"I don't hate you, Perdi. You wonder why we're rarely together? Whenever we're in the same room, you poke and push every chance you have. Each time you jab at me, I walk away because I can't handle any more of it. For one night, could you just stop with the picking? For a few hours, just give me a chance to breathe and think without having to fight for it. I come here to get away from it all, not fight another unwinnable fight."

"You may not hate me, but you surely can't call this love," I countered. "You, Solas, aren't the only one who is fighting an uphill battle. But at least you see what you're fighting. I haven't a clue, and I'm swinging at everyone."

"I'm not trying to control you, nor do I want to. But the danger still grows. It isn't safe. Those who want you dead, I can't stop them all, Perdi. The war didn't stop the hunt." He dropped his head and groaned in frustration. "You killed a king. Do not forget that, because his people never will. You closed the Gate, and not everyone was thrilled about that. The fact that you're still alive makes others question how. How could a little Crow survive?"

I stifled a laugh. "Rest assured, I remember every single minute of my time in Elphame. No matter how hard I try, I'll never forget what I've done to be here at this table, eating the scraps of freedom you feed me."

"You have freedom. Just remain within the boundaries of the Dark Court, where I can protect you. You'll be safe here. And once I've hunted down every enemy you have, you'll be free to move throughout all of Elphame. I give you my word. When I have extinguished all who stand against the Dark Courts, you'll be free to do as you wish…with or without me."

I opened my mouth to ask what his last comment meant but closed it and nodded instead. My words were caught in my throat. I wondered what he meant, '*free to do as I wished, with or without him.*' That would be difficult if I were dead.

"I don't think you should be going out without a guard," Solas mentioned casually, like rain being wet or needing the salt passed.

"No. Absolutely not. You don't get to take everything from me, including the little I do have. I've earned it. I've done everything you've asked of me. You will not punish me for it, now." My tone dropped along with the temperature in the room. I was firm and feral about what little freedom I had. I didn't have much, but that was mine, and he could pry it out of my cold dead fingers before I gave it up willingly. "You won't like who I'll become if you cage me. You've seen what I will do for freedom."

He lifted his hands, surprised. "It was just a suggestion."

"I won't leave the Dark Courts, as you've requested. But I won't be followed and restricted." I finished my tea and thought of a hundred ways I'd cut him down if he so much as tried to jail me. "You don't own me. I won't be your prisoner any more than I was willing to be your fucking Crow."

He moved with incredible speed and was at my side within a breath. He grabbed my hand, and I jerked. My heart pounded and threatened to rip from my mouth in a scream. And for a brief moment, he could see how scared I was. My creature, Orrian, burst from my pocket and darted out of the room. I made a mental note to ask her why she ran. At one time, she cared for Solas deeply, and now she feared him. Solas slid into the chair beside me, and I flinched. I could have sworn he looked sad by my reaction, but I did nothing to hide it. His careful mask slid back down, hiding the beast that lurked within.

"I've never jailed you." He let out a strangled breath. "If you do not want a guard, so be it. But at the first sign of danger, you will run. Promise me, you'll run, no matter who is bringing the danger."

I looked him straight in the eyes. "At the first sign of danger, I will run. I give my word."

"No matter who it is, Perdi. Say the words."

"No matter who it is, trust me when I say I will run."

The only danger I was currently facing sat at the table with me. I felt it in my bones. The only question was, when do I run, and where do I go? How would I get away from the very darkness of Elphame?

"I pray you do, Perdi. I really do. Because one day, you will have no choice but to run."

I nodded. "I feel like I should already be running."

"Yet, here you are, not running," he answered.

Before either of us could continue chipping away at the other, Zephyr picked the perfect time to show up. He always showed up when I was scared. He didn't have my pearl, but he always knew. His eyes darted from Solas to me, unsure of what had just unfolded. He didn't take a seat, which meant his words were not for me to hear. Zephyr stood at the entrance to the dining room and hovered, his arms crossed. He waited for me to leave. Within a week of the war, Solas stopped allowing me to hear the news of the court. Zephyr, the consummate royal subject and friend, always looked like he was caught between a rock and a hard place.

Solas kissed my hand and smiled. "Good night, Perdi."

I pulled my hand back and leaned into his ear. "I see your mask, Solas. You may be able to hide from everyone else, but you can't hide from me. I taste your lies. If you won't tell me the truth, I'll find it on my own."

"I'm counting on it. We all are."

I stood without saying another word and wiped my hand on my thigh. I was dismissed as quickly as I usually was. The war was over. I had played my part at the Gate. There was no need to include me anymore. They had gotten everything they needed from me, and they didn't care if I knew it.

"Hi, Zeph." I smiled faintly.

"Perdi..." Zephyr looked from Solas to me. His smile was small, hidden. "Good night."

I stood at his front with pleading eyes, but he still stepped to the side. I shook my head as I left. Not even Zephyr would go against Solas. Zephyr, the only one who had a chance in hell of escaping Solas' temper, didn't chance it. What did that say about my own?

Chapter Four

In my bedroom, I pulled the bubble of magick around my room, out of habit, to block out the ears and eyes of those I'd wish not to know my secrets. I paced and played back every conversation I had with Faolan. Every threat he had made had been a warning, a plea for me to listen, but I didn't understand. Even if I had believed him, I was now stuck behind enemy lines with the very terror of Elphame. No one would come for me here, not with Solas and Zephyr standing between me and the rest of the world. Not even the Gods dared to come here. But if no one could stand between me and Solas, who the hell was strong enough for him to fear they'd come for me? Who was scarier than the very blight of this cursed land? I closed my eyes and pushed my Malice around the room. We were alone, but I couldn't shake the feeling that both Solas and I weren't entirely alone for dinner. I hadn't seen anyone, but I could feel a taint of energy in the air that didn't belong in the Dark Court.

"Perdi." Nix came in from the balcony and climbed onto my bed with me. He had spent the day poking around, listening in, checking on the court and going places I couldn't. "Everything is as it should be. I mean, nothing stands out. Whatever Solas has planned, it doesn't look like anyone else knows about it. There's no mention of the Gate or of a pending war or risk to you. Whatever is going on with him, the rest of Elphame is blind to it."

I nodded. I doubted Solas would leave clues behind. "Before, you had said Solas sent you to the mortal realm, to me. Why, exactly, did he send you? And why you, of all his people? Not that I regret meeting you, Nix. I'm just wondering about the details."

"You were a child at the time, and a gnome is not nearly as terrifying as others Solas trusts. You didn't fear me when we met. And once I was there, I could hide and not draw the same attention to myself as larger Fae," he replied. "When he came to me and asked if I'd go, he said that Aoife told him about your Taking. I was to protect you and get you to the Dark Court when it was time."

"Why did he want me in his court?"

"He said you were the one who would close the Gate. That he was the only one strong enough to protect you from all other courts and, to be honest, he really is stronger than the rest. It's the only reason why I went, to stop the Taking."

"Did he want the Gate closed, or did he want me to do something to them, so he could open them for good?" I muttered, more for myself. "And how did Faolan play into this?"

Nix shrugged. "I don't know about the Gate part. All I know is what he's said, that you'd close it — and you did. With Faolan, I didn't know you knew him until he chased me around your garden."

I groaned. I didn't even know what questions to ask. I was grasping at straws, trying to piece together a truth that no one wanted to fill in for me. I wasn't foolish enough to think I could trust Faolan, but I couldn't trust Solas either, not how I once did. I had to decide which enemy would keep me alive the longest. I picked through the questions I had, and there were many answers I needed.

"Did Faolan ever meet Aoife?"

"Yes, many times. Before she came to the Dark Court with Solas, she told Faolan the same thing she told Solas. I think, to guarantee someone would save you when it was time."

"Did she come here willingly?" I asked.

"To my knowledge, yes. But remember, I am not Dark Court. I am courtless. We are part of the Dark Court, but more under the protection of them, not active in Dark Court matters. We go to the Court of Less to get away from all that, not deeper. Solas and I were friends, and I have always looked to him as my king. But I didn't know what was happening here. I wasn't privy to all the inner mechanicians of Solas' court, but no one had ever said Solas took her or any other."

"Before you became courtless, what court did you and your people come from?" I asked.

"I was born into Royal Fae, a descendant of King Lubdan. Our clan's territory was in the mountains of the Winter Court…Faolan's court."

"Faolan banished you?"

"No. I'm much older than that." He smiled. "His father was king at the time, and he banished me."

"Why?" I asked.

"At one time, Solas wasn't the most feared in Elphame. Faolan's father, Amphion, was." Nix shuddered when he said the name. "He was feared for reasons Solas wouldn't dare to do. He was cruel in the most deplorable and creative of ways. Remember when I told you that there were places that made the Golden Court look like a picnic? You'd have run from Amphion's court and happily stayed in the Golden Court, welcoming the respite from Amphion. Torture at the hands of that man was hell. It truly was hell. Nothing you've experienced to date would come close to what Amphion was known for, not even the lashes. I can't even bring myself to describe most of what that man did to others, especially those weaker. Before my banishing, I was in good favor with King Amphion. But when I wouldn't delight in the torture of my people, of women and children, I was banished. He said I was a bore."

"How did he die?"

"Amphion, in a fit of rage, killed Faolan's sisters when they were trying to escape. They were running away to the Court of Less to get away from Amphion. Amphion butchered them. Faolan killed his father when he found out. Amphion was still wet with the blood of his sisters when Faolan took the life of his father."

My eyes got big. "I didn't know that."

"This isn't new in Elphame, death at the hands of someone who loves us. We are a harsh and unforgiving bunch. That was the one and only time Faolan lost his temper, but it was enough for us all to remember his rage. He killed his father and those who supported him in his wicked delights. Those who Faolan knew had tortured women and children, he didn't just kill them.

He slaughtered them for all to see. It was a public event, and he ripped them apart slowly. Those who had been held captive were given free rein to do their absolute worst to those who had held and tortured them. It ended so badly, in such rage, that Faolan doesn't allow himself to anger easily anymore," Nix said. "From that day forward, Faolan forbade the very mention of his father. Every reference to the man was stripped from their history. Every painting burned, books were torn and teaching of Amphion's name became criminal. Faolan wanted to wash his father from history. And aside from those of us who are old enough to remember him, Faolan has succeeded. Eventually, Amphion will be gone for good."

"What about his mother?"

"Ethine, his mother, took her life long before that."

"She just left her kids with that man?" I was surprised. "What mother does that?"

"*Tsk*, Perdi. You shouldn't judge so quickly. Ethine was forced to choose who would be punished for actions of her own. Amphion used to do that, make her watch others being punished to death whenever she did something wrong. The entire court was the whipping boy for Ethine — not because she wanted it but because she didn't. She would have taken the beatings for everyone else if she could have. And with Amphion, no one could do a damn thing right, and the punishments were daily. Only this time, he made her choose one of her own children for punishment. Instead, she chose herself and jumped from the tower." Nix's face dropped. "Ethine was loved by all who knew her. Even I loved her dearly and mourned her death. She did what she could to help her people, all while Amphion bled his way through his court. He beat her senselessly whenever he caught her helping her people. He stripped her in the town square and lashed her until her bones showed. The worst part was that it wasn't a lesson for her. It was a lesson for her children. Any form of weakness would be punished."

"It's a wonder Faolan turned out the way he did."

"I think that's why you were lashed at the Golden Court. Aelfdene only lashed people when Faolan was around. The lash was Amphion's favorite punishment. And in the Golden Court, it was used to test Faolan's loyalty every chance he got."

"I'm surprised Faolan isn't more...cruel. I mean, disturbed like his father and not cruel as in he broke my heart."

"Before all this, the hell of his father, Faolan was much like his mother. His father broke something inside him, but he's still loved by his people, as his mother was. Stories of Faolan's fierce loyalty and love for his people are known by all in Elphame. Although, so are the stories of his dark side. When this all happened, your Taking, I thought perhaps the stories of his bravery and kindness were a lie. I don't know... Like you, I thought he sold you out. I thought he was responsible for all of this. If he isn't, then Perdi, maybe Faolan was trying to stop it all from happening. But if he is lying, he helped cause this all, and you're still in danger anyway. It doesn't seem to matter which way you turn. But it is a wonder why he's decided to say something now. I question what he gains from it."

"No one here does a damn thing for free, do they?" I muttered.

"Sadly, no."

"I'm so tired of this." I groaned. "I spoke to Solas about Elswyth. I think Faolan was telling the truth about her, and she's been killed. Can you find out if Elswyth is still alive or what happened to her?"

He nodded. "Then what?"

"I think there's more going on than we know. At dinner, I could feel something, someone's energy, in the air, like a hint of perfume lingering. It felt like being watched in a crowd. You can't see them, but you can feel their eyes. Once I couldn't feel it anymore, Solas stopped picking at me, and for the briefest of moments, I could see who I remembered him to be."

"Do you recognize the magick?" Nix asked.

"No. It's familiar, the same way all magick is familiar, but I couldn't say who owns it. I've felt it here before but can't attach a name or a face to it."

"Great. What the hell do we do now?"

I released a long breath, ending with a groan. "I don't know. But either way we look at it, I think we're in enemy territory. I just want to know if I'll be running into the territory of another enemy."

Nix stood at the balcony, ready to go back underground for me, and paused. "If Elswyth is dead, we're soon to follow. I have a feeling, in my bones, we're ears deep and sinking."

"I know," I answered. "But I don't think it matters where we go. I think fate will still deal the same hand. It'll just be someone else taking the life that fate does not want me to have."

"I don't envy your choices. If we stay, you're going to die. If we leave, you're going to die."

I nodded. "The only choice I really have is, do I want to die in the dark or in the light, without the lies and secrets."

Nix jumped from the balcony in search of answers I'd never find in this Court of Darkness. I curled into the shadows, free from threat and fear. It didn't seem to matter what happened outside of my cocoon. I never felt the blowback of it.

"Why seven years, for Crows?" I asked the shadows. "Why are we kept for exactly seven years?"

"We don't know."

"Perhaps that's how long it takes for a Crow to show their full abilities. How old was Zephyr when his Finis abilities presented?"

"Within a few years," they replied. "We see where you're going with this, and it makes little sense, given the majority of Crows die before their seven years are up."

"But those who survived their Taking before Aoife cursed the Gate were returned home at exactly seven years."

"Maybe they were not who She was looking for? Before Aoife, they were returned with child, to maintain the halfling population in the mortal world. But these are better questions for Zephyr. We simply do not know."

I groaned in frustration. Finding any shred of truth in Elphame took me in circles. "Am I being watched?"

"Always."

"Am I being watched by someone outside of this court?"

"Perdi, over half of Elphame wants to see you dead. You are being watched from all corners of hell."

"At dinner, I felt magick in the air. Do you know who owns that magick?"

"Solas' priestess," they replied. "She is never far from him now."

"Why?"

"We don't know. He doesn't speak out loud about it and doesn't confide in Zephyr. We know as much as you do about her."

"Do you trust Solas?" I asked.

"No more and no less than we trust Faolan, given that is your next question."

"Is Faolan telling the truth?" I asked.

I felt them twist at my question. "We don't know. We weren't there for any of what he has spoken of. Just as we do not know if Solas is being honest with you. We know, like you, he is hiding something, but what that is, we don't know. Nor does Zephyr. We, as you would say, are in the dark."

"Damn it," I grumbled.

"The only way you will know is if you go to Faolan for the answers that you cannot find here. He seems more willing to share than Solas, for reasons we don't know."

"Running from one enemy to another... Isn't that counterproductive?" I asked.

"It doesn't really matter if you're in danger here or there. At least there, you'll know why."

"Or he could kill me."

"You'd die with the truth — or you can stay here and fight against it."

"If I leave, I can never come back," I answered.

"You don't want to be here right now. What makes you think you'll want to come back?"

I shrugged. "I don't think I could leave, even if I wanted to."

For the first time, the shadows laughed, and it startled me. "You aren't a child anymore. It is time you stop acting like one. He only owns what you provide for ownership."

"It's not that simple."

"It is as easy as it is hard. The issues are not whether you can go. The problem is that you don't want to. All these games are easier if you tell yourself the truth of it. You cannot complain of lies if you are telling them to yourself."

"I think living in a lie is easier than hearing the truth," I finally answered.

"That's the most honest thing you've said to date. Are you willing to die on a hill of lies or in the valley of truth? Do you want to know why you are always looking over your shoulder, or are you content with waiting for it to finally attack you?"

Chapter Five

"You're not alone," Seth, my gargoyle, said, perched in a tree over my shoulder.

"Maybe not here while I'm dreaming, but in the real world, I feel very much alone." I looked up and softly smiled. I sat on the edge of the field, overlooking the Court of Less, watching the silent war play out before me. Even as men fell to their bloody deaths, I heard nothing but the wind and birds. "How do you walk in and out of my dreams, but no one else can?"

"That's not wholly true. Zephyr comes and goes as if he owns the place. But he and I come for different reasons. He fears you'll kill someone and is making sure you're not taking souls as you slumber. And I am here only for you. Whether you eat souls is not something I worry over. I dreamwalk for you and not the souls who may fall at your feet as you pass." He moved his wings awkwardly. The tips touched the cherry blossom flowers in his tree, sending a flurry of petals to the ground like rain. I caught the petals as they fell, and even in my dream world, I could smell their sweetness.

"Why do you dream walk?" I asked.

"Long ago, long before my father's father or me, we were trained as Royal Mares. The Gargoyles of Elphame are known for war, but those battles weren't always in the waking world."

"What's a Royal Mare?"

"We were trained to protect the Royals in both their waking lives and their dreaming. We ate nightmares, fought in the battles of their dreams. We ate their fears."

"I'm not a Royal, though," I pointed out the obvious.

"No. But you are who I choose to bond with."

"Why?" I asked.

"Because, Perdi, one day, you will war, and it will be magnificent. I will die gloriously, and it will be worth it."

I recoiled at the thought. "Morbid, Seth, even for you."

"Oh, it is very much a dream for us to die in place of someone of worth. I will go on to my next life with honor. My people will remember my name. There is nothing morbid in that."

"I don't want you to die," I finally said. The thought of him gone thumped a beat of sadness in my chest.

"Nor do I. But like you, I choose to fight for what is right, no matter the pain or loss it may cause. You will need me, and we will suffer the war together," he answered. "Until the Fates choose a different path for one of us, I will come whether you are awake or asleep, at peace or at war. It is what being bonded means, together until the end of one or both. It will hurt to part, but it will be glorious for the one who falls."

"I wish I had your outlook on death." I looked out over my dreamscape battleground and cringed. I always dreamed of horrors, and they were never within my control. Nothing I could do or say or think would change the dream. "Do you see Solas' dreams?" I asked as I stared out over the soundless war, at Solas cutting a path through those who dared stand against him. I had seen him in battle before, and this was every bit as scary as reality.

He nodded. "His head is not a place I enjoy venturing into. But by remaining with you, I catch snippets of all who are near you. His dreams, I dislike the most."

"What does he dream of?"

Seth paused for a moment as though he contemplated telling me secrets that I had no right to know. "Mostly, he dreams of you."

"How is dreaming of me a nightmare?" I asked. "That's not insulting at all."

"You know the answer. I feel what you feel right at this moment. You know exactly why you are his nightmare. You are his life and his death. You are his very will to live. That, Perdi, is terrifying. For a man of war to be brought to his knees by one single person is the reason his mind is an awful place to be."

"What exactly does he dream about me, Seth?" I asked again, unsure if I knew the reason or if I feared the reason.

"He dreams that you kill him or will be responsible for his death. He dreams of the Gate most nights. Some nights, the Gate is destroyed, and he dies at your feet, with you looking down on him. He dreams that you will stop him. But the dreams that wake him are the ones where you don't stop him. I believe he sees it as a foretelling that you will either help him or hinder him. He's still trying to figure out which path you will take and which one you both must take. His path has already been chosen for him, but yours is willed by only you. I worry for you and him – him, because he cannot command you, and the end result is deadly, and you, because you'd rather die than follow a simple instruction and hear with your heart and not your ears."

"Why do I dream of this moment so often? It always ends here?" I asked. "I don't even remember any of this."

"This is not your memory, Perdi. This is his. You, like Zephyr, can find any soul, awake or asleep. You are dreaming, but it is not your dream you sit in," Seth answered. "You were *heading to the Gate at this point. Solas was fighting to get to you. This moment, this exact moment in time is when Solas realized you weren't coming back out alive. That is why the dream is so horrible. It is his worst nightmare. It plays over and over in his mind the moment he lost you."*

"If his worst nightmare is losing me, why is he pushing so hard for me to leave him?"

"That is the question, isn't it? Why would a man who loves you to his own death, be so willing to lose you, to chase you away, to force you to run from him?" Seth answered. "He has given you all of these answers, but you've heard nothing beyond your own hurt."

My ears filled with a high-pitched ring that popped the silence from the war, and my head was flooded with screams and pleas for life. In the distance, a horn softly hummed over the carnage. As it had played out every other time, I felt the power rolling over the bloodstained grass and into the Gate. The old metal shuddered and screeched and tried to fight against the tearing at its seams. As the Gate cracked, so did my soul. The horn, no longer soft, blared to life and trolled over the hills. It was a warning no one but I could hear. The Gate had fallen. I swallowed a lump in my throat and forced the vomit back into my rotting stomach. I had watched this play out over and over, yet it made me feel sick each and every time.

I watched as Solas turned from his men and ran toward me, his sword lifted. I stood and closed my eyes. I grounded myself in the knowledge of what I had forgotten, my will to live was stronger than his will to dominate. In every dream before, I knew his blade would pierce my chest, and I wouldn't make a move to stop him. And in every dream, there would be no stopping the pain I'd feel in my heart. The cold iron would plunge and slice it in half. My dreams had been telling me the truth. If I did nothing to stop it, I would die here. Until now, I had failed to see it as anything more than my fears playing out.

And for the first time, I looked him in the eyes. "Stop, Solas."

"You can't even leave me be in my dreams, can you?" Solas shouted from a dozen feet away. His voice was twisted with anger and fear. "You won't stop me. You can't."

"Yes, Solas, I will," I answered. "It'll hurt like hell to do what I need to do, but I will do it just the same."

"Would you kill the man you love so easily?" He smirked.

Without a thought, I smiled at his comment. It was cruel, like the rest of Elphame. But it was not him, not the Solas I knew was still buried inside. "You, the man before me, are not the one I love, so this should be quite easy for me."

"I'm counting on it," he answered.

"What are you hiding from me?"

"Our fates," he replied. "This only ends in death."

His truth surprised me. I lifted my hand and pulled on his soul. With wide eyes, Solas dropped to his knees and clawed at his chest. I squeezed my hand shut and pulled it back toward me, yanking the darkness from his beating heart until it was mine, all mine. I ate the wickedness from within his soul while he stared me in the eyes. Once the hatred was gone, the wall he had built between us crashed down around us. He had nowhere left to hide. I let my Malice roam through his body, and as he fought against it, I picked up bits and pieces of who he had once been and tried to fit them back where they once were. A Soul-Eater could either eat it all or build what was broken, giving life back to the fallen. While I held his soul in my hand, I felt something more, something that should not be there. I plucked at a dark string twisted around his soul.

"No!" He struggled against my touch.

"The truth will come out long before I'm willing to give up and dig my own grave. It either comes from you, or I will find it on my own." I looked into his eyes, right into his

breaking soul. I felt him fight against me. His rage gripped my Malice, and I almost pushed it, in spite of him. Beyond his shattered soul, sat the blistering touch of something more, something that wasn't him at all. Whatever I touched, I should not have. I pulled back from his soul and let him wallow in his ache. "I don't know what you're doing or why, but I didn't make it this far to die on Elphame soil at the hands of the man who swore he'd protect me. And I sure as hell didn't fight to come back just to watch you wither away in front of my eyes."

He rolled to his side and climbed up to his knees to kneel on the grass. He held a blade up to me. "End it. But look me in the eyes while you do."

I knelt before him and drew the blade from his hand. It carried the weight of choices I couldn't make. Since the decision hadn't come easily, I dropped the knife. If I couldn't do it quickly, without a thought, he didn't deserve to die. "Solas, whatever is eating you to your death, you're going to take me with you."

"I have tried to find a different way, Perdi, but there isn't one," he answered. "She won't allow it."

I leaned into his ear. "Please, stop, or you will die at the end."

He nodded. "I know."

"It'll be at my feet."

"There isn't a place I'd rather be when I die," he answered.

I could smell Zephyr, not with me, but with Solas, as he dragged Solas from his dream. I heard Zephyr's voice on the wind. "But it will not be today, Soul-Eater."

I smiled. "There's always tomorrow."

I jerked awake to Nix standing on my pillow, his little hands shaking my shoulder. "Perdi, you're dreaming. You smell of Solas."

"Nix!" I sat straight up, sending him onto his back on the bed, with one hand over my mouth to keep myself from screaming and one hand on my heart. I could feel it pound, but it still took several deep breaths for me to understand I was awake and alive, and my heart was in one piece. Out of my window, Seth sat on my balcony, his eyes silver in the moonlight. With one nod, he was gone.

"She's gone," Nix said.

I frowned, confused. "What? Who?"

"Elswyth, she's dead." His answer felt like a hot slap.

I swallowed hard. My mouth was dry, and it felt like my tongue was swollen from being chewed on in my dream. "Wait. What? How?"

"It's as Faolan said. Her husband killed her three days after they wed. They say it was…brutal."

I blinked against the tingle in my eyes, a threat of tears. My breathing came out hitched. "How could Solas do that to her? He had to have known this would happen."

"He did." Nix wiped his tears that smelled of creeks and moss. He was sad, but more than that, he was angry. Elswyth was his friend. She was *our* friend. I felt the same anger in my bones. "Solas was told she would be put to death and did nothing. Even the servants here are talking about it. We were the only ones, it appears, who didn't know what happened. The whole damn court knows, except us. They were probably too scared to say anything. Solas did nothing to protect her and has admitted as much."

I paced at the foot of the bed. Each time I tried to spit out words, a strangled moan escaped. I put my hand on his shoulder and gave him a slight squeeze. "I'm so sorry, Nix. I don't know what to say. I'm so sorry for your pain."

"You didn't do this. He did." His shaking hand pointed to my door. Just down the hall was Solas. His voice was heated. "Now, what the hell do we do?"

"I need answers. Before I burn his court to the ground, I need to know if it's worth lighting the fire. Of course, someone will pay for what has happened to Elswyth, but I need to know if Solas burns with the rest." I continued to pace. "What if Faolan is using me as a pawn in some war against the Dark Court? Or worse, he's telling the truth. I'm a prisoner here and don't even know it."

"I would wager that both potentially are true."

"If Solas is damaging the Gate, the mortal world will be invaded. What if my dad is still alive, and there's a way for me to get home?"

"Even if you could get a warning to them, you couldn't stay there. It doesn't matter what Faolan says. If you leave and don't come back, you'd be an oath breaker. I'm sorry, Perdi, but you can't risk being an oath breaker. They'd invade for that reason alone. It would be a death sentence, especially if not even Solas is willing to protect you. But, a warning? We could do that."

"There are things I need to know and no way to find out without Solas knowing. I'd end up like Elswyth, rest her soul. I need to know what's going on with Solas, why I feel like I am at risk here and who the hell is behind it all. I can't keep running blindly. I'm going to end up dead. I'm stuck between a possible death and a potential one. Unfortunately, we have to let it play out a little more and be ready to move when the time is right. Maybe Solas' grandmother, Elda, would answer questions without telling Solas—although I doubt that I could step foot there without him showing up and hauling me away."

"There may be a way, but it is forbidden. If Solas found out…" Nix blurted and covered his mouth.

"Spit it out, Nix."

"The seeing pool. It is where all truth is held. Well, the people there are Seers and use the magick of their land to see futures asked. It is a forbidden place to all, including Solas. If you can get in there and they agree to see you, you'd be able to ask them any question, and they would tell you the truth. You could ask why your life is in danger, and it would probably answer a lot of other questions, as well."

"How do I get in there?" I asked.

"First, you'd have to get out of the Dark Courts undetected and in one piece. Then, you'd have to get by the Sluagh, the entire Aos Si army and whatever lurks beyond. If you got in, you'd have to survive whatever was held beyond the walls. I don't even know what's there. I imagine it would be deadly, as if there is any place in Elphame that is not."

"Where is it?"

"The Court of Blood and Bones," Nix answered.

"A Dark Court?" I asked and paused, replaying memories.

She is Blood and Bones.
She, the opener of the Gate.
She, the bringer of Blood and Bones.
She sang the song that opened the Gate.
She is the one who picks the Crows.

"It's not really a Dark Court. It is where the Aos Si originally came from. It was the first court, the first territory. There were no Unseelie versus Seelie. There were just Fae until the uprising. Factions of Fae no longer wanted to be part of the entirety, ruled by one queen. They called for a hierarchy of their own and waged war against the queen, thus, branching off from the one court. The war divided all of Elphame—some out of fear, others for power. The Court of Blood and Bones closed themselves off from all Elphame to protect the power of their court, their people. Those who are descendants of the originals, the first Fae, are what roam Elphame now. But they are but a drop of power compared to the originals. The original Fae are the most deadly, and that is why they are off limits. Kings fear any meddling with Blood and Bones would result in another realm war, which is why it's heavily guarded."

"Can Zephyr get in there? He's Aos Si," I asked.

Nix shook his head. "No, no one is allowed in."

"Do people get out?"

"No one has gotten out that I know of. But if you want answers, that is where you will find them…if they're willing to help you. If they're not, we're dead like the rest who tried before us, and none of this will matter. I'd rather die in search of the truth than rot here in comfortable lies."

"They're not even comfortable anymore," I countered. "Elda mentioned that this is what we get for building thrones of blood and bones. Is that what she was talking about?" I remembered my talk in the caves with her.

"I've no idea what Elda ever means. She speaks as the rest of Fae, in riddles."

"Why don't you speak in riddles? I mean, I've only ever heard you say what you mean and not play word games."

"I used to, long ago. But after a decade and then some with you, your bluntness has rubbed off on me," he replied with a smile. "In truth, I grew sick of these games so long ago that I wouldn't remember a riddle to save my life. When the truth works faster, why bother with the rest?"

After I paced a little more and weighed the only two options I had, stay or go, I made up my mind. I knew I was crazy to go into a place that sounded about as inviting as sitting in a room with Solas. But if there were answers behind that wall, it was worth the risk. I had nothing to lose that I wasn't already risking by staying put. If death is what I got for it, at least my problems were over. The dead didn't care about the truth. They didn't care about anything.

"I need to go there, to Blood and Bones…and soon."

"Perdi, do you really think you should be going in your condition?" he asked. "Maybe wait it out a bit. A couple of weeks, maybe?"

"Condition? What condition?"

"I'm never that far away. I've watched you vomiting every day. You're having a hard time keeping down food. You don't sleep, you're barely eating and you cry every single night. Your voice is rough from screaming in your sleep and puking when you're awake. You look like you've already scheduled an appointment with death, and you're waiting for him to get here."

"Maybe it's a stomach sickness." I fidgeted and couldn't meet his eyes.

"When was your last bleed?"

I shrugged and immediately felt awkward. "A few weeks ago, I think."

"Try six."

I glanced up and groaned. "Yeah, that's about right."

"Are you pregnant?" he asked.

I shrugged again and my face fell. "I don't know. I assumed it was the stress."

Nix sighed. "You should see a healer. You didn't miss your bleed while you were at the Golden Court, and they tortured you there. You're under less stress here, even with Solas the way he is."

"I don't want Solas to know. He already keeps me on a leash. I don't need to be locked up. We haven't been together in over a month, anyway. I think it's the stress, nothing more. I have to go to the Court of Blood and Bones," I answered and paused at the look of concern on his face. "I'll see a healer, just not now."

He finally nodded. "*We*, Perdi. We go together. It would kill me if something happened to you. I don't have anyone left, just you. I can't lose you, too. If you die, I'm going with you. If I lived and you didn't, Solas and Zephyr would eat me for dinner."

"Okay, we go together, but let's try for survival."

Nix smiled at my answer. "This isn't going to be easy. You'd have better luck taking Solas' throne from him."

"Sounds like a piece of cake."

"Made of blood and bones," Nix replied.

We agreed we would go together and plotted our route and how we would approach Blood and Bones. It sat to the east of the Gate, on a stretch of land blocked off by miles of trees and caves. As Nix taught me the polite court customs of a place named after death, my mind was on a challenge that could be around a different corner. I had been sick for weeks, violently. My stomach swirled and kept nothing down. I felt off and couldn't focus. Something was wrong, and I had known it for weeks. If I were pregnant, without a doubt, I'd be trapped here. I'd never leave, even if I were allowed. I couldn't leave my child behind, and he'd never let me leave with them. I couldn't imagine what Elphame would do to a child of my line and Solas'. They would be hunted. I pushed the thoughts from my mind. I'd worry about that fork in my path if I ever came to it. But I sent up a small prayer that it was an illness and not a pregnancy. I wonder how many times the Gods heard that prayer before or if they even bothered to listen anymore.

Chapter Six

Leaving the Dark Court was not difficult. No one stopped or questioned me. I wasn't seen as a threat...not yet. But the farther we got from the safety of Solas' lands, the more I wondered how I had made it this far in life, given the chances I took and the decisions I made. I was a ticking bomb of poor choices. One day, I'd face a decision that would blow up in my face. I knew it. I could feel it. Solas had warned me to remain within the borders of the Dark Courts, and here I was, marching my way out. I'd add this to the list of reasons he'd be angry later. It didn't matter if I deserved his wrath. He still would take it out on me.

We moved through the forest of darkness, as uninviting as the rest of Elphame. The shadows twisted and turned over every rock and behind every tree, adding another layer of disconcerting to the pitch of the forest. I felt like I was walking through someone's bad dream. The potential of it pressed down on my shoulders. We saw nothing, but we could feel the menace. We pushed through the Court of Less and inched our way to the Court of Blood and Bones, all while being hunted by something unknown. Nix said it was fear and paranoia chewing at the back of our brains. I said it was more likely to be a monster. In Elphame, paranoia kept you alive, whereas monsters always did the opposite. I wasn't looking forward to meeting whatever stalked us.

We had eaten the day away with our trek. Being out as the sun set wasn't a good idea, but we had no choice. I wasn't as fast as Nix, nor could I run the length of the journey. I had done better this time compared to the last run I had made through the same forest. I didn't tire as easily and could keep a pace that surprised even him. Still, I held us back, and we'd be walking back in the middle of the night. I had no doubt we'd be nibbled on upon our return trip.

"Can you feel that?" I asked Nix. The hair on the back of my neck stood in a warning.

Nix pointed ahead, the tree line coming to an abrupt end. "We're about to get an introduction. There's the wall of no return."

I froze at the slight snap of a branch to my right. My breath caught in my throat as I strained to hear beyond the now-eerie silence. The natural sounds of a forest, even the darkest, always blistered with life. Sometimes that life felt like a reminder of death, but it was still there, under the hush of darkness. And now, there was nothing, as if every drop of life had been eaten at once. There weren't many things that could eat life in one fell swoop. There were many beasts in Elphame that silenced even the dark, but none that ate it completely.

"Sluagh," I whispered to Nix.

The beast stood hunched in the brooding darkness between the known and the unknown, the wall of no return, the Court of Blood and Bones. He stood, black as night, twenty feet tall, wings and all, between me and my answers. I could feel the energy roll off him in waves of heat. Even with the distance between us, it felt like standing too close to a fire. Each pulse of power gave off an aura of pure horror and hunger.

"Into the thick brush." Nix snapped my attention back.

I had saved my energy for these final moments. We knew it would be a fight to get in and risked having nothing left to get back home with. It was worth it. Even if I died on the way home, I'd die with the truth. The shadows wrapped around us both and pulled us along, hidden. We had saved the shadows for the end run. Zephyr would feel what was happening and eventually would come to see what trouble the little Crow was stirring up. I was hoping it would be later rather than sooner, or he'd derail our plans before they came to fruition.

When the shadows dropped us beyond the trees, they could go no farther. Zephyr had forbidden them to leave the lands of the Dark Court with me. They were tied to the earth with roots we could not dig up. Unless Zephyr was with them, they had to go back. They took my jacket and left. They would carry my scent to every part of the Dark Courts in hopes of buying me more time. If someone came looking for us, they'd track me everywhere else first.

I didn't have time to say thank you. I ran behind Nix. The soft and mossy ground had been replaced with dirt and sharp rocks. One misstep, and I'd break bones. This was not a place I wanted to be with broken legs. I ran with caution, slowing my breaths, willing myself to remain calm when all I wanted to do was scream. Even in the warmth of the season, the air grew colder, uninviting. Wherever we were going, the Sluagh did not follow. Behind, at the edge of the grass, where the world turned from lush to deadly, dozens of them stood, pacing. It was as if there were a glass wall where no Sluagh flew beyond a line I couldn't see.

"It won't take long before the court knows we're gone," Nix said. "If they don't know already."

Littered along the rocks were beasts and creatures with rotting flesh, broken beyond repair. Those still fresh looked like their carcasses were melting, limp against the sharp stones. The older ones were nothing but jutting white bones, ready to impale whoever was unfortunate enough to fall on them. Smaller creatures poked their heads up from small gaps in the rock but quickly pulled back down with wild eyes. I chanced a glance back and saw Seth coming from the Dark Court. The sight of him made me both sigh in relief and panic at what we would face next.

"Aos Si," Nix yelled and glanced up ahead to the left.

"This is going to hurt," I answered. "They have perfect aim."

"They won't kill you," Nix answered. Arrows dug into the earth around us, and we each shrieked. "I take that back. Run, Perdi."

Zephyr's men had been kind enough to give us a warning, but I was desperate enough to ignore it. The world spun as an arrow soared by my head. They hadn't missed me by accident, and I knew it. The next would land where it was meant to. I veered to my right and stumbled, skinning my hands as I kept myself from hitting the ground. I knew they would have killed us had they wanted to, had they been allowed. Zephyr, from wherever he was, still protected me. Zephyr was the only one I couldn't hide from and the only one I wouldn't need to do so. Although, when he heard about this night, I'd wish the Aos Si hadn't missed.

Nix cried out as three small creatures jumped on his back, ripping at him with razor-sharp claws. Blood colored the white rubble at his feet. His screams attracted more hungry critters. I lifted Nix from the ground like a ragdoll and pulled the little brutes from his body. Slowly, the world we had entered surrounded us. For a moment, I couldn't think. My brain scattered its thoughts, and all of them were of us being eaten alive. I spun in a circle, trying to find a way out.

"You are not alone!" Seth screamed as he and his people flew over me.

I swallowed my panic and ran. Nix's blood covered my hands. I didn't look back. I pulled Nix tight against my chest and maneuvered over the rocks and broken bones of those who had tried to come, and failed, long before me. The creatures who had once been brave enough to attack ran from us. A familiar high-pitched shrill didn't settle my nerves. I turned to see Orrian and her people picking off creatures as they moved toward us. Bits of bodies and wings and tails fell in their wake like bloody hail. Orrian's usual white body was painted red, stained with the death sentence she handed to those brave enough to come for it. Nothing about her appearance made me feel safer. Her teeth, bared to the world, made my skin crawl.

"We can trust her," Nix choked out. His voice was weak.

"How do you know she won't tell Solas we were here?" I asked. "She's his friend, a lifelong one, if I remember correctly."

"Zephyr will know we're here, so it doesn't matter much, does it?" Nix said. "Orrian is with us, Perdi, not Solas. She is ours...not his."

Orrian zipped to meet my eyes and nodded rapidly. I didn't understand her words this time. The pitch was far too high for me to do anything more than wince from the harshness of her voice. She landed on Nix and pulled salve from a bag tied around her naked waist. She fed Nix a small handful of paste, and soon, his body went limp. She stroked his head before lifting back up and into the air. Her shrill pushed her people out— hunting, protecting, tearing open anything that moved. It was both relieving and startling and reminded me that nothing, no matter the size, was of no consequence here in Elphame.

"Orrian, if anything happens to Nix and you are to blame, I will rip your wings off," I spoke firmly. "He is all I have. He is everything to me. There is no one in this world that means more to me than Nix."

Orrian paused for a moment. I knew she and her people could kill me long before I could do anything to her, but the threat was still a promise of my intention. With my last breath, I'd do my absolute worst on my way out, taking as many of her people as I could. With one nod, we continued on. Only now, nothing came out to snatch us off the path. I had found an ally in an unlikely place, with a creature I thought was tied so tightly to Solas that I couldn't trust her with the simplest of secrets. But here she was, ready to fight, prepared to die yet again. Her willingness to pay the price when Solas found out made me question how much she enjoyed having a beating heart.

* * * *

The Court of Blood and Bones was everything it threatened to be. Before us, stretching as far as I could see, a black obsidian wall flanked the border. It looked as though it had been carved from a mountain, encircling the court from all sides. Each step I took crunched stones under my feet. The rocks were made of bone, both old and new. It made me think of the Golden Court and the path I'd walked on when I'd first arrived. I let the memory wash through me rather than fight it. It came and ripped at my heart on its way out of the door. It hurt, but it didn't hurt as much as when I fought it. Solas had been right. I'd never forget my first day in Elphame. It would haunt me until the day I died.

I followed a path of long-ago bodies, now broken down and picked apart, that made the road to ruin. As we came to the wall, I could see it wasn't black. It was blood, years of blood — and war and death. It was coated in the lives of those taken. The Court of Blood and Bones was the boldest of statements within Elphame. Nothing about this court said others were welcome, yet it invited the most daring to die at its feet. It was temptation and fate and endings — and promised nothing more. But I was not brave. I was just foolish enough to think I had a chance in hell.

I followed the path and stepped through a slice in the stone, no bigger than three feet wide but hundreds of feet high. Ahead, the path curled coldly away into infinite darkness and painful possibilities. My skin crawled each time I touched the rock. I could hear the aged blood flake off like paint chips. My brain began to lose focus on why I was there and started to search for a way out, a way back to safety. I turned sideways in hopes of convincing myself that it wasn't as horrible as I knew it was. Yet, each time my body touched the centuries dried gore, I wanted to vomit.

With Nix tight against me and Orrian in my pocket, I inched my way through the darkness and flinched each time my arm or leg rubbed against the stone. The path remained tight, which was more reassuring than terrifying. It told me that whatever monsters lurked, at least they wouldn't be the Sluagh. Whatever would grab me, I'd have a chance. I risked a glance above, instantly scared there would be hordes of flying beasts inching their way down. There was nothing but more darkness. No eyes stared down at me. No claws gripped the stone above me.

"You should not be here, Perdita Darkmore." A single voice echoed and bounced down the walls. It was both quiet and loud, like a whisper spoken in excitement, a little too close to my ear.

"I need your help," I called out to the unseen woman.

"No. You need our knowledge. That is not the same as help."

"Depends on how you look at it," I answered back and groaned my frustration. I told myself to remain calm and make no demands. This was not a place that would welcome an ego. This place would not suffer a fool easily. "Please... I've come a long way."

"Then you should know your way back," she answered. "Leave."

"Please, I need to know..."

"They all needed to know, and they all now pave our walk."

I winced at the thought of being ground up for gravel. "I mean no harm, no disrespect. I come not with force." I hugged Nix's sagging body, curled in my arms. "Can you help him? I'll leave, but can you help him, please?"

"He needs no help. He is in slumber as his body heals. It is his natural state. He will awaken once he is healed. He is a gnome. They are difficult to end with mere sticks and stones. His people are heartier than yours."

"Tell that to his family," I mumbled.

"Come forward," she finally said.

The shining black walls moved outward, releasing their hold on my shoulders. And for a moment, I realized that any beast, no matter the size, could have rampaged down on me, the walls opening for their attacks. Trickles of light poured down a vast corridor. I carried Nix for what felt like a mile, into a perfectly square stone room. It held no windows or lights, yet the room was as bright and warm as a summer's day. In the middle, a small hole was carved from the rock in the floor, holding water as swift as any river. The raging river gave out no thunderous noise, although I could see it rage by. A hooded figure stood, dressed in white, to the side of the water.

"Welcome." Her voice bounced off the walls as she pulled the hood from her head, exposing her face. Her pearl-white skin and hair looked out of place in the blackness of the room. But it was her eyes that grabbed all my attention. I had seen them before and had spent almost a year looking into those eyes. Where she was the light, he was the dark. As the realization of who she was sank in, she tilted her head in a graceful nod. The energy, thick in the air, was familiar. I knew she was the one whose scent and magick tickled the back of my brain with each room I walked into. She was my enemy. She was the one plotting against me.

"I am Solene."

I couldn't take my eyes off her. It took me several tries of opening and closing my mouth before I could speak. "Thank you, Solene, for seeing me." I dropped to my knees in a bow, touching my head to the stone. I was surprised to find the ground warm. "I come, pure of heart, seeking that which I do not know and cannot pay with that which I do not possess."

"Your little friend has taught you of our customs?" she asked. Her voice held a hint of amusement.

I didn't look up. I didn't dare. The weight of being this close to her felt like I had grabbed onto a bolt of lightning. Her power ran up and down my body and threatened to burst out of my head and toes, frying everything in between. I felt her power reach for my soul but knew she'd feel nothing but Malice. My soul was not for the taking — not anymore, not by anyone.

I did my best to steady my voice. "He tried, but we had very little time for me to learn. Any mistakes are mine and not his."

"You may stand. What is your question?" she asked. Her voice rattled inside my chest. "You may have one and only one. Do not waste it, or both your gnome and the fairy in your pocket have risked their lives with you for nothing."

Orrian jerked in my pocket, not hidden as we thought she'd be. I stood and lifted my eyes back to her. "Thank you."

I took a deep breath and closed my eyes. I thought about asking if I could trust Faolan, if Solas was using me and damaging the Gate, if my father was still alive, was I carrying the child of the Dark King, who in Elphame planned to take my life? On the very tip of my tongue was Solas, and where the man I knew had gone? There were dozens of questions, all of which needed answers. But I had all the answers I needed. I didn't need to waste my question on answers I knew but had been too scared to look at them. I'd find the rest once I was brave enough to look.

I stared down at Nix, asleep in my arms. I thought about how many times he's looked death in the face, stared it down by the sheer force of heart and soul. I had never met anyone as fearless or loyal as he was. Even in moments of great darkness, he had stood firm in his resolve. He had run into battle and stained his own soul to save mine. He stood at my side during my most painful moments, and never once did he think of saving just himself. I had never met a soul as pure as his.

"Is there anyone left in Nix's line?"

Solene cocked her head. Her blank face softened into an unexpected smile. "It is rare that I am ever surprised. Most come for riches and revenge, kingdoms and thrones. But this, you, I was not expecting. You come with a mind full of questions about your future, your safety, your freedom, but you ask a question about a being so small that most do not even notice them."

"He's given so much for so long. I can figure out the rest on my own. Fate always comes, whether I answer the door or not. No one can hide from her forever." I looked down at Nix, unconscious in my arms. "He deserves to know if he has family left. He, of all people, deserves this more than I do. He would give his question for me just as quickly as he'd give his life."

"You'd give your question for him?"

"I'd give my life for him," I answered. "Yes, I would give my question for him."

The woman knelt, dipped her hand in the water and pulled it up. The water ran down her arm, leaving a trail of glitter. Whatever she saw, she smiled. "Your friend is not the last of his line, as he feared. His blooded sister is alive. She has children of her own. There are others from his community who escaped."

"Where are they?"

The woman looked at me and raised her eyebrows.

I smiled bleakly and hoped she wouldn't grind me into bits for her walkway. "Can't blame me for trying."

She nodded. "Your friend will find his line in the Unseelie Court with the leprechauns. They can be found in the Hallows, the mountains."

"Prisoners?" I groaned at the thought of facing another leprechaun. I'd do it, but I didn't have to enjoy the idea. "I'd rather deal with the Sluagh than a leprechaun."

She let out a small laugh, and it surprised me. "No, you will not need to face another leprechaun. His people were granted sanctuary."

"Thank you," I responded and hugged Nix to my chest. "Nix, you're going home."

Nix stirred in my arms. His bloodshot eyes fluttered. "Did you get what you needed?"

I sighed and felt only happiness. "I got what was important."

"I need a minute, just a little nap," he answered and passed out again.

"Thank you." I bowed my head and backed out of the room.

Solene made no move to stop us or help us further. My mind raced with how we'd get home in one piece. I didn't know how, but I knew I had no choice but to get Nix back there. I stood outside of the chamber and tried to steady my shaking nerves. The monsters would all know we would be coming back out, and they'd be ready for us this time. I took a few cleansing breaths and steadied myself. This would hurt more the second time.

"Perdita Darkmore." I turned to see a younger woman, robed, standing at the entrance to the chamber I had just left. She was not Solene, but she was just as beautiful. "They escaped when the darkness came for them."

I froze. "Nix's family, they were killed by darkness?"

"A darkness rolled across his village and took them all," she answered. "The questions, all of them, you know the answers deep in your soul. You know all of that which you wished to ask. If you're willing to look the dark truth in the eyes and are willing to go find that which you do not know, you will find your answers. The path will be painful, but you've felt worse. The path will end in death, but you've already kissed the rings on death's hand once before. Be careful who you trust, or you'll kiss those rings a final time."

"Thank you."

"Don't come back here. I grant you safe passage home," she answered and walked down a hall I didn't see.

I turned, ready for the journey back. I was prepared to give it everything I had, to get Nix home. My energy was spent, but I'd spell us back if I had to, and I'd willingly pay whatever the cost for using my magick. I inched our way, no longer afraid of the touch of the stone or the decades-old blood as it rubbed off the walls as I moved. I squeezed between the walls and stepped into the forest behind the Dark Manor. I looked behind me. The wall was gone, and I was safely in the Dark Courts territory. I didn't bother trying to understand how I had gotten home, simply that the Seer had allowed me safe passage.

I rushed through the trees and straight into the house. I headed up the stairs, Nix in my arms, toward my bedroom. Both of us were covered in blood, cuts and scrapes. I knew Solas wouldn't be home, not that it mattered anyway. I rarely saw him outside of meals. But he was the last person I'd want to explain this to.

Zephyr stood at the top of the stairs and stared down at me. "I have already heard."

"I don't know what you're referring to," I answered casually as I got to the top of the landing. He moved to stand between me and my bedroom door.

"I don't want to know, either. Next time, I will inform Solas what you've done. And the next time you wish to tow my shadows all over Elphame, you'll be sorry to see they will no longer come to your call." Zephyr crossed his arms.

"I'll keep that in mind," I replied.

"Count yourself lucky. The only reason the Aos Si didn't kill you is because you have my protection. But my protection only goes so far. Next time, my men won't miss."

"Yes, they will," I countered. "If you wanted me dead, you'd come and do it yourself. We both know you do your own dirty work."

"I didn't say they'd be the ones to kill you. But they'll make sure you live long enough for me to get there." His answer ended with a snarl. His anger was palpable. I could feel it press against my chest. "The Court of Blood and Bones is off limits to all for a reason. Solas will be informed the next time you risk your life like that."

"You do just that, Zeph. I'd hate for you to have to do what is right rather than what is expected." I stepped around him and grabbed my doorknob. "You and I both know that you knew where I was every step of the journey. If you didn't want me at Blood and Bones, you could have come at any moment and whisked me away...but you didn't."

"I shouldn't have to chase you around. You're playing a deadly game." He grabbed my arm. "Deadly games win deadly prizes."

I smiled. I had just finished saying similar to Faolan not that long ago. "Get your hands off me. And don't threaten me again." I pulled away and glared at him. I did not like being touched without permission. "Deadly games?" I laughed. "I haven't stopped playing them since the moment I was Taken by *your* king."

"Perdi, you're going to get yourself killed..." he started, and I shoved him. I put everything I had into the push. He staggered back just enough to give me breathing room but held his ground, as I knew he would.

"It will be your king that takes my life while you watch! If it is not by his very hands, it will be because he won't protect me," I yelled at him and didn't care who heard me. "You once told me that simply existing wasn't enough, that I had to live. But then you've watched him chip away at me until I am nothing more than an anxiety-ridden husk of a woman. You do *not* get to tell me how to live and also how I will die. Now go do the bidding of *your* king. Don't you have someone to torture or souls to eat? Or are you going to pick the rest of me apart until I finally throw myself off the goddamn balcony?"

"I warned you, little Crow. You would not survive. You were merely choosing a different day to die. If you're not careful, that day will come quicker than you'd like."

I stepped to his front and snarled. "And if you're not careful, Soul-Eater, I'll eat your fucking king on my way down."

"This will be my only warning. Take it or suffer for it."

"Suffer? What a unique change that would be from the misery I'm already experiencing." I swallowed a laugh and glared instead.

I closed Zephyr in the hall and pulled the wards up and over my bedroom. I would be surprised if he didn't tell Solas. There was no reason not to. Zephyr owed me nothing, but he owed his king—or so his sense of loyalty did. And if wasn't him, it would be Solene who told Solas.

* * * *

I paced and hovered over Nix. Orrian had returned with more herbs and roots. While I wrung my hands and swallowed my urge to cry, Orrian ground up her ingredients. I watched her limp across my desk. Tiny bruises no bigger than freckles smattered her pale skin. Her wings had small tears, yet she never complained.

"Orrian, you're hurt." I finally sat with her, guilty for her pain.

She shook her head and tried to wave me off.

"Thank you." I said weakly. "I'm sorry I didn't trust you."

She looked up and smiled. Her expression did nothing to take away from how terrifying she truly looked.

"Do you trust Solas?" I asked, remembering her bolting from the dinner table.

She nodded at first, then hung her head and shrugged. She was in the same boat as I was—confused, unsure of who to trust.

"Do you think he's going to hurt me?" I asked.

She shrugged.

"Would you trust him with my safety?" I asked, and she shrugged again. "Will you tell him what I'm doing?"

She shook her head again, and I left it at that. She fluttered to Nix and rubbed salve on his wounds. She watched over him while I showered and gathered up my bloody and torn clothes. I thought about burning the clothes to hide the evidence, then tossed them in the trash. Solas would know what I had done, whether I tried to hide it from him or not.

Once dried off, Orrian rubbed salve on my cuts. But before she could go, I cleaned her of blood and dabbed her with ointment. I pierced my finger and offered her my blood. I knew it would speed up her healing. Once she stopped limping, she took her leave. I knew she had to go heal her people. I gave her my thanks and sat beside Nix on my bed, a small knife in my hand. I knew my knife would do nothing if it were Solas who came into my room, but the false sense of security kept me from crying.

Nix twitched a few times and muttered nonsense until he finally woke. He stretched, and upon realizing he had been asleep, he jolted to his feet, eyes darting around, ready for a fight long gone. "What the hell happened?" he asked, a look of confusion blanketing his face. "How did we get home in one piece?"

"We made it. We saw one of the ladies of the Court of Blood and Bones."

"How terrifying was that?" he asked. "I can't believe I slept through it all."

"To sum it up, I thought we'd end up in their bone garden. It was both amazing and scary as hell. Zeph wasn't impressed when we got home and made his usual threats and a tantrum." I rolled my eyes at the mention of his name. "The priestess, her name was Solene. I think she is Solas' sister. I think she's the one that's been coming to see him in secret, under the guise of being his priestess. I've heard her voice in his office. I've felt her presence, even when she's not here. I think she's the one watching me, watching Solas."

I kept my other suspicions to myself, such as her seeking out my ending. I wouldn't derail Nix's return to his family, not for anything, including my freedom. I, more than anyone, knew how important finding the way home was. I had spent almost every minute in Elphame, wondering how I'd ever get home.

His eyes grew in surprise. "There were rumors long ago, but no one really believed them, and it's not like anyone could go there to confirm them. And who in their right mind would ask Solas if it were true?"

"What rumors?"

"During the war, Blood and Bones closed to protect it. But a small few didn't want to close it off. Solas' father argued to keep the court open and to rule all Elphame from that throne. Solas did nothing to stop his father. His mother, the queen, along with her ladies, banished them both from the Court of Blood and Bones. When they were exiled, they created the Court of Shadows, the first Dark Court. Solas and his father took the land from the Unseelie Court, though it's said no one fought them for it."

"Why does the Aos Si follow him still?" I asked.

"It's not that easy of a question to answer. The Aos Si follow Zephyr, whose loyalty to Solas is absolute, for reasons unknown. But after the exile, Solas' father took responsibility for what happened, given it was his plan. The sins of the father went to the grave with him. Solas carried no blame for what happened — the cause of the war, the closing of the Court of Blood and Bones or for the following wars," Nix answered.

"Was Solas actually responsible?"

"Hard to say. Solas has come from a line of brutal force. Whether he is or not, who Solas was then is not who he is now," Nix said. I gave him an unsure look. "This, who he is right now, is not even him."

"As much as I want that to be true, who he is now is all that matters. It's the only man he's willing to be right now," I replied.

"I agree." Nix smiled, although his eyes said he didn't. "Did Solene answer your question?"

"She did." My stomach fluttered with butterflies. I knew he was about to get really mad, really soon.

"What did you ask? What did she say?"

"I asked about your family," I answered and watched Nix's face grow red.

"How stupid can you be? Damn it, why would you waste your question, Perdi? I already know how they died. We're up to our ears in uncertainty and danger, and you asked that?" Nix paced from the top of the bed to the bottom and back. His little feet stomped as he muttered his disappointment that we could never go back and ask another. "Maybe we can get into the Sluagh caves? Do you think Elda would see you again without Solas knowing?"

"Nix, your sister...she lived," I blurted out.

Nix spun around and stared at me. His mouth opened in surprise. "What? No one lived, Perdi. They said no one lived. Solas went and looked for me. He told me that no one was left."

"She escaped with a few others. She's in the mountains with the leprechauns. They granted them sanctuary. They're in Winter Court territory, in the Hallows. It's likely why no one knows about them."

Nix stumbled until he landed on his knees, and tears fell from his eyes. "She lived? But...I was told they were gone."

"I know. She got out, along with a few others," I whispered and squeezed his small shoulder. "She has children, Nix. You need to go to them."

"I can't just go there, Perdi. It's Winter Court." Nix waved off my suggestion. "She was granted sanctuary. I wasn't. Things don't work that easily here."

"Then we make a deal with Faolan," I said. "You're going home, Nix."

He smiled. But as soon as his happiness came, the sadness set in. "What about you?"

"Hopefully, one day, I'll find my way home, too."

"I can't leave you." He shook his head. "You can't do this alone. You're in danger."

"But you are going to leave," I answered. "This isn't your home."

"You're my home."

I smiled. "We'll find each other again. But here, right now, this isn't where you should be. I won't let you stay. If I could go home, you'd give your life for that. It's time you go. I promise this isn't the last we'll see of each other. The rest will work its way out. In the meantime, we're not going to miss the only happiness found in this cursed land — not for me, not for anyone."

"You shouldn't have wasted your question on me," he said again.

"It wasn't wasted. You deserve this and more. I can find my answers if I'm willing to look hard enough at the truth. If I find myself at too great of a risk, I'll find you, and we can both hide out with the leprechauns. Until then, we both must meet our fates," I answered. "Can you get a message to Faolan?"

"Yes, but do you think that's wise? Can he be trusted?"

"No. But I think we can trust him more than our current options."

"*Rogha an dá dhíogha.*" Nix sighed. His Gaelic was much better than my own. "The choice of two evils."

"We pick the lesser of the two," I answered.

Nix argued his point not to leave, but soon, after many tears, he gave in. He left me to my thoughts to get a message to Faolan. I agreed to see him again if he granted Nix safe passage into the mountains.

* * * *

We waited at our agreed meeting spot. Nix stood beside me with a sack strung across his back. As happy as I was to see him go home, my heart slowly broke with each passing minute. I loved Nix as I would love a brother. He wasn't just my friend. He was the only family I had in these hellish lands, and I was saying goodbye to him.

"He's coming," Nix whispered.

"Is he alone?" I asked.

"No, he has about a dozen of his guards. He's scared. I can smell it."

"I'd be scared, too," I answered. "I live here, and I'm terrified of the place."

Faolan glided through the trees as if he were the very wind. The closer he got, the more pungent the smell of Christmas grew around me. He darted his eyes around nervously. He looked like a starved alley cat being offered food for the first time, ready to dart at a moment's notice.

"I didn't know if it was a trap or not," Faolan finally said. "I'm sorry, but…"

I lifted my hand. "I understand. I wouldn't come here without an army at my back, either."

"Yet, here you are, without an army," he pointed out.

I smiled. "I've learned many tricks since first coming to Elphame, and your army doesn't scare me. Let's try something new, shall we? We'll leave the posturing for a different day. I'm too tired and feel far too old for this right now."

"Agreed." He exhaled as if he had been holding in unwanted bravado for years. "I was surprised to hear from you so soon. I wasn't expecting it."

"Thank you for meeting with me," I started, and my voice caught in my throat. I looked down at Nix and smiled. My happiness for him would trump my grief. I could cry later.

"Why do you need safe passage for Nix?" Faolan asked, but his eyes danced through the forest, waiting for an attack that wouldn't come by any of my doing.

"We found out recently that his sister and some of her people have survived. They're in the Hallows, the mountains of your territory. They were granted sanctuary within the Hallows. What would it cost to grant him safe passage through your lands, so he may reunite with them? I am willing to pay whatever the cost is."

"There is no cost for him." Faolan frowned as if he were insulted by my offer of payment. He looked to Nix. "You have safe passage and anything you need if it means you will find your people."

Nix nodded. "Thank you. I should be there by nightfall."

I lifted Nix and hugged him. "I love you more than life."

"I love you, Perdi. If you find yourself in trouble, call on me, and I will come, no matter what."

"Go before I break down and make a scene." I smiled and held back my tears with sheer stubbornness.

He hesitated at first and looked up to Faolan. "If you hurt her, I will bring back the leprechauns."

"Good luck, Nix. If ever you need assistance or passage back to Perdi, you have my word. I will help you." Faolan touched his chest, signing his oath, and Nix was gone. He, like me, wouldn't look back for fear it would break us.

"Thank you," I whispered, my voice quiet with unshed tears.

"Perdi, I can help you get home, too."

I shook my head. "Thanks, Fao, but I can't leave yet."

"Fao? It's been so long since you called me that." He smiled softly, as if remembering a time before Elphame had cleaved our bond. "Then you believe me?"

I pulled back. "Not quite. There are too many questions and not enough answers."

"If you need me, come back to this spot and hang a red ribbon to this tree. I will know and will come."

"Thank you."

He grabbed my hand. "If you're in danger, come into my territory. I grant you safe passage. If you don't make it to me, I will hear your call and will come. I give you my word."

I nodded. "Why, Faolan? Why help me?"

"I never once stopped loving you. It may not be the love you want or know, but it is the only love I can afford in a world that doesn't allow for such things," he answered, and I knew exactly what he meant. Not all of us can pay the cost for showing how we feel, good or bad. "I know all too well what hell this place brings. It rubs away all that is good. I've been there, Perdi. I've been forced to make decisions that stain me to this day — decisions to protect myself and those I care about. I don't blame you for surviving and all it took for you to get here. This place makes you pay, one way or another, for each day you've had to fight for. We all have had to make choices, and not all of them are understood by others."

"Not even after I drained your guards?"

He shook his head and smiled. "They weren't my people, but I did have to step over them. I believe they were from the Golden Court. But I saw what you did, though."

"That doesn't scare you?" I asked. "Who I've become?"

"Not once," he answered.

I pulled away. "It should."

"I'm sorry, but it doesn't. I've seen and done worse. All truth here, Perdi. I've ordered worse and will continue to do so to protect my people. I hate that I know what I'd do, because it's uglier than what you've done."

"Thank you for helping me, for helping Nix. But I don't think I can leave, even if I wanted to," I whispered, my thoughts on the possibilities in my stomach. If I were pregnant, I couldn't go. Solas would never allow it.

"But you can't stay where you are," he answered.

I stared at him for a long moment. "You're hiding as much as Solas is. I can feel it. I can't leave until I find out if I'll die slower in your court or his."

I stepped away from Faolan and left him standing on the border. I ran through the trees and let my sadness finally bubble to the surface. Nix was gone, and I was now truly alone in the Dark Courts and, quite possibly, my enemy's territory. I would face this nightmare alone, and it hurt more than I could put into words. As soon as I hit my bedroom, the shadows wrapped me up tight and didn't ask any questions. They felt my sadness and let me break open without the rest of Elphame feeling my pain or reveling in it. My pain was my own, and as lonely as that felt, I was glad for it. I couldn't bear the thought that Solas would have been able to feel it and would choose not to come. This way, I could still lie to myself.

That night I dreamed of the Gate. I dreamed of Aoife.

"Run, Perdi," she whispered.
"Why?" I asked.
"You know why. She will kill you unless you run. She's been waiting for someone like you, and if She finds out who you are, She may not kill you at all, but you'll wish for it."
"Where do I go?" I asked.
"As far away from the Dark Court as you can get. It is no longer safe for you."
"It's not safe for me anywhere," I replied.
"Some danger is better than certain death."
"Solas will never let me leave."
She smiled. "Silly child, he is the one pushing you to run. The only way he can protect you is by losing you. You will force him to take drastic measures to force you from his side."
"That's a painful way to show someone you love them."
"This is the cost of love in Elphame."

I woke from the dream. Seth, my gargoyle, was there, but he wasn't alone. The gargoyles were there in masses. The trees were filled with them. My balcony was littered with stony soldiers. They, like me, could hear a horn in the distance. They each turned their heads to it. The war wasn't over, it had only just begun, and the gargoyles were ready before the rest of us knew what would unfold.

Chapter Seven

"Get up." Zephyr's growly voice pulled me from a half-awake state.

The bubble around my room shook me from the deepest of sleep as soon as Zephyr had pushed past it. But it was his voice that lifted me the rest of the way out. I dragged my eyes open and winced at the sandpaper that was my lids. Zephyr stood beside my bed, dressed in full leather combat gear. His brilliantly blond hair was pulled back into a tight braid and exposed an angry look on his face. His eyes were bitter cold, an ice blue he reserved for war. I had seen that look on his face before, directed at those he planned to kill. It should have scared me more than it did.

"Go away, Zeph," I muttered and pulled the covers over my face.

"You have five minutes to be up and dressed."

"You have less than that to get out of my room," I warned and rolled over, away from his early morning call.

"Four minutes," he said and left my room.

I nestled deeper into my pillows and faded back into my dream world. The warmth of sleep that had tiptoed back over me was yanked brutally from my bones as the shadows swirled around me and dumped me on the cold, wet ground. The cool air hit my hot skin, and I instantly chilled.

"What the hell?" I groaned from my back on the forest floor.

Zephyr stood over me. "I warned you."

"Send me back, now," I demanded.

"No." He crossed his arms and smiled but didn't lose the ice in his eyes.

I jumped to my feet and cursed him. "I'm in my underpants, damn it."

"And a shirt," he added. "I told you to get up and get ready. You told me to get out. I got out."

"Yes, as in I wanted you to leave me alone — not haul me into the bushes in my underwear...and a shirt." I tried to cover my arms and legs all at once, shivering as I failed. "I'm cold."

"And I don't care," he answered with anger in his voice. "That's the crux of decisions we make. We must pay for them all, the good and the bad. You could have gotten up and dressed, but you chose to ignore me. You are the one who chooses to stay out all night, running for your life, plotting and planning, scheming until the bitter hours, rather than sleeping. Not me. And if those are the life choices you plan on making, this is where you need to be."

"Why the hell do I need to be up at the crack of dawn, half-naked, in the forest?" I asked.

"Solas wants you to learn how to protect yourself, how to use your Malice to its full potential — to channel it, in case the Gate opens again," he answered, then added his two cents. "If you're going to put yourself at risk, you should know how to get yourself out of it, as well. One day, little Crow, I won't be there to help you. I won't be able to. You will be on your own, and I won't be able to save you from yourself."

Zephyr had shown up in the bitter early hours of the morning and had dragged me to the forest under the guise of my training. But I knew he was still angry at me for going to Blood and Bones and wanted to tear a strip off of me in private, where his words wouldn't echo into the ears of the king.

"Oh, does he?" I asked nonchalantly. I rolled my eyes to showcase I wasn't buying the crap he was selling. "For the Gate? Why? Is something wrong with the Gate, Zephyr?"

"No, but Solas is always one to be prepared for anything and everything," he replied. "You know he plans for every inevitability."

He stretched his arms across his chest and loosened his body. This wasn't going to be training. This looked like he was gearing up for a fight. He motioned for me to mirror his actions. I'd never win in a fair fight against Zephyr, but I'd do my best to make it hurt for him. At least it would warm me up, beating on him. And if he knocked me out, I'd be asleep and wouldn't care how cold I was.

I nodded. "Just like he was prepared for me, huh? Always the careful planner he is."

Zephyr frowned and paused his stretches. "You know, I'm pretty damn tired of always being in the middle of you two. If you have questions about Solas, you need to speak to him directly. I won't speak for him."

"I would if he'd actually talk to me, but he won't."

"Well, you're barking up the wrong tree. Only Solas can speak for himself."

I glared. "Of course not, Zeph, but you haven't a problem speaking for me."

"What are you talking about?" Zephyr stepped to my front and motioned for us to begin.

Simple jabs passed between us. We moved in a circle, him jabbing and me ducking. My striking out at him and him stepping out of the way with ease. It got my blood pumping, but my anger worked just as well.

"*I agree. Perdi doesn't need to hear this. Perdi doesn't need to know that. Perdi needs to rest. Perdi needs to stay here and recover. Perdi is wounded. Perdi needs to heal. Good night, Perdi.*" I taunted him with words he had said in the last week alone. "Shall I go on?"

"You don't need to know how we clean up after a war. You don't need to hear about the dead women and children. You don't need to know that villages have been razed and their young women have been taken. Do you want to know what they'll be used for? Do you want to see the charred remains of a mother shielding her infant child? Do you want to hear about me trying to rescue those taken, only to find them already dead? Is that what you want? Because you can have those fucking memories since you're so good at dealing with your own."

Zephyr grew angrier with each memory he dredged up. His sparring had turned from teaching me how to defend myself to leaving me no choice but to use the techniques I had learned or have him knock my head off my shoulders.

"You *are* wounded, Perdi." He raised his voice little by little. "I hear you screaming every single night. I smell the tears on your face when you come down for breakfast. I feel the house shake when you dream. I watch you when you don't think anyone is looking, and I see the pain on your face every single minute of every single day. Soon, if you don't start dealing with this crap, I will have to deal with it. You don't want me dealing with you, Perdi."

"Are you threatening me?" I asked and put more force into my throws. "Don't threaten me."

Zephyr shoved me, and although I went down, I got back up. "It's not a threat. It's a promise. What do you think will happen when a Soul-Eater is beyond repair? You will be a danger to everyone, whether you love them or not." He jabbed faster as his temper heated. "If you can't see how damaged you are and how badly you need to step back and fix yourself, you're blind — and you are stupid."

"I can see more clearly today than yesterday or days before." I sparred back with the same force he had used.

He circled behind me and smelled my hair. "You see nothing but your own suffering. Your blindness will cause your own death. You stink of wounds on your soul. I can feel the pain in your heart and smell the pain coating your skin. It's strong enough to choke on. It's covering you like a rainy day."

"Nix is gone," I whispered, my voice catching in my throat, stuck on my swallowed tears.

"What?" He stopped in his tracks, no longer circling me.

I turned and jabbed my fingers into his chest. "You tried to kill his family. You almost killed my best friend's family." I screamed in his face and swung. My fist slammed into his temple, and he staggered. I used every opportunity I had, just as Zephyr had taught me, and brought him to the ground, breaking his left knee to get him there.

"I didn't touch his family," Zephyr called out, moving between blocking my attacks and holding the bones I stomped on.

"The darkness came for them, Zeph, and you are the very darkness." I kicked his jaw, and he blocked my foot on my next attempt. "What do you think I asked when I went to that hellhole, Blood and Bones? I asked about Nix and his family. They told me the darkness came and killed nearly all of them."

He grabbed my legs in one swift movement and brought me to the ground, sharp and hard. He rolled onto me and snarled. He hovered an inch over my face. "Do not pick a fight with a Soul-Eater. You will not enjoy how I end it. You cannot win against me, so don't even try."

"Go ahead, Zeph." I smiled and laughed in his face, taunting him. "*Eat my fucking soul. Eat my fucking world.* I'm so over that threat. Go ahead. You'll still be hungry when you're done."

"Don't tempt me."

"Imagine me without the little bit of soul I have left. Think of how damaged I am now, then let me lose upon Elphame, soulless. How many souls would I need to eat before I sated that hunger before you were forced to stop me? Think of every death you'd be responsible for, not like you care. As long as I only eat *your* enemies, you don't give a shit about me! You're just like Solas, only worth protecting when you need something from me."

"You know better than anyone else that if I ate all of who you are, you'd never taste freedom again. You'd never step foot into Elphame to do your worst. Do not ever force me because I'd never be your jailer. I'd kill you before I took your freedom." Zephyr rolled off me and moved away.

"But you'll let everyone else do it." I spat the words at him.

I watched him grab onto his nose and twist it back into place. The grinding bones echoed and crawled up my body like spiders. I gagged at the sound. He glanced back as I stood. "Don't do this. You're going to get hurt. My limits have been pushed, and it's time we end our session for the day."

"Oh, *your* limits? I'm supposed to care that I've pushed *you* too far? Welcome to the club." I snarled right back. "I've been pushed so far beyond my limits, I couldn't muster a care for your comfort right now if I was under threat of death."

Zephyr turned in one fluid movement and rotated his shoulders. "I will heal. You won't."

I shrugged. "Enjoy explaining to your king why I'm dead — although you'd probably be doing him a favor."

Zephyr jabbed the air inches from my face and motioned for me to step forward. "I didn't say I'd kill you. Hurt you? Most certainly. And I have no worries about telling Solas I beat you to a pulp to teach you a lesson. Let's be honest. He'd understand. You, little Crow, never know when to stop. You poke and poke, then cry when you're bitten. You never learn."

I smiled the most unfriendly of smiles. "Old news, Zeph. I've learned every lesson here through pain. You're not bringing anything new to the table. As for Solas, if we're finally being honest, I don't think he'd give a shit what happened to me."

"If you want to learn things the hard way, so be it."

"Are you trying to tell me that there are other ways to learn besides the hard way?" I asked.

"Apparently not for you," he answered.

We fought again. This time, he didn't hold back as much as usual, and every second hurt worse than the last. Each time he knocked me down, he thought I'd stay down. But I had learned that pain could be overcome. Hurt, on the other hand, took lifetimes. I'd rather every bone broken than suffer one more heartache, so I got up when I should have stayed down. I kept fighting when I should have stopped. Nothing here was free. If I didn't fight tooth and nail for it, I never got to have it and never got to keep it.

I called on the shadows and twisted them around my body, moving from place to place before Zephyr could grab me again. It was only with Zephyr that I could be all I was meant to be. It was only here, away from the eyes of the Courts, that I could be a Soul-Eater. When he tried to pull the shadows back to him, they moved slowly, struggling between the pull of two Soul-Eaters, giving me an opportunity to move once again.

"Why would I ever harm the gnomes?" Zephyr asked as he dodged a rock I threw.

"I think you did it to force him, to force me. If he didn't have a family left, he'd stay in Whitwick with me. And you knew I'd follow him wherever he went, that I'd always choose to stay with him, even if it meant staying in this godforsaken Court," I yelled and threw another rock. The death of most of Nix's family had forced him to remain with me. It was the start of my journey into Elphame, long before I knew I was marked for this land.

Zephyr moved to kick my abdomen, and I curled to protect my stomach. My lip split when his fist connected with my unprotected face. I spat blood and groaned but wouldn't give in. Neither would he. I cursed Elphame and my becoming more and more Fae with each passing day. All that meant was that I could take a beating unlike ever before.

"As if I'd need to kill a single soul to control you. I would gain nothing from taking the lives of the gnomes. Of all things to kill, why the wee folk?" he asked. "And how could I even do it? When Nix's family was killed, I was locked in a prison, warded. How could I, even if I wanted to? I couldn't send my shadows to do harm. They, like me, were tied to the Golden Court."

I twirled around his back, and when he moved to follow, my elbow connected with his nose once again, and he cursed my name. He spat blood and roared when he twisted it back in place.

"If you weren't the darkness, who..." I whispered and closed my mouth. I dropped the two rocks in my hands. Zephyr wasn't the only dark beast of Elphame.

"Don't say the words," he commanded. His face held the truth, even if he tried to hide it from me.

"If it wasn't you, there is only one other that is described as the darkness," I whispered. I didn't need to say Solas' name out loud. We both knew.

Zephyr dropped the thick branch he held and sat hard on a log, the wood crunching under the pressure of his force. "Don't say it, Perdi, not out loud."

I dropped beside him. "Swear to me, you didn't harm Nix's family. Give me your word, Zeph, that it wasn't you."

"I swear. If I had, I would have told you. I would have had good reason to do it, far beyond this ideal of control, and you would have needed to know why. If the gnomes had posed such a risk for me to kill them all, I would never have allowed Nix to keep his life. Not a soul would have been saved. You know better than anyone else. I would never have allowed a single one of them to live, let alone sit at the dinner table with me," he answered, and I believed him. "I thought it was Faolan."

"Faolan didn't do it," I answered. "When I went to the Court of Blood and Bones, they said it was the darkness who tried to kill Nix's line."

"Where is Nix? He's not going to confront Solas, is he?" He looked worried.

"No. Some of his family survived, his sister and her children. He's gone to find them," I answered. I thought twice about telling him where Nix went and how we got passage through Unseelie territory. Some things were better left unsaid. And this was how lies began, and I felt like I was now throwing stones at Solas. "Zeph, no more lies. Is the Gate damaged?"

He nodded.

"Why didn't you tell me?" I asked. "Better yet, why did you lie to me?"

"I wanted to tell you, but, damn it, Perdi, I'm stuck between a king and little Crow. He has forbidden us from telling you anything not cleared through him first. He says it's because he's worried about your safety, but I think he just doesn't want you to know. Maybe he's falling back to his old ways, holding his cards too close to his chest? Or maybe he really doesn't want you to know, because he doesn't want you involved again? Hell, just to come out here today, I had to tell him you needed training, that the Gate may need you again, that if you were in danger, we had to make sure you could defend yourself. I had to convince him to allow me to train you in case he was right and your life was in danger. He finally agreed on the grounds that I made sure you could use your Malice at its fullest potential."

"I can. And the longer I'm here, the more it grows," I answered.

"Yeah, but he doesn't know that. A small white lie in the grand scheme of things."

"It's not that big of a stretch. My life *is* in danger. I saw him at the Gate, pushing power into it, damaging it. Is he going to invade the mortal realm?"

He shrugged. "I don't know what he plans on doing. He's not telling me anything of importance."

"You're lying to me, Zeph. I can feel it." I glared at him.

"I'm not lying. I'm just not telling you what you want to hear."

"We have to stop him."

Zephyr laughed at the thought. "Oh? And how do you suppose we approach him on this? He is king."

"He's not *my* king," I answered. "And he's not your king. He's your friend. No one rules you."

Zephyr laughed. "Are you really going to pull that here, too?"

"He's not my king any more than he is yours. Before this, he was just Solas to me, never my ruler. As for you, Finis have no kings or queens. Regardless, whatever he is or isn't, we can't let this happen. I don't know what's going on, but does any of this sound like Solas? Something deeper is afoot, and I don't plan to stand aside and just let it happen."

"I've tried to talk to him, but he won't listen. He takes meetings in private and won't share his plans. I'm outside of his decisions. I don't know what's going on any more than you do."

"I find it hard to believe that anyone could withhold the truth from a Soul-Eater." I stared at him and gave him a place to set down his lies without consequence. But he still didn't take the chance I offered. "Once, before the war for the Gate, you had told me Solas was meeting with his priestess. But you and I both know that she isn't his priestess. I can feel her here, even when she's not around."

Zephyr sighed. "She is his priestess, but yes, she is more. But that isn't my story to tell. He, like you, has many secrets, and I'm not the teller of those. She comes, but he doesn't tell me about the meetings. And nothing short of burning this world will keep her from coming. There truly isn't a single power alive that can stop her."

I nodded. He hadn't outright lied to me, but an omission of the truth was close enough. Did I risk being angry that he kept both my secrets and Solas', or appreciate the awful place we have put him in? I let it go for now. Hopefully, there would be a tomorrow where I could chew his hide for it.

"I've heard him. At night, when he's in his office," I finally said. "The shadows hide me, and I pick up bits and pieces."

"I know. I feel it every time you call on them. You need to stop before he catches you."

"If you wanted me to stop, why do you let the shadows come at all?"

"What if I stop them from going to you, and it is when you need them most? You'll get hurt. It pisses me off to no end, but I'm scared that if I put my foot down, that'll be the time you're in the most danger."

"Thank you." I smiled and touched his hand. "Now, what the hell do we do?"

He raised his eyebrows and shrugged. "Hell if I know."

"For the sake of argument, say he was doing this and wasn't just a puppet. Say this was all just Solas gone wild. Why would he want to invade?"

"For the sake of argument, if I had to guess, to finish what his father started. It was the Dark Court who originally waged war against the mortal realm — to enslave, to own, to rule all. But Solas wouldn't dare. He's done everything he can to protect the mortal world."

"I don't think Faolan betrayed me, as I thought." I said the words that gnawed on the back of my skull.

"That, I don't know. I wasn't there. But I don't trust him." Zephyr stood and held out his hand. "I'd keep your hunches to yourself, as well as our conversation today."

"I'm going to stop Solas," I replied.

"You're going to die if you try," he answered.

I shrugged. "We all die someday."

With my hand in his, he flinched and smelled the air. "I understand why you smell like days of tears, but why all the vomit?"

My hand instinctively went to my stomach.

"I saw you protect your stomach over everything else during our sparring. It is why you have a fat lip. You gave up guarding your face and vital organs and favored your stomach. One punch to your chest would stop your heart. What's going on?"

I groaned. "I haven't had my bleed in well over a month."

"Huh, interesting." He smiled. "I thought perhaps you weren't well and were trying to poison yourself."

"I'd rather have the plague than be pregnant."

"A child is not a bad thing, little Crow."

"A child is a beautiful thing, I agree. But if I'm pregnant, what will happen to me then? He will trap me, and I'll never get away…ever. I'll be stuck here for the rest of my days." Saying the words out loud freed me in some way. I had thought I wanted to spend all my days with Solas, bind our futures together and give him children. But I knew this wasn't how I wanted it. I didn't want to have children with the man he was now. Once I spoke the truth, the pressure was gone from my throat. The noose I thought I had tied around my neck was gone.

Zeph pulled me into his chest and hugged me. I cried, not for the worries I held but because it had been weeks since I had felt an actual hug—a simple touch that didn't ask anything of me, a friend offering me comfort. And it was everything I needed at that exact moment.

"I feel nothing but your soul," Zeph finally spoke. "You're not pregnant."

"Thank the Gods," I muttered.

"You should have come to me right away. I could have saved you a lot of worries." He pulled back from his hug and smiled. It was the kind of smile that he saved for me. Gone was the Soul-Eating warrior legend that was Zephyr. "You should see a healer for your sickness."

"Nix said the same thing. But I don't think it's anything a healer can help me with."

"If it is an illness, you're only going to get weaker. Right now, being weaker is not an option. You can't protect yourself if you're too weak."

I feared it had nothing to do with illness and everything to do with what was going on with the world being off balance. I turned to walk home and stopped. I could hear it again, the faint hum from a horn. I tilted my head and turned. I stared off and focused on the sound.

"What is it?" Zephyr asked.

I shook my head. "You can't hear that?"

"Hear what?" he asked.

"Nothing," I muttered. He didn't hear the Gate like I did. "What would you give me for a pearl?"

He grabbed my arm and shook his head. "Solas will smell the missing pearl. Do you think times are tough right now? Show up without a piece of your soul and see just how hard things will be. This wouldn't be like the last time. He'd go right off the deep end and take us both with him."

"I doubt it would be that bad. He'll be ticked off, but not enough to kill us over it. Plus, you'd always feel me, where I am and if I'm in danger. You'd be able to keep me safe if I needed help. Isn't that part of your duty to protect me at all costs?" I asked. "Zeph, I think you need to take it. I think my life is in danger. One day, I may need it back. If you had it, you'd be able to help me when no one else can or will. I can't explain why, but I feel like I need to give you one. Zeph, I can't shake the need to make sure you have my pearl."

"Conniving, that's what you are." Zephyr grinned. "What would you like for it?"

"Your oath that you will never bring me harm, no matter what," I answered.

"That's a simple deal. I'd never hurt you," he replied. "If you're going to play games with kings, you better be ready to pay the price for it."

"If he isn't going to save me, I'll save myself."

The moment we shook, the oath was in place. The pain flooded me as he ripped a piece of my soul away, but the satisfaction it brought was worth it. No one, not even Solas, would be able to use Zephyr to come for me. And when I did decide to leave, nothing short of breaking an oath would get the nightmare of Elphame to drag me back. That was worth so much more than a piece of my soul. It was worth the entire thing.

"Zeph, one more question," I added, shaking off the feeling of having a piece of my soul ripped from my stomach. "How long will it take for me to become fully Finis? How many years does it take for my Finis abilities to be at full strength?"

He frowned. "Why? Are you planning on eating the entire world in one gulp?"

"Not at the moment," I smiled. "I'm honestly curious. Crows are Taken for seven years. What is the significance of seven years?"

"Of that, I'm not certain. But seven years is usually what it takes for a halfling to become fully Fae. It's why, upon return, your people went mad. They were locked away from Elphame energy, the very thing that keeps us Fae, keeps us balanced. I suspect it's either to punish mortals — sending back a soul who needs to be put down — or it is to see if the halfling is worth breeding with. Before Aoife, the Gate was two-way. Fae would send back pregnant Crows to keep the Taking from ending."

My entire body shivered at the thought of being used as breeding stock for Fae. "That's as sick as Taking us."

"And most Fae are just that, creative to a disgusting fault," he replied. "To answer your first question, for most Finis born in Elphame, it is known at birth that we will become Soul-Eaters. We start exhibiting our abilities when we're still nursing. Once we're a few years old, we can give or take life from small creatures. By then, we attract the Aos Si, and they take over our training."

"What about me?" I asked.

"Since you were born in the mortal world, it'll take six or seven years here in Elphame for you to become fully Fae. It won't be until then that you'll feel only your Finis side. I think, though, because of your Darkmore blood, it may be sooner."

"Will I attract the Aos Si when I'm fully Finis?"

He laughed softly. "Not in how you think. As a female, you'd never be enlisted as a soldier. Female Finis were trained as healers. But the Aos Si are attracted to you and your power. You feel like home, like me. There are times when they're looking for me and end up at the Dark Court, tracking you instead. Eventually, I won't be able to keep them away. They'll bond with you as they have with me." He pulled away. "It's time to go face the music, Perdi. And I doubt very much you'll like the song Solas chooses for you."

"Everything hurts in Elphame, especially Solas."

"He's the only one who won't hurt you on purpose," he replied.

Chapter Eight

Orrian sat at my desk with a pencil and scribbled on paper. Nix had taught her how to write, to communicate with me, but the process was long and drawn out. As I dressed for a dinner that would be explosive, she frantically wrote me a note. Her writing was small, and it took a lot of strain to make out the tiny words. But it was better than staring at her puzzled, not understanding her shrills. I could have called Seth in to translate, but Orrian shook her head. Apparently, what she had to say was for my ears alone.

I took a seat and read her minuscule writing.

This is not a good idea.

I laughed. "I know it's probably not the best one I've had."

She jotted again.

He can kill you both for this. Zephyr will die with you.

"I doubt he'll kill me. Punish me, jail me, peel the skin from my body, perhaps. And I honestly don't think he could kill Zephyr unless Zephyr let it happen."

She sighed and nodded. I waited for her to finish writing a rebuttal.

Whatever you do, do not provoke him once he's over the edge. I've seen him do terrible things for fewer reasons — things I fear him for. Do not needle him. I don't know what's going on, but it's not good. I don't have a good feeling.

"How bad could it be?"

Her eyes grew wide, and she clutched her chest.

Bad enough for me to fear for your life. He has killed those he loves. Why not you?

"Because he needs me," I answered.

No, Perdi, he doesn't. He wants you. There's a difference. He doesn't need you. And what happens when he doesn't want you anymore, either?

I groaned and dropped my head on my desk. I rolled my eyes at Orrian. "If he kills me, burn his house to the ground with him inside."

She smiled and nodded.

He's hiding something, and I fear he'll take it to both of your graves to keep it a secret.

"I know." I sighed. "Who the hell can force him to keep a secret?"

If someone can force Solas to do their bidding, do you really want to find out what else they can force him to do?

"Not particularly, no," I answered. "Just stay here this evening. I don't want you in the middle of this," I told her. She glanced up and grumbled. "I mean it, Orrian. I don't want to worry about you while I'm worrying about myself. If something happens, I'll choose to protect you and will suffer for it."

I finally stood and pulled my hair back with a white ribbon, matching my cream-colored dress and shoes. I looked as innocent as the days before Elphame, when I went to church, long before Elphame had turned me into a killer before I realized the Gods didn't care about any of us. Tonight, though, I would play the part I needed to, the parts Elswyth had taught me — the role, the mask that would keep me alive for as long as possible. And from the outside of Solas' life, I'd wait to see if he hanged himself with his lies or if he'd come clean to save us all. In the pit of my stomach, though, I feared he'd take his rope and use it on my neck instead of his own.

Eventually, with or without his help, I would gain my freedom, even if it was from six feet under. Death didn't scare me as much as life did. Life hurt over and over. Death, it happened, and by the time you noticed it, it was already done and gone. It's hard to regret death when you're dead. The dead have no regrets.

I waltzed with more confidence than I should have through the house. I paused in the hall outside the dining room. The air held familiar scents. Solene was either in the room with Solas, had just been here or was watching closely. Each outcome said I'd not be facing the man I loved. I'd be dancing to a tune controlled by someone else. I squared my shoulders. As Zephyr had said, it was time to face the music. As soon as I stepped into the dining room, I saw he was alone, and I was thankful. My appreciation died when Solas stood from the table. His wine tumbled over and drenched the tablecloth. His eyes cut through me, and he shook his head. It had taken the blink of my eye for him to move from the table to my front, his hand gripped around my arm like a vise. The speed of it shocked me, and I screamed. I wanted to vomit my pounding heart onto his feet.

"I'm sorry, Perdi, for how you'll learn that nothing is free. It's either me or her teaching that lesson. That was the only choice I could buy you. I can't protect you from her." His words whispered over my skin. "And I don't think you'd survive."

"I'd rather it be her."

"No. Neither of us can survive her. I'd rather you hate me than bury you," he replied. His hand gripped harder as he glanced around to an added pressure in the air.

"I can take it."

"I can't," he whispered. "I wish you had run."

The room filled with her scent as if she were standing beside me. I knew I'd pay for this in ways I never would have before her. Before I could steady myself, I felt the blistering heat of Solas' temper flood the room. Static filled every inch and ate up the air. I instantly regretted thinking that I could play court games and was arrogant as all hell to think I'd get away with it simply because Solas loves me. I had expected so many reactions, but this, him holding me in the middle of his rage, was not one of them. I had never experienced being in the center of his storm, and it was worse than I imagined.

"Where is it?" he demanded, and I said nothing. With each word, the room filled with his temper. When I said nothing, he repeated his question with a boom that cracked the very earth and marble at his feet. The room filled with guards, looking for a war that could only be found inside their king.

I smiled through the anger and fear. She would not take anything more from me. "I love you."

"Where is your pearl?" His face was inches from mine, his breath hot on my cheeks. His fingers dug into my arm, but I didn't cry out. It reminded me of how he used to haul me around in the Golden Court like a ragdoll, teaching me lessons I refused, even in the face of death. "How many times do I have to pay for your decisions before you understand that people live and die on what we do, what *you* do?"

"I gave it to Zephyr," I finally answered. My words came out rushed. I couldn't think of anything I could say with her ears this close. Everything I had prepared myself to answer was gone. My clever retorts vanished as soon as I realized my answers weren't safe.

"Leave us, now." Solas waved his men from the room. My eyes darted from them to Solas. "How did you think this would play out? Did you think there'd be no consequences? There is a cost for everything. I see everything, Perdi. There isn't a move you make that isn't seen." He pushed his mouth to my ear, and I cringed against the heat from his mouth. "If you're so ready to take what she can give, is this how you'll let her break you? Force you to become a dog to be kicked? A Crow to be caged? Find your courage before *she* digs it out of you, and you haven't a drop left. If you're not going to run, you better learn to fight. Do not show anyone, not even me, that you are weak. Fight or run. Those are the only choices in Elphame."

"You won't like the person I will become if you don't take your bloody hands off me. *Now*, Solas." I found my courage in the line I would draw in the sand. I'd never be Elphame's dog again. I would not let him or his cursed sister do this to me. There were a million deaths I'd sooner endure over allowing someone to own me in this way. I wasn't brave, but I wouldn't become a dog to kick after a bad day.

"Is that how I am to learn of your mighty power, oh great king of mine? Is this how you will punish the woman you are supposed to love? Are you really the monster you had claimed you weren't? Go ahead, do your worst, but I'll hate you until you squeeze the last breath from my chest. I will never forgive you for as long as I live, however short that obviously may be. Do it. It will be the last thing you do to me, and I pray my face haunts you until your death."

"Why would you do this? Why would you give your pearl to him?" Solas finally dropped his hand from my arm and shook his head. He glanced to the corner of the room behind my back. "Do you and he have plans I should know about?"

"No, Zephyr and I don't have plans. And this isn't about you, Solas. It's about me," I replied. His shoulders relaxed a little at my answer. I hadn't lied. Zephyr had no idea what I had planned. "I didn't think you'd care this much that I took matters into my own hands to ensure my safety. I didn't think you cared much about me at all, and I certainly didn't think you'd react this way. Angry, probably...but not this." I slowly dug my way back out of the hole I knowingly made. I went with the truth rather than a lie. Although with our anger with each other coating the walls like paint, I doubted anyone would be able to tell if I was telling the truth or not. "Someone will always know where I am. Someone will always be able to come for me. Someone will help me when I need it."

"Rest assured, your whereabouts are always known," he replied. "Why Zephyr? Why do you run to *him* whenever you have a problem but don't come to me?"

"Because he's the only one who gives a shit about me anymore. I'm scared, Solas, and that's the truth. I am scared that one day, I will need help, and you won't be there to help me. I want safety, but I won't trade my freedom for it. I won't feel like a prisoner. I wouldn't be one for the Golden Court, and I certainly won't be one for you."

"No, it's just... That was a pretty big decision you made, and you didn't even consult me." Solas closed his eyes and exhaled a shuddered breath.

I didn't bother hiding the shock on my face. "Consult you? Am I to ask you when I want to make decisions for myself? I need permission from you about my body? I need to ask you if I'm allowed to save myself? You've got to be kidding me."

"No, that's not what I meant." Solas grew frustrated and reached out to grasp my hand.

"You don't own me, Solas." I pulled it back. "No matter what you tell yourself, as long as my heart still beats, you will never own me. No one ever will again."

"You are in my court," Solas started, and I moved to walk away. I was done with his speeches. He stepped in my path. "We're not done here."

"Yes, we are. I've said it once. I've said it dozens of times. But you still don't hear me. I am *not* one of your subjects, I am *not* one of your servants, I am *not* your bloody possession." I stared him in the eyes. "You are not *my* king, Solas. You are *a* king of a court that is yours and *not* mine. You have made it abundantly clear this is *your* territory, not mine. This is *your* home, not mine. You are free to ask me questions, but you are not free to demand answers or terrorize them from me. If I cannot have that from you, you do not get it from me."

"Fair enough." He scowled. "Why did you go to the Court of Blood and Bones? There of all places? I am trying to keep you alive, and you march straight to death every chance you have," he asked, and my breath caught in my chest. "Did you think I wouldn't find out? Did you think you control all my court, as well as Zephyr? As you say, this is *my* court, these are *my* people, I am their king. Nothing happens here without me knowing."

"I didn't think I had to ask," I answered. "And I certainly don't believe I control anyone here—not Zephyr, not your people, and certainly not you, the very blight of this land."

He inched closer. The heat of our mixed anger licked against my bare legs. My eyes darted around the room for a way out. He could try to trap me, as so many have before—and failed. He could try to control me, but I'd burned down one court for freedom. I would burn another just as quick.

"You do not lead this court. I do." Solas' words were clipped and heated. "You do not come and go as you please and expect me not to have questions or want answers for your actions. The Court of Blood and Bones is off limits. That is absolute law. Your little gnome would have known this, but you went anyway. Why did you go there?"

His point would be made, whether I wanted to hear it or not. So, he would listen to mine just as clearly.

"Oh, please, let's be honest, Solas. You're not the one controlling this court. You have about as much power here as I do," I spat back at him. "You, like me, are a pawn in someone else's game. If you can't be honest with me, at least be honest with yourself before we *both* die for your lies. If you're going to go down in a ball of flames, I'm not going with you. You can burn alone this time."

"Don't, Perdi. You won't live through your next words." He glanced around the room and warned me with his eyes. I tried to step around him, but he moved with me. His guards stood in the hall behind Solas and blocked any escape I had. "You don't want to leave this room just yet. You're safer trapped in here with me."

My first instinct was to panic. Being trapped in any way was one of my worst fears. I closed my eyes and breathed through my need to run. I told myself to relax. I tried to convince myself that he wasn't the one who would kill me. But I was starting to have my doubts. I knew there was no talking to him any more than I could be reasoned with. I had to be the one to walk away. If I lost my temper, Solas would only leave if he was carried away, dead.

"I don't care if the gates of hell have spat out their worst into the hall beyond this room. You need to move out of my way. I'm angry, as are you, and trapping me in here will only make things worse." I spoke calmly, even though there was a fire burning within me. "You may be fine with being controlled by someone, but I'm not."

"I am *not* someone's puppet." He barked his words.

"Is that a soft spot for you? You keep telling yourself whatever you want. Whatever helps you sleep at night." I wanted to laugh, to say the words I knew would sting, to keep poking him. Instead, I breathed out a shaking breath and stopped myself before I pushed him too far. I swallowed my snarky remarks and focused on getting out of that room alive. "Solas, you need to understand one thing about me."

Something crawled behind his eyes, ate away at his calm and left behind only the rawest of rage. It was something we had in common, how quickly we angered and how it turned to utter fury with minimal provocation—him, because he was being controlled and me, because I never had the kind of control a Soul-Eater needed.

He crossed his arms. "Oh, and what's that, little Crow?"

I flinched when he called me a Crow. My hand connected with his cheek before I knew I had even swung. He hadn't ever used it to hurt me before. It cut me like a knife. His guards flinched from the same blow. "How dare you."

"I didn't... Perdi, I'm sorry." Solas closed the distance between us.

I smiled, and it wasn't friendly. I finally let the door open to my hurt. I had been carrying it around long enough. Whether someone else plucked his strings or not, he was the one foolish enough to be standing in the room with me, poking at a beast that would eat his soul in one gulp.

"I had thought I'd do anything to survive, since the only way you will protect me is if I let you control me, bend me, break me, own me. Whenever I'm near you, I regret living. I regret coming back. I regret not choosing death." Once I said the words, I felt the weight of my shame and regret and pain lift from my shoulders. "And that's what is eating me up inside. That is why I scream every night. Not just for what I did to survive but because I came back for you, and you never did. You begged me to stay and have only given me reasons why I shouldn't have."

"Don't say that," he whispered.

"You weren't helping me, so I helped myself. And this is how you respond? I need you to understand I will die before I let you do this to me again. You promised me that you'd protect me. You swore it. You're a liar, just like everyone else." I backed away from him to look him dead in the eyes. He needed to see the truth I spoke. "Move. Now, Solas. I've had enough. Truly, I am done. You need to get the hell out of my way now before you crawl out of this room."

"Please don't go out there," he said. He grabbed my arm to pull me to him, and I yanked back with as much force. I snarled in his face and shoved him, putting my anger and frustration into it.

His grip slipped as he slid across the floor, and I hit a small accent table, smashing a vase. He reached for me again but didn't catch me in time. I landed in the sharp mess, slicing my hands. Blood coated the floor. Each time I tried to stand, my hands slipped, and I went back down, cutting myself further. Solas stepped forward, and I screamed. My scream bubbled out of me before I had the chance to tell myself to calm down. The familiar rage that soaked the room panicked something deep inside me. I wasn't scared he'd hurt me. I was afraid I'd hurt him.

Once I was on the ground with him towering over me, I couldn't see beyond memories I'd never forget. I was back in the Golden Court, with my skin being belted from my body. The memory washed over me, and the more I fought it, the worse it got. I cried out in waves of pain that wouldn't stop. I couldn't make it stop. I was back at my Taking, and I screamed. I fought with the voice in the back of my mind that told me I could stop him, I could eat the lash before it touched me, I could eat all he was and there would be nothing left to harm me.

"Stop, Solas. This will not end well for you. I'm begging you, don't make me do this to you."

When he didn't back up, when his anger still floated on the surface, I screamed out at the Malice that finally broke free from my grip. It snaked through my body. It starved for vengeance. It, like me, wanted the pain to stop. It wouldn't suffer the lash again.

"Do it. This is the one way you win, Perdi. This is the cost of survival in Elphame. If you're not going to run, you're going to have to fight for your life. Fight, damn it! Get up and fight, or you're going to die here. Do you understand? I can't keep you alive."

My Malice howled its way up my throat and slid from my lips. It met the darkness that was Solas. His shadows, the very night sky, leaked from his fingertips and ate at the world around us.

"If you're not going to run, kill me. I've given you every reason to want for my death," he said. "It is the only way you'll survive what's coming next. Because not even I can stop it, and I'm the very nightmares of this goddamn world. You're so close. Let it out. Please, do it. You're the only one I'd die for."

Shadows burst into the room and surrounded me, forcing me to choke my Malice's desire back down. The pain was gone in an instant. Thick darkness blocked Solas from me. For the first time, Solas couldn't reach into the shadows as he once had. They stood between us, crackling and sparking to life, filling the room with echoes of mountains crumbling. I had never seen them angry.

"She may not be able to stop you, but I will fucking end you." Zephyr now stood in front of the shadows, blocking Solas. "Back away *now*."

"Since when do your shadows answer to her?" Solas asked. Behind his anger, I saw disappointment, as if he regretted not pushing me hard enough to kill him. It panicked an ancient voice inside, tucked deep within my need to survive. What would he do next that *would* make me kill him?

"They protect all this court. The fact that they came to stand against a king says a lot about what was going to happen had we not come," Zephyr answered. His voice was rough, as if he had screamed with me. "That I felt her fear from the other side of Elphame should tell you how scared she would need to be. Since the very day Perdi came, I've only felt her call this loudly once, when she was held between two men and lashed until her bones showed. But at this moment, I felt her fear, and it was so much more than her first night in Elphame. I can feel it now, as thick as mud."

"You were r-right to c-come." Solas stumbled on his words.

I stood and swallowed down my Malice, who was as disappointed as Solas that I hadn't killed him. The shadows let me pass but clung to me like my own flesh until I reached Zephyr. From the look on Solas' face, he was as surprised as I was that Zephyr had gotten between us. The shadows faded, leaving me and Solas, Zephyr in the middle. What a horrible place to be, between a rock and a hard place. Not even I wanted to be there, and I was the rock.

"You had no right to do this," Zephyr snarled at Solas. "She did this to stay alive, not to piss you off. And even if it did, she is a Crow in Elphame. Her very presence is a death sentence for her. She has the right to protect herself. For months we've been telling her that her life is in danger, that Fae are hunting her. Every bloody night she screams from her nightmares, and you do nothing to help ease her fear. So, she did something. You don't even go to her when she cries herself to sleep. It's *my* shadows that hold her. It's *me* that goes to her. And you wonder why I am the only one she turns to? I'm the only one that's ever there!" Zephyr's voice echoed through the room. "She's terrified and is trying to do what she can to survive. And you do *this*? She did it because you told her that she was standing on the edge of life and death. Don't you dare punish her for trying to save herself when you won't help her."

"It's all right, I'm okay. I was more scared of what I was going to do than of him," I mumbled.

"Like hell it's all right," he snapped. "Solas, if all you're going to do is abuse her, why the hell did you even bring her here? Why didn't you release her the moment she closed that cursed Gate? You took her and swore you'd keep her safe, yet you use her as a whipping boy the moment the pressure is on. Whatever war you're fighting in secret, you're taking it out on her. Whoever is pushing you, you're punishing her for it. You are no king. You are a weak man. There is no

145

place on the throne for men like you." He stepped forward and pushed his finger into Solas' chest to make his point clear. "I will *never* follow you if this is who you are when I'm not looking. You are not the man I thought you were, and I'll be dead and buried before you do this to her again." He poked him again, and Solas did nothing to stop it. "Touch her again, and I will leave your side for good. But know this... I will take Perdi with me. You will lose the only people in this goddamn land who will walk into hell for you. Are we clear on this? Do you understand where we stand? Say the words. Tell me you understand, because I won't have you beg for your life later when I take it from you."

"Yes, I understand." Solas finally answered. Solas ran his hands through his hair and freed a tightly held scream that was more of a growl. "I'm sorry. Perdi, you were right. It doesn't matter why. I shouldn't have touched you. I should have moved away and given you space. I shouldn't have trapped you." Solas started to reach for me again. One look from Zephyr, and he changed his mind. "I was angry, and you wouldn't answer me. I thought I deserved to have answers. I'm sorry."

"I did answer you, Solas. You just didn't like my answers. I was trying to tell you, but you scared the hell out of me and I froze. I didn't know what to say that wouldn't make things worse. I got trapped in my memories, and I just wanted to get away from you."

He nodded. "I know. I felt your fear. We *all* did."

I nodded and glanced around the room, swallowing any more truth than what I had given. Some things were better left unsaid. "I went to the Court of Blood and Bones with many questions I needed answers to, but I asked about Nix — to find out if he had any family left. I thought if anyone in this world deserved a second chance, it was Nix. I went there and asked if anyone was left in his line. She told me where they were. When we got back, I sent him home. Nix should be allowed his freedom to start over, to not have to live like this. I didn't want him here for any of this."

"Nix is gone?" Solas was surprised.

"I sent Nix home because it was the right thing to do. All of us deserve to find a home. It had nothing to do with going against you, as much as that would have felt good to do. It was about Nix and my love for him. I knew full well that I was not allowed to leave the Dark Courts, I was not allowed to go there, that it was off limits — and I went anyway. Nix told me it was off limits, we weren't allowed to go there, but I still went. I thought the answers I'd get would be worth the cost of going," I replied and felt my sadness for Nix well back up. "I didn't ask you because I knew you'd tell me the same thing you always tell me...not to leave your territory. It's not safe, nothing is safe and everyone wants me dead. I knew when you found out, you'd be angry. But you're always angry. I might as well do something to deserve it. And that is the truth. I had a hundred other questions, but that is what I asked."

"I'm sorry he's gone, Perdi. I should have been there after he left."

"Thank you."

"I'm sorry for all of this. I didn't want any of this for you," Solas whispered. His words caught in his throat. I half hoped he'd choke on them and save me the trouble of strangling the life from him. The other half of my heart wanted to strangle him because I loved him and wanted to shake some sense into him.

"Thank you, Zeph, for coming when I needed help."
I smiled.

"I will always come, little Crow." When he called me
a Crow, it didn't hurt.

I had nothing to say to Solas and left him standing
with Zephyr with my blood smeared on his cold marble
floor. In the hall, Solas' guards offered to walk me to
my bedroom. I didn't bother. It wasn't like they'd get
in the way of Solas or Solene. I listened to Zephyr and
Solas argue as I walked through the halls. Solas
demanded Zephyr not to meddle when it came to me,
and Zephyr told Solas to go to hell. Zephyr made it
clear it would take more armies than Solas had to keep
him from me. I wanted to smile because of it, but I felt
sad for him. He was torn between two worlds, and I
feared what would happen when those worlds
collided.

Inside my room, I sealed myself in tight. Orrian
helped me pick glass from my hands and arms. I didn't
need to understand her to know she was scolding me.
But she had been relieved when I had walked in my
bedroom door still standing. I had to admit to myself
that there had been several moments in the last hour
when I'd thought my life was over. Although my
Malice was breaching, I think it would have taken more
pain than that to push me to take his life and not just
defend myself. And I wondered what they meant for
my survival or his.

Until tonight, Elphame had forgotten who I was
before becoming a Crow...human. And if there's one
thing humans are, it's that we're spiteful and resilient
pests. Resilience was how we had survived the Fae,
year after year. They took our children. They took our
lives. But I'd die before they took anything more from

me. I would face my regret, my decision to live. I no longer had the option of living in my wounds. Tarnished soul and all, I had to climb out of them.

The shadows danced down my walls and blanketed me. I silently thanked them. For once, the darkness and I had agreed fully on something. If Elphame tried to take my freedom, I would take their lives. If they hurt me, I'd burn their world to ash. Deadly games, after all, came with deadly prizes.

"What is that ringing?" I whispered. "Can you hear that?"

"It is the horn of Elphame," the shadows answered.

"What is it, this horn?" I asked.

"It is Elphame, the soul, the wind, the magick of who we are. It comes from nowhere and everywhere. The first time the Gate opened, the horn sounded for all Fae. It was a warning. And, now, it has awoken once again. Someone has broken their oath, and it's a big enough oath for the Gods to notice."

"But no one else is hearing it," I answered.

"We only hear it because we're with you. The call is for you...but it's too late now."

"Too late for what?"

"Too late for whatever the warning was."

"Why?"

"We think you know that answer. Something is coming, and it's giving a chance for the oath breaker to correct their path before it makes decisions to restore balance."

"You say the call is for me, but why can't anyone else hear it?" I asked.

"The warning is for you. Those who broke the oath heard it first and did nothing to stop it. Now, it is for you, and it will only grow louder as your fate approaches."

"This is going to hurt, isn't it?"

"Everything in Elphame hurts, Perdi."

That night I didn't dream. Solas' screams from his bedroom kept me from my own dreams. I opened my door once to go check on him. Zephyr stood in the hall and pulled my door closed again. I didn't need to ask a Soul-Eater why he was guarding my door from the king. I slinked out onto my balcony and stared down the side of the house to Solas' bedroom.

"Is anyone else here?" I asked the shadows.

"Aside from who should be here, no," they replied.

"Let me know if it changes."

I gripped the wall as I inched across the house. Solas' bedroom was twenty feet from mine and mirrored it in every way. I lowered myself onto his balcony and slowly opened his door, to his surprise. I lifted my fingers to my lips and inched over to his bed. His darkness pushed the world out around us, sealing us off from those who wanted our secrets. I crawled up his bed from the foot and sat on his hips, drawing my king-killer blade and pressing it over his heart. He did nothing to protect himself.

"Two kings within a year. You'll beat my own record." He smiled.

"I planned to come and tell you if you touched me like that again, Solas, I will kill you. But I think you already know that." I pushed the blade a little harder, feeling the skin under the tip open. "If you think death at *her* hands will be bad, it'll never be as awful as falling before mine. I'll take you and your entire kingdom with me."

"Did you change your mind on the warning and skip straight to the death part?"

"No, nothing as simple as death for you. If I suffer, you better believe I'll keep you alive to suffer with me." I leaned forward. My lips were close enough for us to share our heat. "She may pull your strings, but she doesn't pull mine."

"She will." He breathed into my mouth.

My laughter bubbled up and spilled into him. "There is nothing she can dish out that I can't take or haven't already. Trust when I tell you, I can take it."

"I don't think you can — not even I can."

"But you're just a king, Solas, whereas I am a Crow. My purpose was to suffer in Elphame. And there's nothing I do better than suffer for this goddamn realm," I replied and pulled my face back to meet his eyes. "I still see you. She doesn't get to have what I died for."

I kissed him once and pulled back. He gripped my hand with the knife and reached around my back, flipping me onto his bed. He leaned as close as he could without piercing his heart. I released the knife and cupped his face.

"It will get worse, Perdi. This doesn't get better for you or me. I can't stop any of this. I can't protect you." His voice quivered as if an ocean of sadness was held back by sheer will.

"Protect yourself, Solas. I can protect myself." I sighed, feeling the weight of the decisions we were being forced to make. "I've taken worse from better."

"I'm sorry, Perdi. I'm so very sorry." He hung his head. "I pushed you as far as I could to make sure Zephyr would come for you, no matter what, against even me. When She comes, he will be the only one who can protect you."

His kiss was rough at first, starved, softening only to pull away and leave me missing him even more than I had ten minutes before. I picked up my knife and left out of the door I had come in, with him following. I pressed a note into his hand, and I left him standing on his balcony.

No one takes from a Finis and survives.
Nothing is free. She pays like anyone else would.
I'll burn her fucking court to the ground before she takes my family.
Let the games begin.
I love you.

I climbed back up onto the ledge between our rooms and shimmied back to my balcony. I stared at him across the darkness and watched his shoulders shake. He held my note against his chest and stared up at the sky as if sending a thank you to the Gods. He turned with glittering eyes and nodded. He mouthed his love back and wiped his eyes. We both stepped back without another word exchanged. I kept the doors closed and locked and slept with a knife. The shadows didn't leave, not even once. I should have been more scared than I was.

Chapter Nine

Inside the Gate, it looked as it should, as I remembered it. I stood in both worlds, here and there, dead and alive, light and dark. Each pulled and pushed against my mind, and neither wanted me to be on the cursed ground any more than the other. The white mist swirled around me, whipping my hair into my eyes. Behind me, beyond the shimmered wall, stood Elphame, a place I considered more cursed than the Gate. The last time I had stood before the Gate, I hadn't left with a beating heart. I stood in the very spot my life had been ripped from my willing arms. Flashbacks of my end assaulted my senses. I could taste my tears, hear myself cry out in the knowledge I was dying, and feel the pressure building in my lungs as my light faded from within. Rather than fight the grief of the memories, I let the pain roll through me and focused on what I could control, what was real, what I could now see and feel and smell.

Little specks of black soot, thick dust, circled in the wind around me. It hadn't been there before. The world inside the Gate was unlike Elphame or the mortal realms, yet, today, it was unlike the Gate had once been. The power was off, and the energy moved as if it were limping. It clawed but couldn't hold on to me. It reminded me of a tarnished soul belonging to a witch. Each time we practiced dark magick, we were left with a stain on our aura, our souls. Eventually, with enough darkness, we'd have to be hunted down and killed. It had been decades since a witch needed to be killed. The fear of it kept us all on the straight and narrow. But I'd be lying if I didn't admit how very tempting it would be to become a dark witch. Life would be so much easier without a soul.

I lifted my hand to inspect the powder in the air and rolled it between my fingers. "Rust?"

Ahead, the two trees that had once stood on either side of a single black Gate were dying. Its limbs sagged, and its small branches and leaves littered the ground at its base. The grass, once lush and green, was patchy and brown. The very earth I stood on was holding on to what little life it had left. The Gate, the very cursed object of my people, rusted and cracked, barely latched, was breaking. I watched bits of rust and metal catch in the wind and leave it weaker than moments before. Whatever was happening to the Gate would destroy it and leave my people for the birds to pick clean. I didn't try to close the Gate. I wasn't powerful enough for that. I was barely strong enough to do it the first time, and it cost me my life. But I was strong enough to pour bits of power into the cracks and damages to begin to heal what Solas had done. It would be enough to set him back, but it wouldn't be enough to stop him. It would take me decades to fix all the brokenness if all I did was little snips of power. For now, this would have to be enough.

Wrapped in shadows and magick, I left the Gate, a faint horn on my heels. I didn't go many places without hiding myself away from Solas' prying eyes. I was sick repeatedly on my way back to the manor. Fear, anger and confusion emptied my stomach and left only an acidic burn behind. If he questioned who had been at the Gate, he could have simply followed the vomit trail back to the manor.

As I walked by Solas' office, I caught the brush of magick against my skin like a ghost. I closed my eyes and pressed my hand against the wall. Inside, he was arguing with a woman. *The* woman—the one who had grown in her spite for me. His arguments were not uncommon, but it was who he argued with that was of interest. The same woman I had heard before, who I had heard many times since the closing of the Gate, was back with her anger. Although I couldn't make out every detail she was saying, I did hear my name off her lips several times, each time more heated than the last. For a split second, I wondered if Solas knew I was at the Gate and what I had done—or if he knew I had met with Faolan.

"Why was she there?" Solas asked her, and my heart skipped a beat.

"She asked about the family of Nix and if there were survivors," she answered.

"Why would she risk her life to get those answers?"

"She had many questions, Solas, but that is what she asked," she answered. "You will not purchase another favor to save her. It will be me, next time, punishing her insolence."

His anger flared, rattling the books on his shelves. "You won't touch her as long as I have a beating heart."

Solene's laughter made me hate her even more. "You have been sloppy with her, and soon she will learn the truth of all you are, and you will lose, as you always do."

"One of us is going to lose in the end, anyway. That is the way of Elphame. You've seen to that."

"You have two choices. Repair the hostilities between you both or kill her. Either way, fix what you have done before I must do it for you," she replied. "God, she even looks like the last one."

"Aoife—" Solas started.

"This Crow is just as weak," she interrupted him.

"No, Perdi is different."

"Are you sweet on this one?"

"Go to hell, Solene," Solas replied. "Why the hell do you hate her so much?"

"I have my reasons."

"She will be your death, and your hate blinds you from the risks." Solas' laughter curled under the door and rolled into the shadows. He knew I was standing there and had let me listen in.

"She will not be allowed to meddle with the Gate. If she does, I will kill her next time."

"You'll die with her," he answered.

She laughed. "Nowhere in Elphame is there enough power to kill me."

"But one day, there will be. I pray I'm still alive to see that day."

I bolted from the hall to my bedroom, horrified. Solene, the Seer, the sister of Solas, was the one who had come to him many times, who had argued for my death, was directing Solas on how to use me, how to bring down the Gate. My stomach, empty from my visit to the Gate, brought up nothing more than bitterness and anger and bile. Had it not been for what hung in the balance, I don't think I would have walked away from his office. And for the first time, I suspected I would not have been the one to die.

* * * *

The shadows had returned before dinner. They had followed Solas to the Gate and returned to tell me that Solas was perplexed at what he'd found. He inspected the repairs but did no more damage while there. They didn't know if Solas could tell it was me, but Solas wasn't a fool. I was the only one who could have done it. He'd either ask me about it or he wouldn't. I doubted he'd come right out and say it, or he'd have to admit to what he had done. But I would give him every opportunity to speak his truth…if for no other reason than to clear the air.

Before I stepped into the dining room, the shadows twisted against the entrance, blocking my path. I breathed in the smell of Blood and Bones, the faintest hint of Solene. The shadows moved once I nodded. That would be the only warning I'd have. To needle him with her near would hurt. I straightened my shoulders and prepared to play the game of life or death—because that's what I was playing for, keeps. Stepping into the room brought Solas' eyes up from his paperwork. He glanced around the room, and I nodded. His attention went back to his papers.

Between Solas and I sat Zephyr, caught between two hells, as usual. He stiffened when he saw my marked arms from my last argument with Solas. Zephyr said nothing, but his glare spoke loud enough. I made small talk with him while Solas sat, frustrated, at the other end of the table. Zephyr, awkwardly, sat to my right, his focus darted from one end of the table to the other.

"Zeph, why are you here for dinner?" I finally ended the small talk. I wondered if Zephyr had come simply because he thought I was in danger and he was oathed to help me or if he really did care.

"Am I not welcome at your table?" he asked. Although his eyes had danced between both ends of the table, his hurt was only for me to see.

"You're always welcome. It's just been a long time since you've come for any other reason than court business. I'm surprised, that's all."

"You seemed lonely," he answered. "How are you doing?"

I sighed. "That's a long conversation. Maybe it's best to be left for a different night."

"Have you heard from Nix?" he asked, changing the subject.

"No, not yet. I don't know how far of a journey he has, but I'm sure I'll hear from him as soon as he can get word back to me," I answered. I looked across the table at Solas. "Solas, you seem somewhere else. Is everything okay?"

"Yes, just court business," he answered, short and curt, his usual response.

"Of course. Is there anything I can do to help?" I asked.

"No. I'd rather you not get involved if I can help it," he replied.

"It's a little late for that, no?"

He shifted in his seat and shook his head. "Not yet."

"I'm sorry about the fire." I smiled.

Zephyr smelled the air. "What fire?"

Solas fought not to smile. "She hasn't set one."

"Yet," I replied. "But the day is young."

"This is an uncomfortable conversation," Zephyr chimed in.

"How's your training going?" Solas asked, changing the subject.

"What training? That pretty much stopped the moment I closed the Gate," I replied, and Zephyr's groan told me to stop poking the beast. I let out a frustrated breath. I didn't need to prod him to the point of needing a Soul-Eater to rescue me again. "I've only just restarted, but it's going well. Honestly, though, I may just take your advice and start a garden or maybe redecorate my bedroom before I burn it all to the ground."

"From hating yourself and all of Elphame to simply hating me... I'd say that's progress," he replied. "Are you planning to lock me inside when you set it to burn or warn me first?"

"I already apologized for the fire. If you want it penciled into your schedule, get a secretary."

"I'll keep that in mind." He smiled, his voice edged on a muffled laugh. "Both Zephyr and I think you should keep training. The Gate may need you again," Solas answered.

"Why would the Gate need me? It's closed, isn't it?" I asked.

"Just in case."

"Always the careful planner," I replied.

"Always."

"I'll think about it. But I think it's best to heed your advice, for once." I lifted my glass and saluted him. "I am, after all, just a Crow in a world of Fae who want me dead."

The edge of Solas' mouth jerked. "You…listen? How rare of an occasion."

"You've got my full attention now, Solas," I replied.

"Not all want you dead," Zephyr interrupted. "I don't."

"I'm glad for that." I smiled and looked at Solas. My words were purely for him. "Unfortunately, some do want to see me buried six feet under. And if I want to survive those who do, I need to stop lying to myself and depending on others to tell me the truth or I'll never survive this place. One day, very soon, if I'm not careful, I won't make it out of my own bed alive."

"A garden… Well, that sounds…nice." Zephyr tried to smooth out the uncomfortable wrinkles in the conversation. Zephyr was not as entertained with Solas and me baiting each other. He was stuck between the two deadliest places in all of Elphame — at one end of the table, his king and friend and at the other end, me, who he had a blood oath with. I wasn't sure yet if he thought of me as his friend or foe. Truthfully, when it came to Zephyr, both could be just as dangerous.

"Unless you don't think that's a good plan?" I asked. "I could go to the Dark Court and see if I'm needed there?"

"You're at risk, Perdi. I'd rather you not bring that to the doors of my people."

"Whatever you think is best, Solas," I replied. "My prison gets smaller and smaller each day. Soon, I'll be in a cell."

"The Dark Courts do not have prisons. We kill our enemies," Solas countered.

"Yet, here I am, being housed and fed, alive and well. You're getting sloppy in your old age."

He leaned back in his seat with his wine. "That's twice I've been told I'm getting sloppy."

"Don't you have some villagers to terrify or scheming to do?" I asked him.

"Likely, but you know I always make it home in time for dinner."

I listened to little clips of information from Zephyr and exchanges between Solas and him, but nothing was said of any importance. I smiled and nodded and agreed. When asked my opinion, I played the foolish Crow who knew nothing and left the table, left them to discuss court business. There was no reason to be there. As entertaining as it was to poke him, I grew tired of it just as quickly.

I spent the rest of my evening on my balcony, overlooking a land I had loved. I didn't hate it, but I didn't appreciate it as I once had. The games of kings and courts rubbed the beauty of the world away. I wondered what life was like before the Gate, before the wars and infighting. The snippets the shadows had given me while in the Golden Court showed me nothing more than Elphame being on the balance of war. Could there have ever been a time of peace?

I felt him before he spoke. Zephyr emerged from the shadows. "You can't have peace without war. There always was and always will be balance."

"Not here," I answered. "There is no balance within these walls."

"There is. Just because you can't see it or don't like it doesn't mean it's not there." His answer was very much Zephyr.

"And stop listening to my thoughts," I replied.

"I wouldn't hear them if they weren't screaming at me through your pearl."

"At least pretend you can't hear me. It's rude."

He nodded. "Why were you at the Gate today?"

"You always make the kind of entrance that rips off the band-aid—skin, scab and all. There's nothing all that subtle about a Soul-Eater." I smiled and offered him a glass of wine. He shook his head. "I was checking on it."

"Don't do this. For once, take some of my advice. I don't give it because I like the sound of my voice. I talk now to save you from hearing about it later when I'm dragging you out of whatever mess that mind of yours creates."

"Are you going to tell on me?" I asked. "I think I'm running out of places to bruise. Between training with you and Solas' temper, I'm fresh out of skin that isn't black and blue and a nasty combination of yellow and green."

"You know I'm not, given it would lead to Solas harming you. And as it turns out, I can't bring myself to do shit, directly or indirectly, if it ends in your suffering," Zephyr growled his words in anger. "You've put me in a position where I can't do my duty."

"I'm so sorry that I've interrupted your job of getting Crows tortured. Whatever will you do with your time?" I rolled my eyes at him. "After hundreds of years, Zeph, how could one Crow cause you so much distress?"

He stood and smiled, but it was more in warning than anything else. "Eventually, you will goad him to the point I won't protect you. I will save myself and leave you to figure the rest out on your own."

"No, you won't. You're built of better things than that," I replied.

"Sadly, for you, I'm not. There is no place in Elphame for better things."

"I disagree — or I'd already be dead."

"You're heading to that grave, fast. For someone who doesn't want to die, you're spending an awful lot of time poking a beast who has no control. You see him on the ledge, and you shove as hard as you can, then complain about the claw marks."

"I am not responsible for who Solas is becoming. I've done nothing to deserve any of this," I replied. "I have given him endless opportunities to talk to me, to share his burdens, but he's chosen to become a man who hangs out on the ledge, then snaps when he gets bumped. He is deciding this, not me. He chose this path and to be on it alone. Not me."

"You don't know what you're talking about."

I stood and moved to his front...angry, frustrated and tired of the games. I did not fear Zephyr, with or without an oath. If he had wanted me dead, I'd simply be dead. Whether I feared him or not, nothing would prolong my life when it came to him.

"You've said that before. But how could I know? No one talks to me. You don't even talk to me without endless riddles. I'm in the dark. I've been here for so long that I can't remember what the sun feels like. I twisted an oath with you, so Solas wouldn't kill me in my sleep." I tried to keep my voice down, to keep what we said a secret, but doubted very much that there was a place in this world where Solas or his sister didn't have ears. "If I stay here, I will die. You know this, and to say differently is a lie, and I'm so fucking sick of the lies. I will die, either by his hand or a hand that he won't or can't stop. And yet, you defend him. *You*, Zephyr, have no idea what *you're* talking about. You have no idea who he is anymore. But I do. I know more than I should, and to get the rest of the truth, to save us *all* from what he's hiding, including him, I will become everything I've fought hard never to be, someone I've always feared."

"And what's that, little Crow?" he asked.

"My wings may be tattered, but this Crow will become someone neither he nor I will ever love again," I answered. "Now, if you're not here to help me, fuck off."

Before he left, I saw his smile—his first genuine smile in so long. It made me nervous.

Chapter Ten

I felt Solas' eyes on me every day. They felt like they added an invisible weight that I lugged around on my shoulders. A week passed, and he watched me like I was made of precious jewels or toxic waste. I don't think he knew which one I was. I didn't mind. If he was too busy watching me, he was too busy to destroy the Gate. When I didn't see Solas, I saw Zephyr. He, like Solas, didn't trust that I wouldn't be lighting fires. Both had different reasons to worry. I didn't blame either of them. I wasn't exactly trustworthy anymore. It was almost amusing in some perverse way, where I had ended up and with whom. The three of us, the deadliest in Elphame and also the least trustworthy, were all stuck within the same walls, each holding secrets that could take the life of the other. We held unbelievable amounts of power, yet neither of us could save the other without risking the third. We were stronger together, but each other's greatest weaknesses.

Rather than worry about their prying eyes, I planned my garden and dug them six feet deep, a statement for Solas to see. It was not lost on him. He watched from his balcony as I measured out a plot exactly his size. I planted flowers, all toxic and deadly, just as I planned how I would bring him to his knees if forced to. Sure, the destruction of the Dark Courts would be equally as satisfying, but Solas was the one who needed to be stopped. To not stop him meant my people would die. It wasn't a difficult decision to make. Solas plotted and schemed behind closed doors, and each time he stepped into his office, he brought my people one day closer to death.

I could forgive the calculating and conniving ways that were who Solas was. I could even forgive his plot to bring me to his court. He had made no promises to me before he had offered me his hand in that cave and safety within his land. But what he had done once I got here, once I accepted his protection and gave him my love, I couldn't forgive. What burned me, what truly shook me to my core, was that the man I loved would be the one who brought the entirety of Elphame to the door of the mortal world. Sure, it may not be his choice, but he'd still be the one knocking on the doors of Whitwick.

"Your garden is looking" — Solas stood close enough for me to feel the heat from his body. I turned with a smile to see his face twisted into discomfort — "really, interesting."

"I'd like to plan a party once this is finished." I turned back to my flowers. "You've not yet held a ball, and I think it would be nice. I would rather enjoy, very much, for your people to see just how far you've fallen, oh great king of ours."

"Spite is a good color on you," he answered.

"Do you think so? Personally, I think it clashes with your deceit," I replied.

"Maybe it's something we ate."

"I don't recall ordering the life on the run until I die."

"We never really do get what we want, do we?" He smirked. "And for someone who is running for their life, you seem mighty content with standing around planting a garden."

"It has come to my attention that I learn the hard way in all things," I answered and finally turned to face him. "Out of curiosity, how far do you think I could run before you caught me?"

"You'd never get out of the yard unless I willed it so," he answered. "I've already told you once, you could never run fast enough or far enough."

"Right, the day you stole me into these cursed lands," I replied. "I'll make sure to break your legs before I leave."

"That'll give you a few minutes head start, from me, but not from those who haunt the sky."

"Good to know," I answered. "So, the ball?"

"A ball? I thought you'd be done with those."

I flinched at his words, the memories of the Golden Court, and I wondered if he had said it on purpose. "Apparently not."

"I'm sorry," he said quickly and almost looked like he regretted the words.

"We can't really cut each other up unless one of us is left bleeding. How would others know who has won without the blood trail to prove it?" I turned back to him with a pleasant smile and let it go. "A ball would be nice to replace the memories. I don't want something unless I can think back on it with fondness."

"To look back on?" he asked. "And when will you need to do that?"

I shrugged casually. "We all need something good to think of when the rest of life is hell. Wouldn't you agree? I'd like to see everyone at least once more."

"Once more? Are you planning a trip?" he asked.

"Before I'm dead." My words came out flat and lifeless.

"Very well, I'll send word." He reached out and, for the first time in a long time, I didn't pull away, but it took a world of effort on my part. He squeezed my hand, and I watched him relax. "I wish things were the way they used to be between us."

"Things aren't this way because I willed them to be. You did this with your lies and secrets, not me," I replied. "This place is no different than the Golden Court. Your dungeon just smells better."

"The Dark Court doesn't have dungeons," he reminded me.

"So you've said."

"I'm worried."

"And I'm a prisoner." I pulled my hand from him and hugged myself, because I knew he wouldn't.

"Perdi, you're making choices that could kill you. More than that, they could kill my people. I'm asking you honestly, how would you respond? How would you keep your people safe?"

I stopped my planning and scheming and thought for a moment. Instead of needling him, I gave him honesty. "I'm supposed to be one of your people, too. I'm supposed to be as important as everyone else you're protecting. You could have simply talked to me. You could have asked me, instead of ordering me about. You could have told me the truth instead of weaving so many lies that they cast a shadow over everything you say. You could have given me a chance to help rather than resent you."

"You resent me?"

I nodded. "In ways you couldn't imagine. This, what we're doing right now, leaves a bitter taste in my mouth. You stopped caring about me in any way that doesn't hurt. How could I not resent that? I understand some things are not within your control, but slowly killing me is no different than taking my life this instant."

"Let's try this again. Remain in my territory. I can't budge on that one. I've spoken to Zephyr about this. If you'd like to leave, please take Zephyr with you, if not me. He will let me know if you're in danger or have ventured out of the Dark Courts," Solas explained. "And when it is safe, you can go to the villages and offer your aid to the people."

"And when will that be?"

"When Zephyr tells you that it is safe. You don't trust me to tell you, so I've tasked him with it," he answered. "I know you feel like I'm keeping you here, trapped. But since he has your pearl, he has agreed to be responsible for your safety. It is a big thing for a Soul-Eater to carry the pearl of someone still alive. Until that pearl is used or returned, you and he have a bond. I'd be lying if I didn't say I wasn't jealous the moment I felt your pearl gone, that you would have something with someone else that I couldn't have."

"You did. You once had every piece of my soul. You chose to return it. You chose this, not me," I answered. He could have delivered the world to me on a silver platter, and it wouldn't matter. He was too powerless now to give me anything more than empty promises.

"I'm sorry. One day I hope you'll look back and know I didn't do any of this to hurt you. I hope you'll see I had no choice, and this was the only way I could protect you. Everything, good and bad, was done to keep you alive. You truly have no idea how deeply I love you and how utterly ruthless I will be to protect you."

"We still have that in common, at least. We're both willing to be utterly ruthless to protect me," I replied, pushed a smile to my face and ignored the rest of the same story he had given me before. "I'll do as you say until I can't."

"I have court business this afternoon. Meet me for dinner?" he asked.

"Of course. I've nowhere else to be," I answered. "Anything else?"

He squeezed my hand before he stepped away from me. "Your garden, Perdi... It's very dark and morose."

"It's not done. There are some little flowers in the trees beyond the manor that I'd like to bring in."

"I thought for sure you were going to say you were missing bodies." He smiled.

"That's in the far garden. Who puts bodies under their bedroom windows?" I smiled in return. "That's so...Golden Court."

"Perdi, your protection is not a waste of time. It never was and never will be."

"Although I agree, this is a waste of time for them. If we're still not safe, they should be hunting down those who meant to bring harm, not watching me garden," I replied. "Solas, I don't want to tell you how you should run your court, but if I may be so bold as to suggest something?"

"I'm listening."

"I will keep Orrian at my side while I am out. She and her people can protect me until you and Zephyr get to me – and probably a lot better than your guards. Zephyr will feel me, and you can come at a moment's notice." I sighed and tried not to make demands. "The trees are filled with Seth and his people. Nothing will get to me without a full-on war starting. I doubt very much that kind of commotion would go unnoticed. And as I've already promised, the first sign of danger and I will run to safety."

"So, you've agreed," he replied. "Yet, here you are, not running. The danger is over your head, blinding you from what's right in front of you."

"Oh, I see the danger, perfectly clear," I replied. "Let's be honest for a moment, at least once. If someone comes and makes it all the way into your territory – through you, Zephyr, his shadows, the Sluagh, the Aos Si, the guard, gargoyles, Orrian and the creatures I've yet to meet, it won't matter who is standing with me. I'll be dead, and this conversation will be our last," I answered. "Even if I'm alone, you and I both know unless I want to be taken, I will do more damage than any of your guards."

"I'd be careful with that truth before someone you don't want to know hears it all," he warned me. He thought on it for a moment, then nodded. "I will take that deal on one condition."

"Which is?"

He leaned into my ear. "You either learn to fight harder or learn to run faster."

I smiled for the world to see. "I'm ready for both."

"If you're not careful, the choice of what to do next will be made for you. You do not want to be forced into war. You will have no advantage at that point. Always make the first move and be five steps ahead — or you're six feet under." He pulled back and squeezed my hand.

"I'll keep that in mind."

One chaste kiss, and he was gone. Orrian fluttered out of the manor in a huff as if Solas had commanded her to take up a post at my side. She lounged on a rock as I planted. Slowly, over the course of the afternoon, the guards disappeared from sight. But one look from Orrian told me they weren't that far from me. It was an illusion, like everything else about Elphame. On the outside, Elphame had been a temptation to every mortal. But on the inside, it curdled like rotting milk and poisoned whoever drank it down. I wanted to be mad about it, but there were so many things to be angry about that his guards didn't make it to the top one-hundred list. Under the anger was understanding. If he really thought my life was at risk, nothing short of his death would keep his watchful eye from my back.

That night, before dinner, my sickness returned, and I clutched my toilet as if it were my lifeline. Solas' court business was nothing more than a return to the Gate. I could feel it. My suspicions were confirmed by the shadows, who rolled around me as I vomited until I shook, and I screamed into the toilet. I heaved until there weren't even tears left to come out. When I was done and truly empty, I curled on my side and pressed my face into the cold tiles. My hair was matted to my face, and my lips were swollen from biting down as I tried not to scream. My bones rattled against the floor as the final tremors left my body. I tried to block out the constant hum from a horn I couldn't see but could never seem to get away from.

"Stop fighting the waves of tainted power. Every time he touches the Gate, the energy lashes out, and it hits you with such force, it's going to kill you." The shadows danced around me, jerking in worry. "Instead, accept the power, drink it down. Perhaps it is the fight that is making you ill."

"I've tried. There's too much of it." I groaned and pressed my cheek into the cool floor tiles. "I'm going to die here, on the bathroom floor, before I even have the chance to save myself."

"No. You're going to die here because you don't think of other ways to save yourself."

I finally pulled myself to the sink. "Has anyone ever told you, you have poor bedside manners?"

"We're dead. We don't care."

"I should think I won't either when I'm finally dead."

"You'll find that out soon if you don't stop this charade with Solas and actually fight for your life. You left the fight at the Gate when you died. Even we can feel parts of you missing, and it feels awful."

"I don't like the choices that are left."

"They're still the only ones you have. If you don't choose, others will choose for you. I fear you will not like those outcomes any better."

"I know, all right? I know all of this." I groaned as the last wave of nausea rolled out of me. "I already know what I have to do, and I'm going to do it."

I washed my mouth out and cleaned the vomit from my hair. I stared at myself in the mirror and didn't like who I saw staring back. My eyes were bloodshot, and my skin was pale and red, all at once. My once-vibrant red hair was washed out into copper, stringy and fell like tossed hay. I looked scared and weak. I looked sick. I had lost weight from the constant sickness and not being able to keep down food. I couldn't survive on grief and anger. I saw a shadow of who I had become at the Golden Court—frail, scared, alone, broken. I wanted to smash my mirror and every hint of broken Crow that looked back.

I dressed and mentally prepared myself for dinner with Solas. The walk from my bedroom, down the stairs and through the halls felt like it had aged me. I sat across the table from him and spoke nothing of my illness. Pale as a ghost, he asked no questions either. He flipped through his paperwork and said nothing. Even I could still smell the vomit on my skin, the sticky sweat that clung to my body after spending hours on the floor in the bathroom. My stomach twisted, and my Malice reached across the table for him. She wanted to rip his mind apart and puke his truths onto the table for me. It would have been easier than playing the silly, yet deadly, games of the courts.

"You know, in some customs, that would be considered rude." Solas looked up, and my Malice slinked back. "You don't want in there, Perdi, trust me. My mind is not a place for little Crows."

"Who said sitting around in your head is what I had planned on doing while I was in there?" I asked.

"There is nothing you could do in there that hasn't been done one thousand times over." He leaned back and opened his arms. "Do your worst. But I warn you, once you're in there, you'll not like what you see or what you'll have to do to get back out. If you think you can swallow the memories I have, allow me to give you a tour."

"Aren't you tired of these games?" I asked. "I am."

"For your sake, I hope you're not. We've only just begun."

I held a butterknife in my hand and remembered the day I'd stabbed him. I dropped the knife on the table and stood. When I had stabbed him in the Golden Court, he had healed before my eyes. If I wasn't ready to kill him, stabbing him was a waste of energy I didn't have. "The next time I stab you, I'll be sure to use iron."

"I'm sure you will," he answered. "I'd expect nothing less from you."

"I expected *more* from you, though," I replied.

"Everyone expects more from me. Get in line. Although, you'll not enjoy the company as you wait your turn."

"Smug bastard." I glared.

"Smug, I am. A bastard, my mother would disagree."

Instead of marching from the room, as every fiber of my being had told me to, I stood inches from his front with curled fists. I stared into his eyes and dropped every pretense I had. I let him see the fire in my soul, the rage I carried on broken wings. I pulled on the shadows, and Zephyr let them come. They curled around my feet and inched up his legs. Solas didn't flinch. He didn't so much as bat an eye. His grin said he didn't fear me. And if he did, he simply didn't care. I pulled them as tightly as I could around us both, pushing preying eyes and ears away from us.

"We've tried doing this your way, but your way will kill us both," I said, my voice calm and even, but under the calm was rage I was holding down with a death grip. "The next time, *Soulless*, you come to me, you come with the truth, my death or my freedom. Those are the only options left for you."

"You're not in the position to make demands, little…"

"It is *you*, little King, who is not in the position to make demands. I have eaten all the lies I can possibly swallow. This hellhole you've trapped *us* in, I'm done with it. I want the truth, or I want freedom. I don't care if your version of freedom comes with a hole dug for me alone. I've had enough of the games. Just dig the goddamn hole already." I pushed my Malice into his chest and grabbed his heart as though it were in the palm of my very hand. "Don't. Push. Me. I won't die in your hell alone. I won't die for this goddamn place again."

"Do it," he finally whispered. "You're so close. Please, just do it. You're the only one who will. You're the only one who loves me enough to end it — the only one worth dying for."

I released my hold on his heart and pulled back. "If I suffer, so do you. But rest assured, I'm looking for places to burn on my way out of the door."

"Good night, little Crow," he called out to me as I walked away.

"Go to hell," I called back.

"I never left hell to begin with. I can't. I stayed here for you."

Chapter Eleven

The horn blasted through my bedroom and yanked sleep from my wishful hands. The walls shook, and I jumped out of bed. The shouting in the air rumbled the very foundation of the manor. Temper rented the air and ate the calm in my gut. If rage could be seen, it would be reaching over the room and strangling the life from me. Anger rolled through across the floor like mist, and the moment its blistered touch licked me, it was sucked back, and the air popped. Someone had snapped magick around the heated words, and it smelled of Solas.

Orrian stood at the door and waited for me to open it. I was already dressed to run, should I have no choice tonight. The shadows were ready and wrapped tightly around us both as we slinked down the stairs and stood by the door to Solas' office. The guards were gone. I knew who was behind the door by that very fact. They only left when Solene was present.

I closed my eyes and listened intently. The heat that poured from under the door did not belong to Solene. It was as if her heart beat so steadily, filled with her own versions of truths, that temper didn't come for her, ever. But I could feel her power, and it rivaled Solas'. If he was pure power, she was the fountain it came from.

"War is the way of doing things, Solas. You have known this since the day you stopped suckling from mother's tit," Solene argued with him.

Solas, who lived and breathed his fiery temper, had been pushed to the edge of flames. "Why must you come here and bicker? I'm doing what you demand of me. I am doing as I'm oathed to do. I am fixing the Gate, nothing more."

"The Gate is in your territory for a reason. You were oathed to maintain that Gate, and now, you are cursed to fix it."

"As I told you before we closed it, it doesn't have to be this way, Solene. It never has. How many more mortals need to die for you to let the fucking thing go?"

"No!" She screamed at him, rumbling the walls with her anger. "The Gate stands, and you will fix it—or I will take everything you love and destroy it."

"Perdi will do everything she can to stop this from happening. You're a fool if you think you can control her."

Solene's laughter turned my stomach. "That Crow will be your end."

"Is that what you see? Because I'd welcome it to be done with you, to be done with these games."

"No. That is what I feel. I cannot see your path or my own. We never see the fates of our own—and mine is tied too closely with yours to see anything beyond your rage."

Solas' laughter came out strangled. There was something in that laugh, a pain behind it that made my stomach clench. "You care about only yourself, which is why you see nothing."

"A war is coming, Solas. You must be prepared. Instead, you are planning parties?"

"If you won't let me love her, I'll do everything I can to fix her," he countered. "Besides, you are the one who told me to fix things with her. What did you think would happen when I gave her back her freedom?"

"I told you to fix it, not uncage the blasted Crow."

"A caged animal knows nothing more than the thirst for freedom. It only bites and attacks, Solene. I, for one, do not want to be on the receiving end of her attack, and neither should you. I think you've bitten off more than you can chew, and she's going to watch you choke on it. I may not be able to stop you, but no one controls her, and no one controls Zephyr. Mark my words, Solene. She will be the death of you, and Zephyr will be at her side. For once, heed my warning. If you don't, you'll lose everything."

She laughed. "No, Solas. The Crow will try, and she will die for it. And Zephyr wouldn't dare stand against me. He will taste his own death."

"For a Seer, you're certainly blind."

"I see war. It will be at your doorstep in a manner of weeks, and she will stand in the middle of the battlefield. If you can't be sure she will be on your side of the fight, then she is my enemy."

"There is a resolve in her that wasn't there before, Solene. She has always been and always will be the only mercy shown in these lands. Perdi will always sacrifice herself for those who are weaker."

"You're not weaker than she is," she said.

"My soul is."

"You sold your soul long ago, Solas, and now I've come to collect. You have one week—after which, I will take over."

"Then what, Solene? Once she's dead, what power do you have then?" he asked.

"*We* don't need her alive. *You* do. If you can't bring her to heel, she's nothing more than a distraction that I can't afford. The Taking of Crows is not over. If she gets in my way again, I'll kill her before you see her hit the ground."

"You'll need to kill me first," he answered.

"So be it. You are my brother, and I will mourn your passing."

"I will not mourn yours, and I doubt very much anyone else will, either," he answered.

I slinked back to my room, angry. I knew my anger was nothing more than a shield from pain, but that knowledge didn't stop the burn. I had been a pawn since the day I was born, but this somehow felt worse. I felt like the animal Solas had called me—cornered, alone, desperate, all over again. It didn't matter that I had died for this place. It didn't matter that I had fought tooth and nail. It was all for nothing. The Gate would remain open no matter what I did to keep it closed. It wasn't so much a matter of how to close it but what to do once it was open again.

"I think this is going to blow up in my face, and it's too late to do anything about it," I whispered to the darkness wrapped around me as I crawled onto my bed.

Orrian, inside the shadows with me, stirred. "Then it blows up in their face, too."

I jerked. "Orrian?" At least she wasn't shrieking this time, so I could mostly understand her.

She stood on my knees and smiled a toothy grin that made me turn my face from her. "The shadows dull the world. They calm the chaos around you, including me."

"If it blows up for Solas, too, what does that mean for his people?" I asked.

"You cannot worry about them, Perdi. They will fare as all of Elphame has, again and again. Tides change. Rulers come and go. Courts rise and fall. It is the way of this world, as well as the mortal world. But you are responsible for yourself, no one else," she answered. Her voice was still high-pitched but blunted just enough for me to make out her words. "You need to leave before you have no choices left."

"What will happen to your people?" I asked.

"We will leave with you."

"Why? Why would you leave him?"

"I have known Solas and his line since before he was born. I had once believed in Solas, his want to close the Gate. Although I still believe he didn't want it open, he was also not able to stop it. He cannot fight against his sister and win. She is too powerful for him to stop her. Until now, I hadn't known there was a plan to break the Gate or to invade." Her shoulders sagged. "I played a role in that, Perdi. I helped get you here, thinking I was doing the right thing. I thought it was worth it to close the Gate. I would have done anything for that to happen, but now, looking at the cost, I wish I could take it back. I was wrong and will not play a part in the rest of his story. I won't watch as he becomes everything he's fought not to be."

The shadows rolled around us and spoke. "Solene will kill you, Perdi, if she thinks she can't control you, if you anger her or if you get in her way. I don't think Solas will save you. I don't think he can. He will allow your death. You must know that."

"Then we all die together," I answered.

"She cannot simply be killed or Solas would have done so," the shadows replied. "He would not have allowed anyone to control him, not without a reason. And his reason, unfortunately, is that he has no choice."

"In the Golden Court, you found your way out. Now, you must do it again," Orrian added. "If you want to save yourself, Elphame, mortals, Solas, you must search for the truth. You must find a way to stop her. If not, you still must leave or you will die."

I nodded. I wanted to burn the place to the ground but knew I'd be setting a fire with me locked inside. The pressure in my chest was a tangled knot, and nothing I could do would release it. All my planning, my starvation for vengeance, was about to explode and take me with it. I had to do better or I'd be dead, and the mortal world would follow. I either had to become who Solene had demanded or leave before they realized I'd never be that person. The harder I thought about it, the louder the background noise became.

She left me to toss and turn. I stirred in bed until I couldn't take it. My thoughts wouldn't shut down, and my anxiety raced in my chest like wine-drunk butterflies. The panic of my death at his hands clung to every shaking breath I took. I climbed back out of bed and went down the stairs to the kitchen to eat my unease away. I didn't know how many more meals I'd have before I was either dead or running from the man who would kill me. Maybe I'd eat enough to get a sugar sickness and could deep sleep myself into a new life.

"Can't sleep?" Solas called from the doorway.

I jumped and yelped at once. The cookies that filled my hands soared through the air in his direction. I moved quickly to put space between us. He caught one and laughed as he took a bite. I stared across the room at him. The last time I had seen him, I'd threatened him, and now I wondered what his plans were with me. As if reading my fear, his face dropped a little. I reminded myself that he could have killed me a dozen different times with less effort than scaring me in the kitchen.

"Solas, you scared the hell out of me." I rubbed the center of my chest. My heart pounded against my palm. "No, I couldn't sleep."

He picked the cookies off the floor and set them on the counter. "Want to talk about it?"

I started to laugh. "Really? You want to talk now? The last time we spoke, we didn't exactly see eye to eye."

He nodded. "Humor me, just for tonight."

My instincts told me to leave, to hide, to run from him, but I forced myself to stay. I couldn't run fast enough to get away, anyway. "Very well. What would you like to talk about?"

"Anything, Perdi. I just want to hear your voice."

"I don't even know what to talk about that doesn't end with us hurting each other."

"You said to come to you with truth or freedom, so here I am."

"Which one will it be, Solas?" I asked. "Truth, freedom or my death?"

"Fair question. Truth. What has you up so late?"

"Neither of us really sleeps anymore. We're either up conspiring or quaking this house to pieces with our nightmares." I thought about talking in circles, as we usually did. Instead, I'd try for a little bit of truth. "I can't shake this feeling inside."

"What feeling?"

I took my hand off my chest and placed it on his. I still remember the days when I wanted to be near him before a wall crashed down between us and I couldn't reach him anymore. "That we won't ever go back to the way it was. That we're stuck between decisions neither of us wants to make. Like we're back to the games of the Golden Court, trying to keep our heads above water."

He nodded and leaned into the counter beside me. He pulled my hand to his lips and breathed me in. He placed one kiss on my knuckles and dropped it away as if it were the last one he'd give to me. "I have the same feeling."

"How can I fix it?" I asked. "Tell me how I fix what's happening. We can keep cutting each other up, or you can tell me how I can help."

"Do you even want to fix it? Even if the cost is greater than either of us would ever pay?" he asked, then turned his face to me. I felt Solas' dark magick slide into place around the kitchen and pull tightly around us. It felt like standing at the end of a very long tunnel that had fallen in on itself. The world around us slid away, leaving just us in the kitchen and any prying ears on the other side.

My eyebrows rose. "I thought you killed your enemies? Who could possibly have their ear so close you'd want to block them out?"

"You know who. I've made sure you would know. Every time Solene comes, I've made sure my anger woke you from your sleep. It was the only way I could tell you without breaking my oath to her," he answered. "All truth here, Perdi. No more lies or tiptoeing around truths. No one will hear us in here. Just talk to me as a person. For once in a very long time, talk to me as you once did. Your truth is the only truth I ever hear now, as much as you use it to cut me up with. Trust there are answers I'm not free to give, but I'll do my best."

I huffed a small laugh. "Easier said than done. When I talk to you as a person and not as the king you've demanded, you lose your temper and I pay. I don't care for the reasons why, not when you're the one doing the cutting. Do I really want to wake up in the morning to see this carefully won freedom gone because I've made you angry again?"

"And when I talk to you, and you don't like what you hear, let's just say I have some pretty bad heartburn this evening."

I couldn't help but laugh. "Should I say sorry?"

"Only if you are, but sorry is not what I feel from you," he answered. "I give you my word, truth between us without punishment. But that must go both ways. Don't slice me up because you don't like what you hear."

"Very well. Some days I don't want to fix things. Sometimes I feel so utterly alone that I wish I wasn't here. It gets so bad that death seems like the only break I'd get from this nightmare. You say I'm in danger, yet the only danger I ever feel comes from you. I tell myself, you have a good reason. You'd never just arbitrarily hurt me. And even as I learn of those reasons, it still hurts," I answered. "But then I see you when you don't know I'm looking, and you're the man I love more than life. Once I remember who you were and what we were, I want nothing more than to go back to that.

Every night, I still crave the person you want to be, not the man you're forced to be."

"Forced... How perceptive of you," he answered. "I never forgot about you. But I wasn't the only one who didn't. When you closed the Gate, it opened up an entirely new problem, one I didn't foresee. I've tried every which way I can to protect you, to show you that you're not safe — and to ask you to do what needs to be done puts you at great risk if you fail."

"I'm not safe *here*, is what you mean. And my life is *already* at risk. The lies are the only thing making my risk grow," I added. "I know, whether you say the words or not, *she* is at work here, and neither of us has control over her. I'd be lying if I didn't say that it pisses me off that we have to let it play out and pick up the pieces once it's over. *If*, and that's a big if, there are pieces left to salvage." My answer stung both of us, but the truth often does. "I'm fighting with someone you're forced to be, and I don't think I'll win. And you're fighting something and someone I can't see, and you won't ask me for help."

"You will not like the help I'll need or what will need to be done to win. I'm supposed to protect you from the monsters, not turn you into one," he answered, then changed the subject. He either couldn't ask for help or didn't want it. "What about Whitwick? Would you go back there if you could?"

"I wish I could lie and say no, that I want to stay here with you. At one time, I couldn't ever see myself willingly leave here, leave you. But now? The truth is, I'd like to go back. I'd like to have the life I once had, to be the woman I was supposed to be. But I wouldn't want to risk my people any more than you want to risk yours for that to be possible. Whitwick is at the mercy of Elphame, and I know, I *really* know, Solas, how close to peril they are. I've seen it with my own eyes."

He nodded. "I'm sorry, but the Gate is not one of the things I can freely discuss."

I shifted the conversation. There was no point asking him if he was harming the Gate. I had watched him do it. "I don't have time to worry about things that have already happened. But when this is all said and done, and I've crawled back out of hell, *again*, because of the games you all play, I'll have a great deal more to say on the matter."

"I'm happy to see you've found your wings again, little Crow." He paused and thought about his next words as if he were weighing each one carefully. "If you could warn your people, would you?"

"Wouldn't that break the oath?" I asked. "If I left, the entire mortal realm would fall."

"You're already called an oath breaker for killing King Aelfdene. Since it was not your oath, there are only threats right now. That is what I've been dealing with—the arguments, the infighting, the threats to hang you, Fae trying to find a way to invade the mortal realm." Solas' explanation made me squirm. I knew it wasn't all the truth, but it was more than I had gotten out of him in months. "You can't be accused of breaking the same oath twice, Perdi. If you were careful enough, conniving enough, you could protect them all, and the oath wouldn't mean a damn thing. Oaths can be worked around if you're brave enough to try. If you're brave enough to do what needs to be done."

"Are you brave enough to work around yours?"

"I'm standing here, aren't I?" he replied.

"What would you do, Solas, if you were me?"

"If I were you, I would warn my people — but only if you could get back before anyone knew you left, or you would sentence all mortals to the whim of Fae."

"But you would know. The Gate is on your land."

He shrugged. "I'm a busy man. I can't always watch the Gate."

"You see everything, Solas."

"Yes, I do see everything little thing you do, Perdi, even when you don't feel me nearby. Winter is a smell one doesn't soon forget." He tapped his nose, and I cringed. I didn't dare ask questions about what he had seen me do or heard me say, because I already knew the answer. When my pulse skipped enough beats for me to stagger, the air cooled and pushed the kind of calmness I had been used to when standing this close to Solas wasn't like standing near villages being burned to the ground.

"Was it Orrian that told?" I finally asked.

His laugh made me smile. It was everything I remembered it to be. "As if she'd sell you out, and I'm not stupid enough to ask her. She is no longer mine. She is yours, and she's more loyal than my threats could ever be. But there is not a moment that's gone by where I don't know exactly where you are, who you're with, what you're doing and what you're trying to fix."

"Good to know. Friends are hard to find nowadays." I skipped past the parts about me trying to push power back into the Gate.

"You have more friends than you realize." I opened my mouth to disagree, then nodded. "Remember, little Crow, you had fewer friends when you got here and fewer when you terrorized the Golden Court. Friends or not, you have more enemies that you can use now."

"What a comforting thought," I replied.

"It's not meant to be. It's simply the truth," he answered after a silence that stretched for what felt like hours. He finally dropped the mask he had been wearing for so long that I had almost forgotten what he looked like beneath it. It crushed my soul to see the fear in his eyes. "I've missed you so very much. I can't begin to tell you how broken I am for who I've had to become. Watching you fade in front of me? It's killing me inside to have nothing to give you."

"I never asked for anything other than your love. I don't need your protection. I need you to love me. I can protect myself." My eyes watered, and I begged myself not to break down. "I miss you. I want you to come home, come back to me. Too many pieces of you are still at war. Come home."

"I can't, Perdi. Trust that it isn't because I don't want to, but because I don't want to be the cause of your death. I want to tell you all my secrets, but both of us would die for them, and everyone we love would die. I can't sentence everyone else to death because I miss you and can't live without you."

I nodded. "Where do we go from here?"

"Would you bring your father here if you could?"

"He's alive, for certain?" I asked. Solas' silence was enough of an answer. Had they used my father as a way to keep me in Elphame? If I thought he was dead, I'd stop trying to get back to an empty home. "Why would I want to show him the delights of Elphame?"

"If coming here was safer for him than staying there, would you?"

I stared at Solas for a long minute and tried to find the message in his questions. It wasn't mere curiosity. Solas had a purpose in all he did. He was warning me of invasion in the only way he could. "I don't know how to answer the question. I wouldn't want my father to come here."

"Here, as in Elphame, or here as in the Dark Courts?" he asked.

"Here, as in close to you."

"I wouldn't bring him into my lands, either. This is not a place for innocents anymore." Solas nodded, but it was jerky, like the words stung and he was shaking them off.

"War is coming again," I whispered, and he nodded. "Where would I even bring my father if not here?"

"You know, in all the wars, all the grabs for land, all the death and horror that I've dealt out, there is only one territory I've never conquered. I've never taken Faolan's land."

"Why not? We both know if you wanted it, it would be yours. So, why haven't you taken it? He's your enemy, after all."

He sighed. "I was told long ago, the enemy of my enemy is my friend. It is more true today than ever before."

"I thought you didn't trust him?"

"I don't…nor should you. He is bound by the same oaths as I am. But I don't need to trust a tool to use it— and neither do you." He closed his eyes and looked like he was thinking of his words carefully. "Do you really think he could come that close to my border, on more than one occasion, to meet you alone unless I allowed it? Unless I saw him as a tool we both could use?"

"If you want to survive using those tools, should you not trust them?"

"No, Perdi. Even those you trust can end your life. Whether they want to or not, they could still be the cause of the ruin. Trust only in yourself and your ability to use the tools at your disposal to keep yourself alive. You cannot be so blind as to see that even those whom you trust and love are the ones who can exploit it the most," he answered. "It wouldn't be called 'hurt' if it didn't come from the heart."

"I'm not. But I do think my desire for freedom sometimes blinds me to what is going on around me, from what dangers lurk in the shadows."

"I suspect you see it perfectly well, but what you see is not where the problem lies." His voice said one thing, but his eyes held a warning. "It is as it has always been with you. You don't want to make the decisions you need to make, and you're eating yourself up inside trying to avoid them. And there are so many we need to make if we want to win. We don't want to be the monsters, but we haven't a choice anymore. In all my warnings, you've not listened to what I've been trying to tell you. We are at final moves, Perdi."

After his words settled into my bones and I had turned them over in my mind, trying to make sense of why he would come to me now, I shuddered at his last remark. *Final moves.* I cut the silence. "And you, with all these riddles, what's your truth for the night?"

He dug out more cookies and passed me one. He waited until he had eaten the entire thing, savoring it like it would be his last, before breaking the silence with his voice. I watched him think of what to say, what he could say. "That's a tall order and an even longer story."

"We've got all night." I hopped onto the counter. "Why the sudden care for my thoughts? You never seemed to care before."

"I've always cared." He turned and stood between my knees. His mask was still down, and I got to see the man I love. I hurt less when the mask was on.

"There you are," I whispered, touching his cheek. "I've missed you."

"You never stopped seeing me, even when I tried to drive you away." He turned his face into my hand and breathed me in. "You smell of darkness."

"And you smell of nightmares." I pulled him to my lips and kissed him softly, for no other reason than to chase away the roughness of the world, the cruelness he's been forced into time and again.

Solas pushed his forehead into mine and sighed. "I'd love to go back. I'd give anything for that. To return to the day I came for you in Whitwick and just left you there. Pick someone else and leave you for a life you deserved to have. Although you could never fate someone else with becoming a Crow, I could have, and I'd have slept perfectly fine with that decision. I'd love to have never known you or your line, if only to save you from this world."

"You're the only one who regrets me coming here. It was happening, no matter what. I'm glad it was you who came. I'd have died without you. And if by some miracle, I'd lived, I'd never know love."

"No one controls fate any more than one could control Aoife and the choices she made long before you." His face was everything I remembered it to be — just Solas and nothing more. "But I am a king who answers to many, and I've had so few choices in life, including that one. Some days, I wish, more than anything, that I wasn't king, that I was as free as you wish to be. Perhaps then, when I had plucked you out of the forest, I'd be running with you instead of being the one to chase you."

"You can't outrun fate," I replied, feeling the words press down on my shoulders.

"I thought I'd have all the time in the world to tell you of Aoife and your destiny. I thought, once you healed, I could tell you everything. But I ran out of time. I'm always running out of time," he whispered. "You asked me how your father knew you would end up here. He was told by your mother, who dreamed of Aoife. The moment you were born, her curse twisted into place, and your mother knew you were fated to become a Crow and would become the last Crow. That is why your mother allowed you the Darkmore journals, taught you the spells you shouldn't know and tried to prepare you the best she could for when you'd step foot onto our lands. They knew who you would become once you came here. When your mother tried to intervene, she was hanged. Wildlings were specifically targeted for who they could become. And since you were the last, the Caller of Crows would not allow the chance of you getting away."

"I didn't know that part." I groaned.

"Don't blame yourself for her death. You didn't cause it. I don't have to tell you, for you to know who's to blame."

"Why all the secrecy?" I asked.

He tilted his head as if I had asked a silly question. "Secrets have power. Truth is power. And for your truths to fall into the wrong hands could mean your death. To know that you're cursed to protect Whitwick could end your life before you're given a chance to try. But to know you'd come here, as the last, and close the Gate? She would have killed your mother before you were even born. And if she had found out what you are, she'd have used you up, and you'd be dead."

"Used me for what?"

"That, I don't know. We suspected who she was looking for, but not why," he replied. When I opened my mouth to tell him of my suspicions, he shook his head. "Your words aren't secret with me when it comes to her. What I think is true of you is one thing. But if you tell me, I can't hide it."

"There aren't many who stand up to you, Solas. Why all the fear?" I asked. "I can see it in your eyes. I feel it roll off you in waves of heat."

"You and Zephyr stand up to me every chance you get." He smiled, then sighed. "I'm called the nightmare of Elphame, yet I can't leave the nightmare that is my life. I can never be scary enough to protect those I love. I want to go back to so many other places and times in my life and make different decisions, but those decisions were never really mine to make. And the harder I rail against it, the more pain and suffering it causes. Every single day, Perdi, is a fight, a new nightmare I must battle. It doesn't matter. One way or another, whatever decision I make leads to war. The only thing I have left to decide is how many I am willing to let die."

"Have you decided?" I asked.

He shook his head, but not in an answer. It looked like he was trying to change his own mind, trying to shake the truth and possibilities away. "I wish we could go back."

"What happens if we can't go back? If we're just stuck in this loop of cutting each other up and growing worlds apart? I want the truth, Solas. What happens? You speak of not having choices of your own. I am in the same place as you. I am a Crow who answers to many and has so few choices of my own."

"Good question. You tell me. If you were me, with the weight of this world on your shoulders, what would you do? If you knew war was coming and nothing you did could change that—and trust that I've tried everything I could to change it—what decisions would you make? If the fate of your people and those you love were in your hands, and those more powerful controlled who lives and dies, what would you do?"

"Kill her," I blurted out.

"You sound like Zephyr." He laughed, then leaned in close enough for me to smell the man under the soap. "If I could, don't you think I would have already? I can't. And the answers to who can stop her do not rest within these borders, nor am I able to seek them out or tell someone else about it. So, what do I do when I have no options? When I'm oathed not to find the options available?"

"I want to tell you to set me free, but knowing what I know, I know that's not entirely possible. The only way I am leaving here is if I run, because *she* won't let me go. And if I run, I'll be out there, where I have a few more enemies than I already have within these walls. But if I stay, I know that those who stand against me could use me or use me against you and your people. So, I'd kill me before they could use me. Before someone else made that choice for you, I'd make it first." I almost choked on my words. They tasted of bitterness, but they were honest. And there was only room in this bubble for hard truths. "I can't allow anyone to use the Gate to invade the mortal lands, so I'd kill the person who stood to be the most risk against it. I would kill the person who held the fate of my people in their hands."

He laughed. "Somehow, I don't think that last part is about how I should handle you and is more of a threat against my life."

"Take it however you'd like, but it's still the truth. You know me, Solas. You know I'd rather die than have someone own me or make decisions for me. I'd leave long before I let you use or abuse me…" I paused and looked him in the eyes. Without having to say the words, I knew he had done it all on purpose. All of this was to force me to leave. When his eyes dropped, I saw his guilt, his shame.

"I told you to run, Perdi. If you were in danger, I told you to run. Why didn't you? I gave you plenty of reasons to leave and cleared your path, but you never left. You were so close the other day, and you still came back. Why?" he whispered. "I am nightmares and fear, and I choose what you feared most — being caged, being owned, being back in the Golden Court — and yet, you still didn't run? I thought if I hurt you bad enough, you'd leave. But you never did. I have taken everything you love and twisted it, but you're still standing here."

"Why didn't you just tell me to run? That I wasn't safe here with you?" I asked.

"I tried many times. Each time, you weren't listening to me. So, I did what I could. I tried to drive you away. Still, here you are."

"I know you, Solas. In some way, I feel like I've known you my whole life. Under all the games and masks, I still see you. I wish I didn't. I wish I could hate you. This would be so much easier if I did."

"I hate myself enough for us both," he answered. "But with choices at a premium, I can't afford many of my own."

"I know you hate the thought as much as I do of not having control over your own life. Now, we're both on the edge, stuck with someone else pulling the strings, and the remaining options are going to burn away our souls."

"So now you see my predicament. What eats at me every time we're close or you do something that risks countless lives, including your own. Hell, you went to the very place that wants your death." He groaned his frustration into my hair. "Now you see the position I'm in and how very few choices really are my own or ones I want to make or even consider. But soon, Perdi, those choices will be taken from me, and I won't be able to stop it or protect you from them. I can't stop her."

"I've always understood the position you're in. I feel the pressure of it all push the breath from my chest and grip my heart every time I hear you say my name. I weigh the tone of your voice in my mind, wondering if that is the day you decide you're done with me. Day after day, I wonder how long you'll keep me around," I answered. My eyes watered.

"I'll never be done with you, little Crow. But fate doesn't care how I feel or what I want, any more than it cares what you want."

"Will you warn me before you kill me? Or will you do it in my sleep where you don't have to look me in the eyes?"

Solas kissed my forehead. "You will know because the world will tremble if I'm forced to take your life."

"How much time do I have left?" I wondered.

"That is up to you and the choices you make."

"Final moves?" I asked.

"There are fewer and fewer to make each day."

"I love you." I closed my eyes and let the tears roll. The words, although spoken to Solas, were not meant for the version of him that he had shown me for months.

"And I, you. That day hasn't come, not yet…but it will," he answered with a strangled voice and pulled back from me.

"I would, you know, shave off my soul to help you," I whispered.

"I know. And if I were to put myself in your shoes, I would finish whatever it is that you're doing, and soon. Whatever plotting you're doing, finish it. Act before your options are gone, as mine are—before not even I can stop what's coming. You will not find answers here. You cannot help from here. Fate decided our paths should cross, but I wish we had never met. I wish I was not deciding when your heart should no longer beat."

"As do I," I answered. I grabbed his arm as he moved to step away. "Solas, what if there is another way?"

"There isn't, not by my hand."

"But by *my* hand, there may be. If there was, would you listen to me?" I inquired. He lifted his finger to his lips and nodded. "Do you trust me?"

"Always," he whispered and raised his finger to his lips. "Don't say the words out loud, not here, not ever, not to anyone. She will hear you."

"How will you know?" I asked.

"I know you, and that is enough. I've watched you master these games, and you can play with the best of us. The question is, could you do it again? Because that is the help I need, the Crow from the dungeons, the one who will suffer as greatly as I will. If you play this game with me, we're playing for keeps, with everything to lose. If we fail, we both die. Can you risk your soul for me?" He finally asked for my help. "Know, the games we will play will be against each other for all to see. It can be no other way, and it will hurt just the same."

"I still have my mask," I hinted.

"Put it on, little Crow. You need it more than I do, and take it off for no one. Absolutely no one, especially me. Once you put it on, we go back to cutting each other up. After tonight, you will have only enemies in this court." He sighed and blew out a breath he was holding in. "This is going to fucking hurt, little Crow."

"Everything in Elphame hurts," I answered.

"I will miss you when you're gone," he answered. "Pack for winter."

"I can do this." My breath hitched in my throat as I felt a new wave of worry squirm into my bones. I'd have to leave my home to save my home. I grabbed his shirt and pulled him into my chest, kissing him as if it would be my last. "I'll never be done with you."

As he pulled the bubble down from around us, he was gone as quickly as he had come. I had expected us both to continue slicing chunks of soul off the other. Instead, I stood in silence. On shaking legs, I returned to my bedroom. My mind reeled with questions, and I searched his every word for the answers. For the first time in a long time, I knew where we stood — and we stood perilously close to death again.

Now, all I had to do was find another way before he had no choice but to end my life. There weren't many certainties in Elphame. But I was sure I'd be pulling out the mask I had worn to survive the Golden Court. It seems I'd need it to survive the Dark Courts. If I wanted to live, I'd need to be the old Perdi, the old Crow, and suffer just as much as I had the first time I had worn it. As much as I loved him for the truths he had given me, I hated that he waited until only final moves were left. I hated that he tried to protect me into my grave.

Chapter Twelve

I had slept like a rat in a storm on a sinking ship in the middle of the ocean. Every muscle burned and felt cramped from sleeping in a tight ball. My dreams of death, war, battles not yet fought and losses not yet had had woken me throughout the night. Like many dreams before, I stood on the edge of them and watched. I had been a spectator into the nightmares of others, over and over. And when I thought they couldn't get any worse, I was ripped into another and another. It felt like a punishment, a consequence, some sort of spiritual sentence for crimes I had not yet committed. It was as if the Gods wanted their pound of flesh up front in case I was too busted up in the end for them to get it.

When Zephyr had come for me to train, although I had been thankful that he had broken me out of the prison in dreams, I didn't want to get up. I was already spent and hadn't done a thing to show for my exhaustion. I thought twice about refusing. I jumped and dressed. I didn't need to be dragged into the forest in my underpants again. He wouldn't care if I was tired or why I was tired. When my five minutes were up, he wrapped me in shadows and took me as I put on my boots.

"Where are we?" I asked as we landed in grasslands and not the forest where we usually trained. For as far as I could see, there was nothing but grass, flowers and untouched land.

"The Wildelands," Zephyr answered with a smile. It was a genuine smile, the kind reserved for moments no one could see. "It's the only place in Elphame that is owned by no king, no Royal, no Fae whatsoever — a land no one can war for and no one can war on. It is the only truly free place here."

"Why did you bring me here?" I asked. I started my stretches and winced each time my muscles refused to move without pain. I never looked forward to training until we were in the thick of it. Once I got over the fear of that first punch, it was all or nothing for me. But that first punch? Man, did I dread it coming.

"This land, Perdi, is you. This place is your soul. It is free. No one owns this land."

I rolled my eyes. "Tell that to Solas."

"*You* tell him, little Crow. You are owned by no one. They may fight over you, but you cannot be conquered. You were Taken into Elphame, but you are no one's prisoner. You have earned your freedom. Stop giving it away."

"And how do you think he'd like me reminding him of that? Should I bring it up at dinner, or do you think I should wait for dessert?" I laughed, picturing it in my head. "He'd lose it, Zeph. He's on the edge, and as much as I enjoy needling him, I really don't want to be the one to give him the final push. I think he'd drag me over with him."

"They are not words that he hasn't already heard from your lips," he countered. "You've said as much or worse to his face."

"Only now he's going to kill me."

"No, he isn't," Zephyr replied. He crossed his arms and stared at me as if I were being dramatic. "If anything, it'll be you that kills him. I felt what you did last night at dinner. You're lucky I wanted to see if you were grandstanding and didn't have to get between you two again."

"I wasn't grandstanding," I answered. "I was making a point. If he comes for me, I will protect myself."

"You overestimate his temper."

"And you underestimate it," I replied. "He *will* kill me. He told me last night. But at least he said I'll know it's coming when he does it. I don't know if he told me that as a warning or for me to get my affairs in order. At least, I hope he was warning me and not just toying with me to see me squirm. Who knows with him anymore? He constantly surprises me each time I see him."

"He's not going to…" Zephyr looked surprised. "He actually said he was going to kill you?"

I thought long and hard about what I could tell Zephyr in the open. If Solas didn't want me saying the words out loud, ever, how could I tell Zephyr the truth? I lifted my finger to my lips and glanced around us. I saw no one, felt no one aside from us, but I also knew this was Elphame, and things were never as they seemed. It didn't matter that I saw nothing. Nothing was as it appeared in Elphame. Even salt looks like sugar until you taste it.

Zephyr's shadows crawled from the ground, behind rocks and trees, and dips in the earth. They were always near, hiding in plain sight. Although the shadows looked as the fog did, they never scared me in the same way. They flowed up, and around us, in a wind I couldn't see or feel. Once I was tucked inside, I felt as safe as the first night they had come to me.

"There is no one strong enough to hear us now," he said.

I glanced at him, uncertain. "Are you sure?"

"Not even Solas could get in here," he answered.

"He is not the one I'm worried about. It's his sister." I whispered the last bit, just in case.

"No one, Perdi, not even the Seers. If they tried, I would feel their magick. Know this and know it to be true. There is not a power in all of Elphame that could push without me knowing. And I'll follow it all the way back to whoever had been such a fool. I may not be able to kill her, but she'd suffer for it."

"Solas told me not to say the words out loud to anyone."

"I'm not just anyone, little Crow. He would have known you'd come to me, regardless of what he's told you. He's not a fool. Whatever he's told you, I either already know or he knew the information would make it to my ears."

I nodded. "Zeph, I can hear the horn."

"Say that again?" He looked confused and surprised at once, as if he hoped I had misspoken.

"I can hear the horn of Elphame, or that's what I've heard it called. And before you tell me you can't hear it, I already know that it's because the call is for me.

Unfortunately, the shadows and Orrian aren't great sources of information when it comes to this. Whether you can hear it or not, I do, and I need to know what it is."

"That's not the horn of Elphame…" His voice trailed off. "Are you sure you hear it? Did you only hear it once?"

"Yes, I'm sure. And no, I hear it all the time. The bloody thing has been sounding off for weeks now. At first, it was faint and random. Now, it wakes me out of a dead sleep as though it were resting on my pillow. It is constant," I answered. "What the hell does it mean? What's it warning of?"

"It hasn't been heard since the Gate was created, since it opened the first time. Is this what you and he spoke of?" he asked, and I shook my head. "You haven't told Solas?"

I stared at him for a long minute, surprised he'd ask the question. "In what world do you live in where I can speak freely with Solas whenever I choose?"

"Perdi, this isn't just the horn of Elphame. This is the horn of the wild hunt. Someone has broken their oath."

"Me?" I asked. "Is it coming for me?"

"It is how Fae know an oath they've made has been broken by the other. It signals us to act. Either you act or wild magick will act for you."

"I haven't made any official oaths with anyone but you," I answered. "Did *you* break your oath with me?"

"No, you're still alive, aren't you? You'd be dead if I broke our oath of protection, and the wild hunt doesn't sound for the dead." He shook his head as if it were a dumb question. "Usually, when someone breaks an oath, we deal with it long before the wild hunt can be called. The last time the wild hunt was called was when the Gate opened the first time. I suspect, since you are the last Darkmore, the oath made now falls to you, and someone is breaking it."

"The Gate." I groaned. It always comes back to that cursed object. "Solas is breaking that oath. Only a Darkmore may touch the Gate."

"He needs to know."

"I think it's a safe bet to say he already does, given he's the one doing it," I answered.

"Have you stopped to think that perhaps he's not as bad as you think? Someone else is moving the pieces around on the board. This isn't Solas."

"I know," I answered. "Last night, for the briefest moments, he was Solas, the man we both know. We spoke as we did once before. And yes, in that brief moment of truth, he said he was going to kill me. But at least he said I would know it was coming. He said there was no other way. He said he was being forced." I told Zephyr of my conversation with Solas. His questions were short and to the point, but he tried not to interrupt.

I sagged and rubbed the pain in my chest. The reality of my situation burned deep inside me. "What the hell did I do to anger the Gods this much? When will this nightmare end? I thought when I escaped the Golden Court, I would be free from this hell. Do I have to live seven entire years of this?"

"You think so highly of yourself to be noticed by the Gods?" He huffed a laugh. "You didn't anger them."

"Then what did I do to deserve it? I must have done something."

"You were born, plain and simple," Zephyr answered. "You're not special in this, Perdi. It is the same reason the rest of us suffer and cause suffering in others. We are simply alive and free to do so. But I warned you of this. I warned you of the suffering you'd feel."

"Warned me? When did you ever tell me that this would happen?" I asked.

"The day you decided you'd rather live than die, I told you that you would suffer for it. I wasn't lying to you. I gave you the chance to end it, but you chose pain and suffering. You knew what living would cost you, yet you question the fate that you handpicked?" He laughed and shook his head. He looked amused. "You cannot stand this close to the throne and not feel the pain of it all. Foolish little Crow, you actually thought things would magically get better, even as I was bringing you back from a death caused by the very place you are expecting to be different."

Zephyr's words echoed in my ears. The memory of my death rolled down my spine.

"You will always be a little Crow. You're made only to suffer, and there will be so much of it that you'll curse me for this day. You'll be forced to fight for each and every step. If you live, you'll live the life I never wanted for you. You'll live the life of a Soul-Eater and will pay for it dearly. You'll never be free, not ever… Your fate is bound to mine, and I've never had a single day of peace. Nothing has ever come easy to me, not even you. If you choose this, you are choosing to walk the same painful path I have and still do. You're not going to live. You're just choosing to die on a different day – and every day in between will be a fight for the next."

"So, you do remember." He could taste my memory of him in my pearl.

"I do," I answered.

"You chose this life, this very path. You made the decision to suffer after I told you not to. This is the fate you wished upon yourself. You can only be angry with yourself for it."

"And what of my fate? How the hell do I control Solas from meddling in my fate, from getting me killed, from bringing wild magick down on his own head? The more I try, the more I beat my head against a wall."

"You can't control the darkness any more than you can control the light." Zephyr laughed. It wasn't his usual laugh. He was as uncertain as I was, and it made me all the more uneasy.

"Someone can, and someone is," I disagreed. "Solas made that quite clear."

"I didn't feel your fear last night. I felt your sadness and confusion, but I didn't feel your pending death. I felt Solas cut you off, pull his darkness around you, but could still feel enough of you to know you weren't in imminent danger."

"I know how I was feeling last night. I don't need to recap," I snapped at him, and he shrugged. "Is that all you can say? I just told you someone is going to kill me. I told you he was being controlled, and you have nothing to say about it?"

"I'm sorry. I don't know what to say about any of that. You've just told me. Give me a moment to digest it. What I *am* trying to say is, if he had plans to end your life last night, I would have felt it. Whatever the reason he had to come to you, it wasn't with your death on his mind."

"Then it was a warning and not just toying with me?" I asked. "Can I trust the warning — or is he being cruel?"

"I would imagine so, or he wouldn't have sealed your conversation away in secret. Had he honestly wanted you dead, you'd simply be dead. He isn't one to toy, as you say. But I'll keep an eye on him. I know there are other players in this game and a bigger problem at hand. If Solas has been named an oath breaker, nothing we do will stop what's coming his way," Zephyr answered, and I nodded. "Not even I can force his hand when it comes to you. Perdi, if someone else is powerful enough to control him, eventually, he won't be able to protect you, and the real danger will begin."

"I told him last night that I would find a different way, but I don't know enough about what's going on to figure a way out of it. I don't have enough answers to even know where to begin. If I screw this up, it could mean the lives of so many innocents."

"All I know is that right now, this moment, is all we ever have," he answered. "Before you can save the world, you have to save yourself. You can't save anyone else if you don't take care of yourself first."

"I'll worry about myself later. This is a little more important."

"No, it isn't. It is time you climb out of whatever hell you're living in or nothing you do, not now, not later, not ever, will help anyone. If you remain here, stuck in this perpetual cycle of grief, you'll keep taking it as if you deserve it. Hell, you stood in the kitchen with Solas as he told you he would kill you and someone else was making him do it, and all you did was cry yourself to sleep. Those aren't the actions of the little Crow I once knew. Those were the actions of someone who is willing to lie down and die. We all die in the end, but make sure your death shakes the fucking world with regret for having lost you." I felt like he was giving me the talk he gave his soldiers.

"I feel like you're sending me to war."

"We're always at war, but it's usually not within ourselves. If you cannot conquer your own demons, you'll never live through someone else's." His amused expression faded. "You need to stop asking for someone to save you."

"I'm not."

"Oh? Then why are you spilling this all to me if not for me to help you? I will always help you. But you need to stop looking outside for someone to do what only you can do and start looking within. You can ask for help, but stop depending on it or you will die. One day, I won't make it in time, and there are only so many pearls I can take before I've taken so much you die anyway. You're a fucking Soul-Eater. Start acting like it, and stop asking for everyone else to do what not even you are willing to do."

"And what's that?" I asked.

"Saving you, Perdi," he answered. "Stop giving your power away. You must stop offering yourself up on a silver platter and expecting not to be used. We are all tools, but we must decide how we're used or they will use us up completely."

"Easier said than done, Zeph." I rubbed my chest with the palm of my hand. Every time he and I spoke, I felt the guilt of things I had already done and couldn't overcome.

"It is, but that doesn't mean it doesn't hurt. If you had no guilt, we'd be having a different conversation right now. If you could kill without grief, we'd be talking about why Solas *should* end your life and not how to save it." Zephyr rubbed his eyes. He looked as exhausted as I felt. "It is your choice how you honor the deaths that haunt you and your actions that caused them. But do not allow it to cause your own. We, including myself, have all made choices that we must carry with us for all times. But we cannot let them weigh us down. Grieving and suffering are a world apart, and you're standing in the middle, drowning in it. I've tried to give you space and time to heal, but I fear that time is coming to an end, whether we want it to or not."

"I'm sorry. I'm rather new at killing and maiming," I replied. "Mortals don't bounce back like Fae. We don't have hundreds of years of this crap to toughen us up with."

"I'm not asking you to ignore it. You can never erase what you have done or what has bruised your soul. It doesn't matter how long you live. It still hurts. Trust me. I've tried so many times to forget it. I'm asking you to embrace who you have become and stop living in the gashes of wars already past. If you can't, not even I can help you, and you will be the cause of your own death."

"I know, Zeph. It's just hard not to feel so bloody defeated. It feels like it hasn't stopped since I came here."

"You're only defeated once you're buried. It doesn't matter who brought you here or the reasons they gave you. You can't change it. You can't go back. Stop trying to. And I suspect, even if you could, you wouldn't have allowed someone else to come in place of your own. You never would have fated someone else to suffer a destiny that is yours. You were born for this, and one day, you will be standing at my side and will understand why the pain was worth it, why all of this was worth it. If you can't be a Crow, be the Soul-Eater you're meant to be."

"As if whoever is pulling Solas' strings is going to let me live," I countered.

"Then you die. But you do not see your future, little Crow. Do not give yourself over to the fate others have decided for you. They do not govern your life or your death, and the sooner you realize that, the sooner you'll fulfill a destiny written before you were born," he answered. If I were on the frontlines with the rest of his army, I'd have marched for him. He had a way of cutting off the ugly fat and holding the meaty truth for all to believe in.

"It's easy for you. There is not a soul alive that isn't terrified of you. I don't have that kind of clout. I'm terrified of Fae."

"Easy is not a word I would use to describe life for anyone in Elphame. And it certainly wasn't easy for me." His words felt more like a slap on the hand, like I had said something foolish. "When I was a child, I feared everything in Elphame. I was sent away from my home to become this—a Soul-Eater, a commander, a blight on Elphame. I feared who I was and who I knew I would become. I was born from two great houses, the strongest of my people. I was destined to do great and terrible things. And after I took my first life and first pearl, I left for years. It was in my own suffering that I found my way. It was in the suffering of my people where I found courage. My grief finally left and was replaced with purpose. But even now, knowing there are few who could stand against me and live, there are many times I'd rather feel love than fear. But it was only that fear that kept me alive. And you, little Crow, have the love of many and the fear of none. It's time you change that. Love, as it seems, will not be enough for you any more than it would be for me."

"I think you're wrong on that last part. Fear is great. It would probably keep me alive a lot longer, but I would never fight in anyone's army through fear."

"Then prove me wrong. Prove to me how love will motivate you and will bring you to the end."

"And if I'm killed before I have the chance?" I asked. "Remember… I fear death still. I don't have a hundred lifetimes to quench that thirst."

"If that is what the fates have decided, then you die, and nothing we say or do is going to stop that," Zephyr answered as if death wasn't a big deal. For him, it wasn't. He'd lived countless lifetimes. I hadn't. "You're asking yourself the wrong questions, little Crow. What do you plan to do with the time you have left? Will worry bring you more days? Will fear bring you more time? Each day you have left, each beat of your heart brings you another chance to live the life you choose to have. If all you have is a sliver of time, how will you spend it? On love or on fear?"

"You said one day I'll be standing beside you and I will know why I was born for this. Do you know why?" I asked.

"Only the fates have those answers."

"If I'm standing at your side, does that mean I'll die at your side?" I whispered the last bit. "Are you going to be the one that kills me?"

"It would take a lot to force me to kill you, Perdi."

"That's not an answer," I replied.

"Yes, it is. No one could make me kill you. Not even Solas could command that of me. I am a Soul-Eater. There isn't a force alive that could make me take a soul I didn't want. I have never stepped foot onto a battlefield that didn't deserve to have me there. So, if you died at my hands, it would be because I saw no other way than your death. You would have deserved to die with me looking over you." Zephyr squeezed my shoulder, and I laughed to myself. He wasn't very good at the comfort thing. He could rile an army but struggled to find words to soothe the soul. "Of all the souls I've tasted, yours, little Crow, is by far the most complicated. It also is the strongest I've had the pleasure of knowing — not once, but twice now. Some days, I feel like I'm choking on it. Others, it feels like home."

I smiled at the last part. We're all looking for a home in our own way. "This is a lot, Zeph, for just one person."

"No, it isn't. You have faced worse and have been more scared. You're stronger than this. You just have to make decisions you don't want to make, and it's forcing you into inaction. Rather than making them, you're dragging it out until someone else forces you, and you can blame them for it."

"What would you do?" I asked.

"I'd eat the fucking world before I allowed anyone the chance to decide my fate. There isn't a prison made that could hold me unless I wanted to be there. And you, little Crow, want to be held in prison more than you want to be free. Because freedom comes at a cost that you're unwilling to pay." Zephyr wrapped himself around me, and we were gone from the Wildelands and landed in the forest beyond the manor. "Whatever comes of the horn, we'll all pay tithe to this God."

"Sounds like every God in Elphame," I answered.

"You can't hide from the wild hunt. There are no lies or bribes that'll keep Elphame from getting her pound of flesh."

I nodded. Whether I understood the wild hunt or not, I understood Elphame collecting debts. She never left an unpaid bill to go unchecked. "No training today?" I asked.

"That was your training. When I woke up this morning, the world felt a little smaller. I needed you to understand you are more than this suffering. You needed a reminder of who you are and what you are. You talk about how much Solas has changed, yet the woman I met is not the woman standing before me. You've lost that spark, the fire which is who you are. It is gone. You are free, no matter what others may say. You have your freedom if you're willing to take it. You have everything you could ever imagine, at your fingertips, if you're willing to fight for it. And if you're not, you never deserved to have it."

"And what about the consequences for taking that freedom?" I asked.

"What about the consequences if you *don't* take it? There are only two questions you must ask yourself. Do you want to die in a cage or die free? Do you want the answers that will save your life, or do you want to die waiting on someone to tell you that which they'll take to their graves?" he asked.

"What do I do about the horn?" I asked.

"That, I cannot tell you. You can answer the call, or you can ignore it and allow fate to sort it out," he replied. "And before you ask, I don't know what I would do. That's the truth. No one who has ever broken an oath they gave to me has lived long enough for the wild hunt to track them down. I've always done it myself," he answered with a casual shrug.

"You sound like Solas."

"Thank you." Zephyr smiled and left me in the forest, alone.

I sat on the pine needles that carpeted the ground of the forest and watched the sun dance through the treetops like artwork created by the Gods and Goddesses. It reminded me of home, Whitwick, and the evergreens that surrounded a place too often touched by death. It reminded me of every afternoon I had tried to run from my fate, the very fate I now sat in. If I could be any other place than here, that is where I ached for. Not just home but the places where I could pretend that I made it past the Taking and was finally able to breathe. I had spent hours upon hours sitting alone and imagining life as an adult, free from Fae and the risk of being pulled into Elphame. And now I did the same thing. I imagined a life beyond my fate within the Dark Court.

The forest silenced the chaos of my mind, slowed it to an understandable crawl. This place of root and branch carved a wall between them and me, those who wanted my death. In the lush greenery, I could be someone else. I could be free and without responsibilities or fear. But from under the cover of century-old trees, I couldn't help. I couldn't get word to the mortal realm. I couldn't warn anyone of what was yet to come. I was still in a cage that wasn't even locked. If I didn't open the door, I would die as I watched my people fall. I could leave, warn them. But I knew that if I left, I would never be able to come back. As Solas said, there were only final moves left. And if that was the move I made, I would be on my own. But he couldn't help me in the Dark Courts any more than he could if I left.

The Gate was weakening and, soon, would be wide open, destroyed. With each new wave of power, I ate it down, but I couldn't keep it from happening. If I did nothing at all, if I sat by and watched, I wouldn't be the only one to die. If I were to do something about it, I'd have to do it soon. I had to get word to the human realm.

Orrian landed beside me as the shadows curled at the base of the tree. She perched herself on a rock and basked in the sun. She had once said that the warmth was the only thing she had missed from the Golden Court. But I'd sooner be sitting in the snow than spend even one more minute there. That place was the very beginning of this nightmare I called life, and I'd do anything never to go back.

"Orrian, it's almost time to go," I whispered to her. She lifted her head and nodded. For now, we'd bask in what was left of our lives in the Dark Courts before we burned it and the rest of Elphame to the ground.

Damn the consequences.

* * * *

I stood beside Solas as he paced outside of my home in Whitwick, anticipating the Taking of a new Crow. His dream played out the same way each time. His darkness swirled around him, doing little to dampen the screams rolling through the hills of my mortal town. Each new ear-piercing cry sent a shiver down his spine. He shook his head and covered his ears. He pushed more of his dark inky magick into the bubble around him, but it still didn't block out what his kin were doing to mine. I felt his emotions twist around us in a wind I couldn't feel. On the tip of my tongue, I tasted the saltiness of his tears.

I had stood in this moment with him dozens of times. I watched him force himself to open my front gate and, with boiling rage, blow my front door from its frame. Aoife had died hours ago, and Solas thundered inside, both sad at her passing and angry that he was forced to come for a Crow. He whispered to himself that Aoife had fated him with this day, that this would end the Taking of Crows. He had choices, and he wanted to make a different one. He was tempted to take someone else, to force the hand of fate onto another.

"You dream of this day often," *I finally spoke. I hadn't spoken to him in this dream until now. Like him, this was a painful memory and not one I wanted to relive or dissect.*

He breathed in. His breath hitched in his throat. "It's my least favorite memory of you. If not for this day, everything else wouldn't have happened. All the other bad memories I have of you wouldn't have happened if not for this moment."

"Knowing what I know today, I'd have still come to Elphame."

"I know, and that bothers me the most. You're a bleeding heart, and it's going to be your death."

I laughed, void of anything remotely friendly. "No, Solas. I will kill to stay alive. I won't die for Elphame again. Fae land is not worthy of another drop of my blood."

"I'm counting on that," *he replied.* "Final moves. Are you ready to make your move?"

I nodded as my shoulders sank. "I am. Are you?"

"No. I will never be ready to see you leave." *His voice was soft yet held thunder and lightning of decades of pain.* "I won't be able to come if you need help. You have to be willing to do what you must to stay alive. I can't protect you."

"But I can protect you, Solas. I'm ready," *I answered.* "I love you."

"And I, you," *he answered and pushed me out of his dream.*

Chapter Thirteen

Wrapped in a darkness of my own creation, I slinked through the forest. Years of hunting Whitwick forest and tiptoeing the courts of Elphame, I was nothing more than a shadow. I had learned, many years ago, the art of not being seen. Back home, that meant the difference between fresh meat and going home empty-handed. Here, on the other hand, being caught made *me* the fresh meat, and I'd have no last meals. It wasn't Solas I feared. It was every other beast on his lands who wouldn't stop to ask questions.

Although I sneaked along to what could be certain death, there was a particular thrill to it that made me smile. It was not the risk of being caught or lashed again for being a wicked little Crow. It was in the independence of it. I had to prove to myself that I could move through the court on my own without the aid of Zephyr's shadows or my Malice. I could if I needed to, protect myself. And if the situation became dire, I knew I could call out for help, and I wouldn't be on my own.

They were two lessons Zephyr had tried to teach me, being self-sufficient and knowing when to ask for help. Today was about saving myself, even if it hurt.

I tied a red ribbon to an oak tree, the same tree I held Faolan against with the tip of his own blade. I waited in the trees, under the cover of natural shadows and darkness, for Faolan and wondered if he'd come, if he'd care or if I was some end game he had, and I was about to be hung out to dry. Orrian and the shadows were busy leading the eyes of the guards away from my escape to the border in the trees behind Solas' manor. They saw me go into the shadows but never watched me climb back out. I felt uneasy with my ask for them to risk getting caught, but neither hesitated.

"I didn't think you'd come back." Faolan moved to my front, and I jumped.

I looked over my shoulders and hesitated. No one had followed me, yet I was more nervous than ever. I didn't know what would happen to me if I was found with Faolan. I wanted to believe Solas or Zephyr would simply rant and rave, but I also knew Solas couldn't protect me as he once had, and Zephyr hated Faolan more than I ever had. I knew I was risking my life to meet him. Equally, I risked Faolan's life in the process and didn't quite know if he deserved that death. Whether he was a friend or foe was yet to be seen, but allies didn't deserve to be strung up and hanged.

I paced while I tried to calm my rolling stomach. "I know I have no right to ask you this, but I need a diversion tomorrow," I finally said.

"Can I ask why?" he queried, which was refreshing compared to the orders I usually heard.

I debated on what to tell him, on if my words would pass from my lips to his and into the ear of Solene. I had nothing to lose, besides my life. But it would be worthless if I chose it over those who had no choices of their own. "I need to get back to Whitwick Gates and warn the Guardians. The Gate is weak, and it's going to fall any day. I can't stop it, and I need to at least warn them of what's coming. If they aren't prepared, the moment Elphame steps through, it will be certain death for all the mortal realm. I will return, but I need to get to my dad."

"I'll be honest. I wasn't expecting that." Faolan's eyes widened in surprise. "What kind of diversion do you need?"

I shrugged. "Anything that doesn't end with innocents dying. Just enough to guarantee it'll get Solas' attention for a few hours, so I can get away and get to the Gate."

"I can do that for you," he answered. "He's always been very curious about me."

"No. It's because he doesn't trust you."

"I've given him no reason to and every reason not to. Tomorrow, I'll give him the diversion you need."

"Thank you." I let out a breath I didn't know I was holding. The bundle of nerves in my stomach released. But the unease for what I was about to do still ate at me.

"Let me come with you, Perdi. If you leave and can't get back, you risk breaking the oath. If you're caught, you will be sentenced to death. This isn't something you can do alone, nor is it something you should have to do alone. But if I'm there, I can keep your head from coming off."

"You'd be risking yourself and your people if you came with me."

"If the Gate falls, Perdi, we're all at war—not just Elphame and the mortal realm. We would fight amongst each other, once again, to protect your realm, to protect our own people from the divide that will happen. All our people are at risk," he replied. "And, you will need someone from Elphame to speak to the Guardians to tell them how to protect themselves. They need to know what is coming. As much as you've seen here, it is so much worse than your mortal words could ever describe. By some miracle, you've not tasted the true horrors of this world. They need to understand what will be sent through that Gate. No one alive in the mortal world remembers the first invasion. They only remember the parlor tricks of the Taking. As horrible as it was, it was nothing more than games to Fae. Imagine what will come when we mean to Take them all? When Fae, stronger than Solas or I, go into the mortal world, they stand no chance."

I nodded. "Thank you."

"Tomorrow night, we will meet back here. You'll know when." He squeezed my arm. "If something goes wrong, I want you to run."

"To the Gate?"

"To Tylwyth. It is my home."

"Tylwyth?" It was the first I had heard of the name. "You've never told me what your home was called. I don't know how to get there. It's not on any map I've ever seen."

"Winter Court. I've never trusted anyone enough to give out the real name. I couldn't risk the safety of my people." He smiled and handed me a small freckled stone. "Once you cross the border, run toward the snow-covered hills. Tell whoever stops you that I've granted you sanctuary, and you are to be taken to Tylwyth. Give them this stone. They'll know it is from me. It will get you to safety, I promise."

"A rock? I'm going to be saved by a rock?" I lobbed it in my hand. "Do you have something bigger?"

"Would you rather you go back to the Dark Court with the official seal from Tylwyth? If you're caught with a rock, no one will question you. If you're caught with a letter granting you sanctuary, you'll see the noose long before I could ever get to you. Whether Solas strings you up himself or not, you would die for treason. There are very few absolute laws in the Dark Courts, but loyalty is total, and the only sentence for breaking it is death."

"Dear God." I shivered.

"Sorry to say, but it's that way in every court, not just his," he added, "including my own. It's the only threat that protects our people. So, do you want a rock, or do you want the flag of Tylwyth nailed to your back?"

I nodded. "I see your point."

"This rock is from my lands and is only found there. Although it would likely be my commander who finds you...Oisin. But show it to whoever stops you. Tell them I've granted you sanctuary. They'll know, just from the stone, Perdi. Trust me."

I sighed. "Trust is an expensive commodity, Fao."

He nodded. "Indeed, it is. Spend it carefully and only when you must."

I pocketed the stone and turned from him. I looked back once, but he was already gone. Again, I slinked through the trees as silent as before. I found Orrian and the shadows close by. Guards were stationed, waiting and watching. They hadn't seen me leave or return. Even with my heart hammering against my ribs, we calmly walked back to the manor, passed the guards who pretended like they weren't there to watch me. As casually as they could, they ate their lunch in the forest, as if that was something they always did. I shook my head as I went by. They had the decency to look embarrassed, both for themselves and for me. But they didn't decide the rules, nor which ones they'd follow. They followed Solas and his word they've lived and breathed for. I wondered why Solas deserved such steadfast loyalty. Aside from the mess we were in, I wondered, under all the masks he wore, what he did to command utter and total devotion. He wasn't Zephyr's king, yet Zephyr referred to Solas as his king. What could he have possibly done to win the deadly loyalty of a Soul-Eater?

Tucked in the shadows, I showered. I kept my comments about Solas and Faolan and the Gate to myself. There were some things I didn't want Zephyr to know. He would stop me. I knew he'd try. I sat with my back against the glass walls of the shower and, like Solas, planned out every possible outcome. I would leave and warn Whitwick, but I'd never be able to come back to my home here with Solas. Once I left, once I sluffed my loyalty to the ground, I would be just another enemy of the Dark Courts. Could I live with it if I actually lived through it? I knew well enough to know that Faolan could not be fully trusted, but underneath the schemes of Faolan held the truths I needed, we all needed. And if I were to become his willing pawn, I'd play the game from inside his very court. The enemy of my enemy was not my friend, and I might regret it, it may kill me to leave, but at least I'd be alive long enough to feel remorse and to burn down what I could before my time was up.

I passed Orrian the tiny stone and pulled my fingers to my lips. She opened her mouth and swallowed it. I fought the urge to grab her and shake her upside down until she spat it back out.

"Spit it out." My whisper came out like a growl.

She laughed. "It's hidden inside me, Perdi. When we need it, I'll bring it back up. But inside, there is never the risk of someone finding it."

"That's disgusting," I teased.

"How else do you think we stole so much gold from the Golden Court to pay the nymphs safe passage? I swallowed it."

"I never thought to ask." I laughed at the picture in my mind of Orrian dragging her full stomach back to my bedroom, too heavy to fly.

The shadows pressed in tighter. "Zephyr is calling us. We must go. The party is to begin shortly."

Orrian left with the shadows, saying something about wanting to see who Solas had invited. Alone, I prepared for what I hoped was my going away party. And like every single ball prior, I selected each item expertly. Each article was handcrafted by Orrian and her people, right down to the tiniest feather details, handstitched to the silk fabric. I selfishly wished Elswyth had still been here…and Nix. They'd have prepared me better. They would have calmed my nerves, and I wouldn't have felt like I was on my own. I could almost hear Elswyth teaching me how to weave a web for those who stood against me. Even in the middle of hell, she would stand tall and instruct me on ways to make the devils bend to my will.

I sat at my desk before my mirror and stared at my reflection. A year ago, I had sat in my bedroom and looked at the same eyes excitedly. I now understood why so many adults I had known, growing up, didn't look in the mirror anymore. It was hard to hide from the truth when it looked back out at you. It was hard to lie to yourself when you could see the lies staring back. And I had told myself so many lies over the years — all of them to avoid the possibility that I'd become a Crow. And now, the lies were told to avoid the possibility of dying as a Crow.

I stood and turned in a circle. My hair was pulled into knots on top of my head, and black pearls were at my ears and neck. A tight black dress clung to my body, leaving little to be imagined. I slipped on black feathered shoes that sparkled with each step. But the statement piece, as Elswyth would call it, were black feathers that wrapped around my shoulders like a shawl. Rather than the gowns I had worn for the Golden Court, I would be the Crow that I had been forced to become.

"Perdi," Solas called from my door with a knock.

I unlocked my door and stepped out. "Good evening."

"Wow." He drew out the word as he looked me up and down. "You look beautiful."

"Just like old times, *Soulless*." I dragged out his name with a smile that didn't falter. I slid my arm into his. "Shall we?"

He didn't take my bait tonight any more than he had before. Like last time, he grinned. "Do you think you can keep yourself from the lash tonight?"

"I wouldn't want to screw with tradition," I answered.

"Alas, I'm without a dungeon. But I'm sure I could scrounge something up. No one forgets their last night in the Dark Courts."

"Competing with my first night in Elphame… How egotistical of you."

"I wasn't wrong then, either."

"When I had first come to Elphame, you promised I'd learn true hurt. You kept that promise." I held my head high as we walked, refusing to allow my pain a place on my face. "But I was also told, if I wanted to survive Elphame, I would need to learn how to be a Crow. I would need to learn to play the game better than everyone else."

He paused and wrapped his darkness around us. "And have you learned to play that game?"

I turned to face him and nodded. "I've found more exciting games to play elsewhere."

"I'm happy to hear you've solved your boredom." His breath caught in his throat for a moment. "Careful of your words. They're not safe with me."

I thought of his riddles and tried to phrase my words in ways he would understand the deeper meaning. "If you could wake up *tomorrow* and could end this all, would you?"

"If I were you, yes, I would. As for myself, I do not have that luxury."

I leaned in and kissed his cheek. "You are king. You answer to no one."

"You were sent to burn this world," Solas whispered back. "We're all waiting for you to strike the first spark."

"I hope the flames find you last," I answered.

"As do I, little Crow. But burn it all, just in case. And this time, don't come back for me."

With Solas leading us to the banquet room, it brought me back to the first night in Elphame — the prying eyes, the judgmental stares. I knew I was nothing but a Crow to them. The only difference was that I dressed the part this night, and I didn't care what they thought. I held my head high, and the rest be damned. We walked into the ballroom, which I had decorated as the terrifying place this court was. Rich textures, black as the night, and red as blood, adorned the tables and walls. It felt like stepping into a nightmare. The very music that played pulled at the edge of your mind and hinted at the dark pleasures found within the room. But unlike the times before, Solas didn't have to drag me in.

He held me on his arm as he circled the room, as he had done so many times before. But it didn't take long for me to leave him and stand on the edge of the room and watch. Once again, I fell back into the patterns learned at the Golden Courts—watching, waiting and regretting. I couldn't muster the spirit I once had, that had kept me alive and in the good graces of King Aelfdene. I flinched with each loud laugh, and my stomach rolled when I watched the Royals carve a path through the room with enslaved Fae on leashes.

"Drink... It'll help." Zephyr slid into position beside me, a place once reserved for someone else. I smiled softly as the memory of Elswyth flooded my mind.

"Thank you." I took the proffered glass. "I'm surprised to see you here."

Zephyr wore his usual black, skintight leather. But tonight, he was armed to the teeth. His eyes didn't stop scanning the room. Any noise that stood out, he zeroed in. Whoever made a wrong move, I pitied them and the results. Zephyr filled a room to the rafters with promise, and none of those promises would one wish to come true. Tonight, though, it rolled off him like steam. His shadows danced high above, watching, waiting. They, like Zephyr, would rain down on whoever stepped out of line. There would be no escape.

I could see Zephyr's men lining every inch of the place, each as threatening as the next. No one ventured too close to an Aos Si. I watched their amusement at the fear of the guests. Part of me pitied the Royals. The other part enjoyed their fear as much as Zephyr's men did.

"Who in their right mind would willingly step into this hall?" I muttered.

"You're here, willingly."

"I suppose you're right. And like them, one wrong move and I'm dead."

"I saw you this afternoon, Perdi. You may be able to hide from Solas, but there isn't a place in this world where you could hide from me." Zephyr leaned into my ear. His shadows slinked from the ceiling and danced around us, blocking my view of the room. I knew, whatever he had to say, was for my ears alone. "Do you think it'll be different the second time with him?"

I froze for a blink. He thought I was going back to Faolan, not using the tools I had at my disposal. I thought of a dozen different ways I could spin it but knew he'd see through all of them and resent me for even trying. But I couldn't tell all the truth — not now, not ever, not out loud. "In the words of your fine king, the enemy of my enemy is my friend."

"Did you enjoy his friendship the first time? He is not your friend, and I've told you as much. The scars on your back should tell you how little he values your life."

"Thanks for that reminder, bastard." His comment made me flinch. I fought against the urge to move my feathers to hide the lashing scars on my back. "Solas isn't exactly my friend right now, either. But Faolan is a tool I need, and he won't kill me as fast as this place will."

"He is using you for something. I can smell it. It crawls on my skin like the disease he is."

I smiled. "We're all tools, Zephyr. Isn't that what you said? And it's my decision on how I allow him to use me."

"You're going to get yourself killed. You ask for help, ask for guidance and take none of what I offer. That, little Crow, is well beyond our oath. You're choosing to put yourself in harm's way, and I can't stop it unless I tell Solas. That would be me living up to our agreement, so don't push me."

I laughed as if he had said something funnier than catching me as a traitor. I laughed because how I felt at that exact moment reminded me that I could be pushed around on a whim, that I was seen as someone who could be threatened. I didn't try to hide my anger — angry at the games, the bravado, the constant threat of death and torture, angrier that he would sell me out so quickly. I knew he was trapped between decisions, but so was I, between life and death. I pulled the mask I had carefully crafted in the Golden Court snug. It would hurt me to hurt Zephyr, to lie to his face. But I would do it to save us all. Hurting him was not a fate worse than death, and we'd both get over it. Even if he didn't, we'd all still be alive enough to hate each other.

"Go ahead, tell Solas what I'm doing. He already plans to kill me, so why not get it done with tonight? It would make for great entertainment. There isn't a soul here who wouldn't clap at my hanging. I can feel it, their surprise that I'm still alive, that I've been allowed to live this long. You would probably be hailed a hero for killing the Crow who killed a king."

"You're forcing my hand."

"Indeed, I am. I couldn't possibly imagine how it would feel to have someone else pulling on the strings of your life," I answered sarcastically and turned to face him. "If you mention it to Solas, I wonder how much more harm would come to me than if you were to keep your mouth shut. I wouldn't hesitate to call you an oath breaker, Zephyr, since we both know my death at his hands this very night is far worse than anything that will happen to me tomorrow or the next day. You do not control my fate or my path. You cannot help patch the wings of a Crow and expect her not to fly. Do not push me, Zephyr. There's nothing I'm not willing to do to protect my people."

He pulled back like I had stung him. I saw the hurt in his eyes as they narrowed on mine. "You and I are in the same boat, little Crow, only you can't swim these waters as well as I can. Like you, there's nothing I won't do to protect my people, including from the messes you always find a way into, even if that means I must deal with being an oath breaker. Never doubt who or what I am. You're picking a fight with the wrong person."

"I'm glad to see I'm not the only one with a plan to save people who depend on us. What else would you do to protect your people? Or are you just talking about protecting him?" I asked and pushed the shadows away. The room was as it was before, and if anyone had noticed, no one was saying a word about it. I glanced at Solas, who was laughing with another group of people. But he could be standing in the middle of hell and adapt. "How many innocents are worth a throne? How many of my kind should die for a crown? You say you're willing to do anything to protect your people.

Just imagine what I would be willing to do to protect mine. I, unlike you, have nothing to lose."

"Your life," he answered.

I shrugged. "If all I have is an hour, a day, a week, I should use that time wisely, no?"

He grabbed my arm as I went to leave. "Perdi, these people are your people as well."

I pulled away. "Pretty thoughts, Zephyr. Maybe at one time, these guilt trips worked, but not anymore. How does one find freedom when they're trapped in grief that is not their own? How do I climb out of these wounds when I let you all bleed on me and drag me back in? I cannot be responsible for saving everyone, only myself."

"You'd let them die?" he asked, almost confused that my heart wasn't bleeding all over the floor for them. "You'd watch them burn for your crusade?"

"Oh no you don't. This isn't my crusade. I'm being dragged behind the boat, and I'm only just learning how to swim," I countered. But the look on his face stilled my nerve. "No, I wouldn't. I'd protect them, as I would any other who needed it. But unlike my people, yours have you and Solas and all you command, the very darkness of this world, to protect them. All my people have is me." I paused and looked out over the room. I wanted to be anywhere but there. What I had thought would be a great way to needle Solas did nothing more than hurt my heart. "Zeph, how did we go from a pep talk to you dragging me back down? You can't have it both ways. You either want me to do whatever I can to live or you want to watch me die. Which one is it?"

He groaned out his frustration. "That's not fair to say."

"Nothing is fair. After all this time, you should know that well by now. It's something you've been beating into my head since I got here. You can either help me or hinder me. The choice is yours to make." I leaned in for only him to hear. "I'm asking that you trust me, trust in who you know I am. If you don't, if you have no faith in me, then I am your enemy, and you can tie the noose yourself. Either way, I will do what I must and hope you'll not bring my end faster than fated. I love you more than my own life but not more than the lives of innocents. I don't love anyone enough to let them all die."

I stepped away, and he didn't reach for me again. I left the banquet, pulled the wards up over my bedroom and locked my door. For weeks, I had locked my bedroom door, and for weeks, I had heard Solas try the knob. I stopped opening it the day he started hiding things from me. I knew then, as I know now, that things were going to end in bloodshed. I may have been sent to burn their world, but Solas ignited the fire that I would use to spread that destruction.

I listened to the party rise and finally fall, ending in the wee hours of the night. After the last of the guests had left, I felt Solas on the other side of my door, as I had so many nights. He usually stood there, contemplating whether he should knock or not. Usually, he didn't. He'd stopped trying long ago. I felt his darkness press down around us, sealing us off from those who listened.

"I'm sorry that you were ever caught in the middle of this. I'd take it back if I could."

I leaned against my door and let the tears fall. "I've found the other way. I've packed for winter."

"I know. Goodbye," he answered. I listened to him walk away and close himself into a bedroom I hadn't gone to since his lies had started.

Chapter Fourteen

At breakfast, I sat with Zephyr and Solas, all of us silent, all of us knowing we were on the brink of something none of us wanted, but none of us were willing to say the words. Like some sort of magical thinking, if we didn't say it out loud, it wouldn't come true, and we'd be able to draw out this moment forever. But eating them down would do nothing to stop them from coming. A pin could drop, and we would have jumped, our minds scrambling to the worst possible scenario. Because that's really all that was left, the very worst of what was yet to come.

So much was wrong with this moment that I couldn't point to just one thing to fix. It wasn't a comfortable silence to be in the middle of. It spoke volumes of the struggle we each felt, the uncertainty with our destinies. Each path overlapped the other in a bloody mess, and it would only get bloodier. We all knew this truth, and no one wanted to be the first to say it out loud. So, as we sipped our morning coffee and nibbled on food that tasted of cardboard, we swallowed down truths we weren't willing to share.

"Did you enjoy the party?" Solas finally spoke, avoiding the silent monster in the corner that bit off chunks of us as we sat and watched. But for the first time, he and I were calm and didn't reach across the table with snide remarks set to wound the other. It was as easy as it was difficult.

I nodded and rubbed my temples. "Too much wine, I think. But you know how I am at banquets, glass after glass. I feel like I slept in a gutter."

"I told you to take it easy." He laughed, and it was the first real laugh I had heard in ages.

"I don't think I know what that means," I answered and joined his laughter with my own. It certainly didn't feel like I had ever known the easy way.

"Well, this doesn't feel uncomfortable at all." Zephyr shattered the façade. I knew he would be the one to do it. He wasn't shy and didn't care how his words landed. He simply spoke his mind and damned the fallout. "We're all dancing around an uncomfortable truth, and no one wants to say it. We may not be cutting each other up, but I can feel the slices just the same. If we aren't going to talk about it, why the hell are any of us even here?"

"No, Solas and I are on the same page," I countered and looked to the other end of the table. "Wouldn't you agree, Solas?"

He nodded. "I'd agree. We both recognize where the other stands and what must be done."

"Am I the only one who doesn't know what the hell is going on?" Zephyr asked.

"It appears so," I answered.

"Does one of you plan to fill me in?"

"No," Solas answered. He rotated his shoulders then glanced around the room, a motion not lost on Zephyr or me. "Some things are better left unsaid."

"No, Solas, they're not. And I don't care who is listening. They are welcome to come and ask me whatever questions they may have." Frustrated, Zephyr pushed his plates away with enough force to send them over the other side to crash into shards. "I want answers, *now*. I will not blindly follow either of you to my death."

"We're not asking you to," Solas countered.

"The hell you're not. Whatever the hell is going on is cutting us up as good as any war."

"Ain't that the truth," Solas muttered. He looked down the table and settled on me. Once our eyes locked, his shoulders finally relaxed. "War in here or war out there. It only matters where you're standing when it comes."

"Don't you dare do this…not like this. I don't give a shit why this is happening anymore. This isn't the way. This will not end well," Zephyr thundered.

"But it will end, just the same," I answered.

Before I could change the subject, before Solas and Zephyr could blow up into a rage that I didn't want to be anywhere near, we were interrupted by a messenger. It was the first time Solas and I were relieved to see the man. Usually, the messenger got a snarl from Solas, and I got a signal that it was time for me to leave the room. He placed a letter on the table beside Solas, who picked it up and flipped it around. He held it in view long enough for me to see the writing. A deep growl escaped his lips. He opened it and scowled.

"For the love of Gods." He groaned. "This shit never ends, not even for a day. It's always one thing or another."

"What is it?" I asked.

He shook his head and pushed it into his pocket. "Nothing, just court business."

But I recognized the writing. It was from Faolan. Instantly, my heart sank. Did he sell me out? Did he do as Zephyr had threatened that he would? Was he saving himself at my expense?

"I have a meeting this evening. Are you okay with being on your own for a few hours? I will be gone for four hours, maybe five if needed." His gaze was as heavy as the decisions that hung in the air. He was giving me my out.

"Yes, if I need something, Zephyr will feel me," I answered. "Meet me for a late dinner, say, in five hours?"

"I have a few things to do beforehand. I'll be leaving after lunch, and I'll be gone for about five hours. I won't be gone longer than that," he answered, and I did everything I could to keep my mouth shut and not cry. We both knew what I was about to do, and neither of us could say any parting words.

After breakfast, I left the two of them alone to discuss the letter. I spent the morning reading in the library — or at least faking it so I could listen in on them arguing in Solas' office. Neither Solas nor Zephyr blocked me from hearing. Faolan had sent him a message, asking to meet, asking to build an alliance, to better their relations. Solas thought Faolan wanted to get near me and was going to go set him straight. I was part of Solas' court, and Faolan would never see me again.

Everyone knew that Solas moved for two reasons — war and a little Crow, and Faolan had tickled both boxes with one letter. Both Solas and Zephyr argued back and forth over why Faolan would reach out, out of the blue. Each reason Zephyr had given, Solas shot down. He would meet with the Unseelie King and set things straight, once and for all. I belonged to the Dark Courts, and nothing Faolan could say would change it. Zephyr thought Solas was a fool, but I knew differently. If Solas was anything, a chump would not be the word I'd use to describe him or any of his motives.

"Why keep her?" Zephyr asked.

"What the hell is that supposed to mean?" Solas asked.

"You don't even want Perdi here. Even I can see that. Why keep her locked up here? Just let her go."

"Faolan doesn't want her there, either. He wants what she can give him. He wants the power that comes with her. To have Perdi in his court, he thinks she'll protect him once this war comes. But nothing will save him from it. He's in as deep as the rest of us. His hands are as tied as mine. He may have more answers than I can give, but he is under the same oaths as the rest of us."

I listened to the clues he'd leave behind for me. I wasn't silly enough to throw my trust in with Faolan, but I did trust his need for me, that was until he no longer had that need. If his hands were tied, like Solas', digging the truth out of that court was going to be more difficult than I had expected. But the answers were there. It was still doable, given I didn't care if I had to dig the truth out of his cold, dead body.

Zephyr laughed. "It's the same reason you want her—her power. And it'll be the same reason you lose her."

"For once, Zephyr, you don't know what you're talking about."

"No, I think I do. And I think it bothers you that I'm trying to extinguish every fire you set before you burn your bridges. As you fight a war I can't see, I'm trying to keep a very real one from burning us all."

"Get out and get ready, Zephyr," Solas commanded. "We leave in a few hours. Go. Be anywhere other than in front of me until then."

"You will lose her, and I won't try to bring her back." Zephyr stormed from Solas' office.

"For once, I pray you don't," Solas said and slammed his door hard enough for me to slink out of the library.

* * * *

From my balcony, I watched Solas and Zephyr leave through the back garden. Every guard in the castle had gone with them. Never had he left me alone until now. At the edge of the forest, Solas looked back once, knowing exactly what I had planned to do. I caught myself waving to him and pulled my arm back down. He dropped his head and stepped into the darkness. He was giving me the only chance he could—for me to save my people, for me to save myself and, if I could, to save us all. Nothing I had told myself prepared me to see his face as he walked away. If I thought I had loved him before, it didn't compare to the love I felt for him right now, as he sacrificed his own soul for mine.

Zephyr didn't bother looking back. He would have felt it without having to see the tears on my cheeks.

As soon as the last guard was gone, I got ready. I stripped out of my casual clothes and put my carefully curled hair back in a braid. I pulled on my training clothes — leather pants, boots and a tight-fitting jacket. I grabbed my pack from the rear of my closet and waited for Orrian. It felt like I had eaten up all my hours waiting for her. When she streamed into my room, the panic started. My heart pounded when she yanked my braid, signaling the coast was clear, and it was time to go. I followed her through the house and out of the back door. We left the Dark Manor on foot, and I didn't look back. I pulled a spell over us to protect and hide us and ran. The spell was weak, just enough for us to blend in. The cost of anything greater would come with a payment I couldn't cover later while on the run. I would never be able to hide from Zephyr. There was no magick I could cast that would be powerful enough to block out a Finis who held my pearl, but I would hide from the sentries on the property.

I was a silent wind. Any sound would call attention, and I stepped carefully, deliberately, cautious of every movement. A single noise could draw the biggest of attention. I kept myself calm and balanced, as Zephyr had taught me. Any rise in my anxiety would tell Zephyr something was wrong, and he'd send his shadows to check on me. But I had just spent weeks in an emotional hellhole. Whatever he was feeling from me now would be no different. He had grown used to my emotional ups and downs.

I tucked Orrian into my pocket and ran through the trees. Nothing followed, but my fear still told me I was being chased. Some ancient voice from a time of caves and monsters had reared up and told me to run faster, that it didn't matter if I couldn't see the monsters, they were there, and they were going to eat me if they caught me. Something terrible must have happened to our ancestors for my rear to be clenched the entire time I ran.

Faolan was waiting at the tree, exactly when and where he said he'd be. I paused for a moment and questioned the little bit of trust I was giving him. I knew he could abuse what I gave, but I had no other option. It was all or nothing now. There was no turning back. I dropped my spell. For my people, I had no choice but to put my faith in a man who saw me as the same tool I saw in him. I couldn't really blame him, given what I was about to do for my own people. If Faolan sold me out, the worst that could happen to me was being dragged back to my prison and hanged. The best, Solas would save me, only to kill me later. Either way, I'd be dead and would have nothing left to worry about. All this hell would no longer be my problem. The dead don't care about such things. How tempting that was.

"Perdi, it's okay," Faolan whispered in the night air. "I'm alone."

I stepped out of the brush and let Orrian out of my pocket. "When you sent the letter to Solas, I worried you were telling him I was a traitor."

"I asked him to meet to discuss strengthening our ties. It should keep him busy for a little while. He always gets there long before he's due to arrive to scope out the threats and position his men. We usually watch him long after we've already done the same. We have an hour lead before he starts to suspect why I'm not there," Faolan explained. "We'll go down through my territory. My men will get word to me if Solas becomes suspicious, then we can head inland."

"He'll come for me eventually," I said. "No matter the reason I've left, he will never let go. He can't. He won't."

"He would be foolish to come into Unseelie territory to find you, and if anything, Solas is very much not a fool. He's never entered my territory, neither him nor his men. He would need to take all of Elphame before he came for my lands, and even then, he'd fail. He is not the only one with higher powers looking over his shoulder, and those powers won't be thrilled if Solas oversteps." He held out his hand. "Are you ready?"

I wanted to tell him he was a fool to think his puppet master would lift a finger to save him. Instead, I nodded and gripped his hand. "Will you take me home? I need to warn my people."

"I told you I would," he answered and pulled me to his side. "If we are stopped, give me your word you will keep running. Get back to my lands. My people will help you."

"What about you?" I asked.

"We're not talking about me. I want *your* word. If Solas or his people stop us, you'll run to my people."

"I give you my word," I answered. I looked to Orrian, who would be remaining. She would be going to Nix to tell him what had happened, to warn him from returning to the Dark Courts. We hadn't bothered asking for her safe passage, as she was a fairy. No one would chance stopping her out of fear, and we would be safe with Faolan. "Good luck, Orrian."

Faolan pulled me into his body, and we ran as if we were the very wind. Faolan moved as though he were a snowstorm, nothing stopping the icy crystals from their landing, and I was along for the ride. He knew the grounds and forests, and they knew him. Trees moved, brush opened for him and rocks moved from his path. My skin tingled as his magick rolled over me and carried me with him. It should have taken the day to move across his land, but we were pushed and pulled and carried to the border of the Court of Less, where the Gate was held, in under an hour.

"Do not stop, no matter what, Perdi. If Solas comes, you will keep running. I will keep your path cleared."

"But...I can't just leave you," I answered.

"If Solas finds me in his territory without free passage, he can stop me in any way he sees fit. I doubt he would kill you, but me, on the other hand? He won't be happy to see me here with you."

"Death. It's always death with him."

Faolan nodded. "It wouldn't be Elphame if we were allowed to live without death always knocking."

He gripped my hand, and we ran. Within minutes of entering Solas' territory, I felt the sting, like something inside me was pulling. *My missing pearl.* On the other end of that tether was Zephyr. I could see the shimmering wall. Behind it was the Gate. But I could also see Zephyr standing in front of it, with his arms crossed and a hateful look filling his face.

"Run!" Faolan called out to me.

"I can't run from him. There's nowhere I can run where he won't find me," I answered and kept moving toward the Gate.

"Little Crow" — Zephyr shook his head — "I knew you would do this. The very moment we left, I knew this is where you'd come, and he" — Zephyr glared at Faolan — "would be the one to bring you."

"Can you blame me?" I asked.

"No, I don't," he answered.

"I need you to step aside," I said to Zephyr.

He shook his head. "You know I can't."

"Yes, you can," I answered. "Please, trust in me, in who you know I am. Whatever doubts you have, remember who I am. Please, I'm begging you, let me pass. You don't understand, Zeph. Just trust me. I've earned it."

"Do you know what you're asking of me?" he asked.

"To look the other way, Zeph. To let me save my people," I answered. My shoulders slumped under the pressure of what I was asking him to do. "Please. Just let me warn them. Let me save who I can. Just this once, let me get to those who need me in time. I need to do this. I've always been too late. Let me save who I can this time," I pleaded again.

Zephyr looked from me to Faolan and back. He finally stepped out of the way. "If asked, I didn't see you. But know this... Countless deaths are now on your hands and not mine."

"I would expect no less," I answered. "Thank you."

"Don't thank me. Solas will raze all of Elphame to find you. The reasons will not matter once you're gone. His soul won't care why you left, only that you're not there." Zephyr shook his head and looked to Faolan. "This, little King, will not end well for you. I hope you know what you're doing. I pray you understand what hell you've invited into your life."

"Not in the slightest." Faolan smiled and pulled me into the mist, leaving Zephyr to fend for himself and the mess I was leaving behind. Whether Solas knew I was leaving or not, the reality of it would eat his soul. Love isn't rational enough to care for such things as life and death. It simply wants what it wants, no matter the cost.

Inside the mist, the Gate barely stood. The earth and trees were dead, rotten to the core. The Gate hung by twisted wires. As I struggled for air, Faolan pulled me to the Gate, and we stepped through together. Smoke filled my lungs and burned away my vision. I was hit from all sides by screams and terror, mixed together into a sludge that filled my mouth and nose and pried my soul from Elphame. The pain, familiar, was everything I had remembered it to be from the first time I had crossed the Gate, dragged me from the place I hated and into the place I had craved for so many months.

The mist stole away my air and popped sharply along my skin, eating away at my life. Although I knew Faolan had stepped in with me, I could no longer feel his hand in mine. It was as if the mist ate every sense at once, leaving me in the between, being pulled by life and death. I inched my way, little by little, unsure of the direction to go. But unlike the first time, I didn't fear where I'd end up, even if the destination was a painful journey. I forced myself to keep moving. Failure was not an option.

The remaining power of the Gate touched me knowingly. It didn't want me there. It didn't want me anywhere near it. It, like me, remembered the last time I had been there.

You shouldn't be here.

The voice snarled, angrier than the last time it had spoken to me.

You bring ruin wherever you go.

It pushed fear against my body, but it couldn't mimic real fear, not the kind I had felt in Elphame. It didn't faze me as it had the first time I stepped along its path. At one time, it was everything I feared. Now, it held back everything I feared.

She will kill you.

"She's welcome to try."

Go back, traitor.

"No."

I couldn't, or all would be lost. Everything I had done, everything I had endured, would mean nothing. I would lose the people I love if I turned around. I pushed forward as it tried to pull me back. I jerked as Faolan yanked me along by my hand. I couldn't feel him but knew it was Faolan, tugging me out of the grips of the Gate. Brilliant light filled my vision like fireworks. The darkness of the Gate was washed away with intense light. I stood in the mortal world, and it was awful.

Chapter Fifteen

My feet touched familiar ground, and I curled forward. My body overflowed with instant pain. It was the kind of pain that told you death had come for tea, and he wasn't leaving until he got his fill. When I tried to breathe the air of home, it felt empty of everything I needed. It was like diving into the sea and trying to breathe between the pounding of the waves. My chest squeezed, and my heart hammered. I dropped to my knees and choked on everything I had once loved. My stomach pushed up every bit of its contents onto the ground of Whitwick. Pieces of Elphame sat on the ground, curdled. My ears rang, and my body twitched, and nothing on this side of the Gate could stop it. This would not be the return to the mortal world I had hoped it would be. This was as dreadful and painful as my first step into Elphame had been.

I felt the sweat begin to bead on my forehead as I choked on home. I had wanted so badly to come back that I had forgotten the madness my return to the mortal world could be. Pain wrenched my body, and I thought I would burst into two — half-mortal and half-Fae. I understood, in the most personal of ways, why those who returned struggled to adapt. They returned with broken minds, only to be met with more pain and suffering. It wasn't lost on me why survivors of Elphame had chosen the bottle as their escape. *Anything to numb this pain.*

"I can't breathe." I gagged on my words. I shook my head at the noise. A high-pitched hum pierced my ears and grew louder and louder. I swore my eardrums would burst at any moment. My blood pressure was threatening to climb out of my ears and spill all I was onto the soil of Whitwick.

"Calm yourself, Perdi. It'll pass. I promise it will." Faolan picked me off the ground and carried me out of sight to a small patch of grass to sit on. "Relax and breathe through the pain. Accept it. Stop fighting it. It's a shock to be instantly cut off from Elphame, from the magick."

"But you — " I barely got out before I puked again. "I never saw this happen to you."

"I am king, Perdi. My link to Elphame dampens but doesn't cut off completely. Now, it makes me feel uneasy, like butterflies in my stomach, but that's about it," he answered and rubbed my back. "I've been coming to Whitwick for a lot longer than you've been alive. My body is used to the feeling."

I wondered, for a moment, about his comment. Why had he come to Whitwick before me? Before I could turn his words over in my mind, my entire body shook as if it were jerked between flame and ice. I knew I had to wait it out, as I had before. This time I wasn't as scared as I had been when I had first left. I knew what

I was stepping into, and nothing here would be as terrifying as the land of Fae. When I walked into Elphame, I was assaulted with a reality my mind couldn't grasp. I was bombarded with a world I hadn't known. But I knew Whitwick. I knew home. I wasn't scared, I was relieved and I'd save his comments on coming here for a time where breathing wasn't a struggle.

"This is what you went through whenever you'd come to me?" I finally asked, my head between my knees.

"The first few times, I thought I was dying. I puked so many times that I went home within minutes. But we get used to it. You'll get used to it."

I gagged at the smells that assaulted me at once. "I don't see how. It's awful."

"I know," he answered. "It does get easier each time you move between realms. But you'll always crave Elphame. Nothing short of death can curb that hunger. It's why returned mortals need to be jailed. They never stop trying to return to Elphame."

"Why are the Guardian bells not ringing?" I asked.

"I suspect they haven't noticed us and don't expect the Fae to come until they've received a message of a dead Crow."

"The Guardians know when we die? I didn't know that. So, they know when another Taking will happen, and they don't bother warning us?"

"They're told when a Crow dies, yes. But no, they don't know when the next Taking will happen. The next Taking is decided by the court, which is next in line for a Crow. After a Crow dies, it's usually within a couple of weeks. Until Fae sends a message, everyone relaxes a little too much and fails to notice us coming and going."

"How do we get from here to my house without being seen?"

"If you stay close to me, my magick will hide us both. Unlike you, I'm not cut off from Elphame. I can still use my magick without an issue."

Once the nausea passed and my ears stopped ringing, I was able to walk. Knowing that we wouldn't have to run for our lives calmed my frazzled nerves. I stumbled and held on to Faolan's arm but made it home, where I had grown up. The moment my hand touched the gate to my yard, I broke inside.

"I never thought…" My words caught in my throat around a sob. "I need a minute."

"You never thought you'd make it home alive. It's a terrifying and wonderful feeling to have." Faolan finished my thought, and I nodded. "I knew you'd make it, Perdi."

"That makes one of us." I smiled faintly.

I dried my eyes and stepped through the gate with Faolan at my back. I tried not to rush, not to run full speed into the house. I was desperate to see my father but didn't want to seem like the child I once was. I didn't want him to see the relief or know, from my urgency, what had happened to me on the other side of the Gate. My father didn't need to know the brutal truth of Elphame. It would hurt his soul to know of my suffering.

Everything was as it was when I left. The flower gardens were blooming. The chimes still hung in the trees and scattered along the front stoop. But it looked empty at the same time, like no one who lived here was living. They, like me, were simply existing.

"Dad?" I called out as I stepped through the door.

My father jumped from his chair, and he stared long and hard at me. Confusion filled his face—first, excitement, then utter disbelief. He rubbed his eyes and shook his head.

"Is this...? Am I dreaming?" he asked.

"No," I answered. "You're not dreaming."

"Perdi?" he looked confused.

"Dad." I broke down and cried. I reached out to him but couldn't move my feet. I was frozen in relief and sadness.

"Perdi," he whispered my name as he rushed forward and wrapped his arms around me. "I didn't think... Oh, my Perdi."

His hug felt like every smashed piece of my soul was put back together in one swoop. The barely holding on twine around my heart snapped as my heart was pulled back from the brink. My legs gave out, and I held on as my father squeezed it all back into place. Breathing him in was the only smell that didn't burn. Feeling his arms around me was the only sensation that didn't feel as foreign as the rest of Whitwick now did.

"How...?" my dad started, and Faolan stepped around the door. "Faolan, you got her back. I knew you'd get her back."

"I never stopped trying, sir," Faolan said from my back. "I gave you my word that I'd do what I could to protect her."

"I truly did not think I'd see you again." My father held me tighter. "Why...? How did you get here? How did you leave so soon?"

I pulled back in a panic. The reason I had come finally crashed back. "Dad, we need to warn the Guardians. The Gate, it's going to open, and it'll never close again. It is on the brink of complete collapse. I tried to close it and keep it closed, but I can't any longer. We need to evacuate Whitwick."

"The Gate is going to open? What do you mean?"

"Someone" — I didn't bother naming Solas because it was not entirely him doing it — "found a way to damage the Gate after I closed it. Soon, very soon, the damage will be too great, and the Gate will remain open for good. When that happens, Elphame will invade."

"What about the oaths that protect us? Fae cannot just come and kill indiscriminately, can they?" he asked.

"Yes, they can, and they will. If the Gate falls, your protection falls with it. And there is no oath stating the Gate shall be open or closed," Faolan answered. "When Perdi killed the Golden King, many believe she broke the truce first. Any standing oaths will be challenged. Whether there are grounds to say the oath is moot, is irrelevant. Fae want to invade, so they simply will do it, and there aren't enough naysayers to stop it from happening." Faolan noticed me flinch at his words. "Those much more powerful than me and many others want into Whitwick. That is all that matters. No oath will protect you from who is coming."

"You killed the king?" my father asked, and I nodded.

Faolan interrupted for me. "Killing Aelfdene was the right choice to make, but since the life she seized was the life of the king who took her, half of Elphame claim Perdi broke the oath first and want to invade. It doesn't matter, though, whether there are oaths. Without the Gate closed, there will be nothing stopping them from coming to your lands."

"Can we stop the Gate from falling?" my father asked.

"All the Gate ever did was limit how many mortals could be Taken at once, nothing more," Faolan said. "The Gate will fall. Of that, I have no doubt. The most powerful of Elphame will see to it, and there will be no one standing between Whitwick and all of Elphame."

My father nodded and asked no more questions. He grabbed his jacket and pulled on his boots. "Let's waste no time then."

We followed behind to the community hall, where he called in the entire Guard. It hadn't taken long for them to arrive. The Guardians were always on duty, always prepared for the Fae returning for another Taking. That was the horror of the mortal realm. Every day could be the last. Each night mothers tucked in their children could be the last night they spent with them. It was a hellish way to live. And now, whether they wanted it or not, that way of life would come to an end. Soon, they would no longer wonder. It would be reality.

My father stood at the head of the room, both me and Faolan at his back. We watched as each Guardian stepped into the hall and eyed Faolan. He, a Fae, was not hard to miss. He stood a solid foot taller than the tallest of men. He was pure muscle and contained violence. Nothing about Faolan would make you think he had ever come in peace. I watched as each man wondered if Faolan had come as a friend or an enemy. The only time the Fae had come was for the latter.

"My friends, my daughter has returned with a warning," my father started and stepped to the side for all to see me. For those who hadn't seen me on their way in, a collective gasp echoed in the room. But when they saw Faolan, the gasp turned into something more of a whimper. They didn't trust him any more than I would trust the Fae.

Faolan stepped forward. "The Gate is damaged. You must prepare for the Gate to open indefinitely. The Fae will invade, and you all face slavery and death."

Whispers filled the room. Questions burst through the murmurs.

"How can we trust you?"

"How do we know this isn't a trap?"

"How can we be sure the Fae won't see this as a breach of our oaths?"

Faolan lifted his hands to calm them. "If this were a trap, if I wanted this, why would I come? Why would I warn you? Why would I bring Perdita here? I would simply do nothing and reap the rewards of your fertile lands, after the war is won—and it will be won. I gain nothing from coming here. I put myself at great risk, along with my people, to bring you the chance you'll need if you want to survive."

The hushed voices were now a thunderous boom of anger, and I didn't blame them. Centuries of hardship, sending children to their deaths, and one Fae planned to walk in and change how they felt about them? I stepped forward and cleared my throat. The silence came after each person had their chance to curse Faolan and his people. They didn't say anything I hadn't said to his face, myself. And Faolan didn't look fazed in the least. He was a man of Elphame. There wasn't much that could be said that would stir him.

"Then do nothing." I spoke loud enough for my voice to carry through the room. I didn't want to shame them, but I would if it meant they'd be disgraced into action. "You can do nothing. You can sit on the side and watch it happen. When the Fae come, you can tell them you played no part in this. And when they slaughter you, which I pray to the Gods they'll be kind enough to do, you can die knowing you did nothing." I closed my eyes and gave them simple truths, because their minds would never comprehend the savagery of what would come should we fail. "The courts, the armies that plan to invade, will torture your families, your children, in ways I care not to repeat. If you are one of the lucky few, you'll be dead before they drag your daughters back to the land that makes you wish for death. You will not survive Elphame, and if, by some horrible twist of fate, you do, you'll regret doing nothing about it when you had the chance. Trust me when I tell you, you will always remember that first day in Elphame, and nothing in this world, the mortal world, will ever come close to the horror of day one. The next day isn't easier. The longer you stay alive, the worse it gets, and the harder you pray to a God that isn't listening, for your death."

"How can we stop the Fae?" one man asked.

"You can't stop them," Faolan answered. "Nothing you could ever do would stop the Fae from coming."

"Then what the hell do we do?" the same man called out.

"Run. That's the only thing you can do," I answered. "Get our people as far away from Whitwick as possible."

The room erupted once again, and I groaned. There was no winning. But I hadn't expected to win here. I was delivering a death sentence for some, if not most of them. I couldn't protect them. I could only bring them the news of doom. The Gate falling was what haunted the nightmares of all mortals. And I stood before them, bringing those fears into reality. I understood every emotion that flooded the room. Like them, I had the same thing happen to me when I was Taken. And my worst nightmare was still playing out.

"Enough!" Faolan finally yelled over everyone arguing and silenced the room. "Whether you trust Perdi and me or not doesn't change what will happen to the mortal realm. They are coming, and no amount of denial or argument is going to change that. You can stand here and fight until they bang down your doors, or you can act. Fighting has never worked in the past, not once. Despite what you may believe, I am not the one with anything to lose here. You are. I only gain from your suffering, and that is the godawful truth of Fae. The choice is entirely yours. But know this... When they get here, those who are strong enough to fight, you will die first, because you are who I would kill first. And that's the easy part...killing. Then, your women will be Taken. Your children will be Taken. There are no oaths to protect them. They will become slaves to Elphame, to Fae, to the very nightmares you fear. If you thought becoming a Crow was the worst thing to be in Elphame, you are sadly mistaken. A Crow, at least, is protected by oaths. You no longer have those protections." Faolan shivered as memories flickered behind his eyes. "You have no real choices in this fight. You either run and hope to live, or you stay and plan to die."

"And be at the mercy of the Fae," my father added.

I shook my head. "No. There is no mercy or pit to be found with the Fae. That is not what you will find there. There is no human kindness on the other side of that Gate. They don't play by our rules. They play for keeps." I felt Faolan stiffen with my reply. But it was the truth, nonetheless. "If you live through it, you'll wish you hadn't."

"But how do we trust a Fae?" one man asked.

"You don't," Faolan answered. "I'm not asking for your trust. Your trust in me won't save a single life. You'd be wise to never trust one of my kind. What I am asking, however, is for you to save your people. Do what you can to get your people out of Whitwick *now*. The longer we talk, the more time we give them and the more victims they'll have."

"What about you? You both came here out of the goodness of your hearts?" one of the guards asked. "What do you get out of this?"

"Peace," Faolan answered. "I want peace for once. I want to live alongside you, without fearing the death that comes when our people come together. I want to stop seeing your children marched into Elphame, only to find them dead within weeks. I'm so sick of seeing my people die, trying to protect yours. This must end." Faolan grabbed my hand and pulled me to his side. "The one you sent to Elphame has paid with her blood to get here, to warn you. She has endured horror after horror to ensure you are safe. Every pain she suffered was to keep you all alive. Everything she has done has been for you all. She could have remained in Elphame, safe within my borders, but she didn't. To warn you, she will now be hunted by the very nightmares of our people. What all of Fae fear most will come for her first. She has given her soul to her people, and you question her intent? How dare you. You have no right to question her or what she's had to do to get back to you. You have no idea what she's done to ensure you've been warned. Instead of thanking her, you throw insults. You do not deserve her loyalty or love."

My father stood and lifted his hands to bring the room to silence. "We evacuate tonight. Those of you who wish to stay to guard the Gate, you would be welcome. A war, I fear, is coming — a war we cannot lose. As Faolan has said, this must stop. I, too, grow tired of sending our children to the slaughter. I will not send another. Stay and fight or get out of our way, but know, we will not suffer fools who wish to stay and ignore the truth of what is coming."

Faolan stood with my father and spoke to the other guards. They planned an escape route and places where my people could hide. Faolan told them how to protect themselves the best they could, the metals to use to ward their bodies, the roots to eat, the flowers to hang in the windows. It would not stop the most powerful of Fae, but it would slow the lesser ones. It would buy them the time they needed to run. Truthfully, when the Fae finally came, running was all a mortal could do. That, and pray for a quick death. Neither, I suspect, would be easy.

I stood outside the community hall, across from the church, and stared at the gargoyles perched as they always had been. Tonight, one stared back and blinked. War had always been coming to the land of mortals. What I could do to protect them was to tell them to run. But I knew, deep inside, they couldn't run from the Fae for long. They were a curse that spread faster than a disease. I had tried and failed, many times, to run from them. If the Gate fell, the entire mortal realm, far beyond our small parcel of land, would suffer as we had for generations.

* * * *

The rest of the night and into the early morning was spent warding every outpost around Whitwick—a complete circle of wards around the Gate to slow the Fae from pushing beyond and into the village in a surprise attack. It wouldn't keep them out for long but would give the people enough of a warning to ready themselves for the fight that was coming. Anyone who hadn't left would be granted precious minutes to get out. For those who did leave, I instructed them not to tell Faolan or me where they'd be going. That information wasn't safe with us. Truthfully, it was because I knew that information wasn't safe with Faolan. He answered to the same person Solas did. I wondered, though, why he was helping me. If his hands were tied like every other king, how could he help me and not pay for it as Solas would have? Not knowing the answers, I'd keep my cards as close to my chest as I could. He was a tool, and I didn't need to fully trust a tool for it to be useful.

I sat on the back steps that overlooked Nix's garden and held my stomach. It growled, not of hunger, but of pain. I was drained of energy, of all my magick. I was empty of Elphame, and it cramped and pulled at my mind like a nagging thought. I couldn't risk a spell since I could risk making the payment for one. Instead, I'd let my stomach cramp. I now knew why the others went mad and fell into delirium. What was left of their body and mind, what hadn't been broken by Fae, was consumed with the need to return, to fill the void that only Elphame could. No matter what I did or how much I occupied myself, I couldn't ignore the itch in the back of my mind. And the more time that went by, the deeper that itch dug.

I held a small buttercup Nix used to snack on. They grew everywhere in the yard, planted with care by Nix and myself, so many years ago that it felt like I was remembering a lifetime belonging to someone else. I twirled the flower back and forth in my fingers. As tiny as it was, it carried the weight of decisions I had finally made. For such a small flower, it was everything to me—all my memories, my past, my future, the lives of us all. I had left Solas in the arms of Faolan and returned to the mortal world, which would have scorched under the touch of Fae, had I not risked it. Solas had tried to keep me on the sidelines, away from the risks and pain, and now I had made myself a key player in a game I didn't know how to win. Solas had fought hard to keep me out of this, and I'd jumped in, head first. He had to have known I'd do this, join the fight, from day one. He counted on me in ways he couldn't say.

Even though I knew there were others forcing his hand, my heart still broke just the same at the memories of how I had gotten here. Thinking back to each conversation, every hint he had given me, I had been so blind. He'd warned me, but I wasn't willing to see the truth until we were nearing the end of a game I didn't know I had been a part of. And now, I was a world away, just beginning to learn how to play. Perhaps, if the Gods and Goddesses allowed it, we would save everyone. But I didn't know if we could save us, him and me. Regardless of the reasons, I think far too much had been done, said and not said, to go back to a wound I didn't know how to close. It didn't matter if he willed the gashes on my soul or not. They hurt just the same. Even if we couldn't go back to how it once was, I still would fight for those who had no one else to protect them. It was who I was, for better or worse. And if we survived what was coming, I'd know then if it was worth it.

When my father returned home, he took a seat beside me and put his arm around my shoulder. We sat like that, silent, for almost an hour — just me and him, overlooking a place my mother had loved to spend her days and nights. As a witch, the earth, the wild, the wind, it all called to her. She would get lost in time, digging the soil, drying flowers and mixing spells and tonics. Hours would pass until she realized the morning had disappeared into the night. I can still remember the smell of magick and soil on her cheeks when she'd tuck me in at night. I wish I could do the same, just sit here until the sun came up and ignore the call back to the wilds of Elphame. *Will the time away be frozen in my memories of better days?*

"I've missed you," my father said, then he sighed. "Even if all we get is this night before the Gate comes down, I'm thankful I got to hold you once again."

My eyes prickled with unshed tears. The tears would come, but I would hold them back until they didn't hurt my father, until I was far enough away that he wouldn't have to see me cry again. "Dad, I can't stay. I have to go back."

"Why? You just got home?"

"But I can't stay. I've been gone too long." I didn't have the heart to tell him I was too much Fae to stay — that the mortal realm hurt me now as much as Elphame had first hurt me. "If I don't go back, they will use my leaving to prove I've broken the oath. I may have killed Aelfdene, but they will use this to storm the Gate, long before it's broken. We can't give Elphame any more reason to come. We will need this time to prepare and save our people."

He stood and held out his hand to me. "Give me a moment to collect some things, and we'll be on our way."

"What?" I asked. "What do you mean?"

"Perdi, you are my home. You are all I have, and I will not lose you again. We will go to Elphame together," he answered. "I will not send my child back to that place. Hell, or high water, you will not go alone again."

"Trust that I'm not alone there. I have Nix, and I have...other friends. I can't ask you to come to Elphame, Dad. If my enemies found you, I don't even want to think of what they would do to you to get to me." I squeezed his hand and stopped fighting him, thinking back to my conversation with Solas in the kitchen. Had he warned me to bring my father to safety? He wouldn't have mentioned it if he didn't think I should have my father close to me, away from Whitwick and the risk of Fae invasion. If Solas had said anything, even in his riddles, he said it for a good reason. Even without direct words, he'd told me to bring my father back to Elphame.

My father pulled me to my feet. "Since I won't let you go alone, we go together. End of story, Perdi."

"It wouldn't be a bad idea to have a Guardian in Elphame, Perdi." Faolan stepped out of the house, as he had hundreds of times before. Seeing him in the light of the house brought back memories of spending countless nights with him. I wanted to shove them out. I didn't want to remember the days when I had trusted him with my life.

"He won't be safe in Elphame," I countered.

"I will grant him sanctuary in Tylwyth."

"And if they come for him?" I asked.

"They'll come for him no matter where he is. As a Guardian, he will be the very first to die here in the mortal world," he answered, and I gave him a stern look. He raised his hands as if to surrender. "It's exactly what I would do and what you would do. We would take out the strongest before picking off the weakest. At least, if he's with us, we can protect him. If we leave him here, no mortal can stand against us and win."

I smiled. "I did."

Faolan nodded and smiled. "You're no mere mortal."

He helped my father pack while I wandered the halls of my family home. I collected photos and little pieces of a life I knew I'd never return to. Part of me screamed to remain, the part of me that didn't want to step foot back into the Sidhe, the part that was still young and naïve and scared. But a larger part of me scolded my fear and weakness and reminded myself of why I had to return. It was true what I had said to my father about the oath. I couldn't give Elphame a reason to come sooner. Every hour it took for Solas to tear down the Gate was another hour my people had to run.

We stood at the shimmering wall, and I held my father's hand. "This is going to hurt, Dad, beyond anything you can imagine. It will steal your breath and your will to live. Whatever you hear or see in there, whatever promises it makes you, do not stop for anything. The only thing that's real in there will be your death. And when you come out on the other side, you'll wish you had died in there."

"When we get there, to Elphame, get ready to run. We are stepping into enemy territory, with war in the air," Faolan added and held on to my father to pull him out the other side.

Chapter Sixteen

As someone who had passed through the Gate twice before, I knew the fear and pain my father would feel, as this would be his first. But when we came out the other side in Elphame, my father was far from my mind as I finally gasped for air I didn't even know I starved for. I filled my body until my hands stopped shaking, and the cramps in my stomach finally subsided. My walk through the Gate had been everything I knew it would be, but my return had come with ease. It felt like I had been holding in my breath in Whitwick and had only allowed myself slivers of air, killing myself slowly and painfully. Stepping back onto Fae ground felt like coming home after too many years away. Relief flooded my system, and for the first time, I was thankful to be in Elphame.

My father, who hadn't the faintest drop of Fae blood in his old bones, keeled over within seconds and screamed wordlessly. He clawed at the air, railing against the pain. It would be a battle he wouldn't win easily. His experience would be worse than mine, and I still remembered how utterly horrible it had been for me. If I had prayed for death, I knew my father would swear it was upon him.

"Don't fight it." I knelt beside my dad. I tried to grab his hand, but he battled me blindly. I looked up at Faolan, who was on high alert, scanning the grounds for Solas and his men. I didn't bother telling him that Solas knew the moment I left and the very moment we came back. "What do I do?"

"There's nothing you can do. But we must go now."

"He can't walk, and I won't leave him here."

Faolan leaned over and lifted my father over his shoulder as though he was nothing more than a bag of flour. My father railed against Faolan's hold, thrashing out in pain and fear. I felt Faolan's chilled magick slide over my father and calm his quaking body. "I'd never suggest we leave him. But we do need to go now."

The ease my return had given me was replaced by nervousness. With my father in Faolan's arms, we began the dangerous task of walking through Solas' territory. We moved slower with my dad, a lot slower than either Faolan or I wanted to go. The journey to the Gate had been swift. The walk back, on the other hand, was like wading through mud.

"What I wouldn't give for a horse right now," I whispered to Faolan as I punched at the burning pain in my tired thighs.

"A horse?" He looked over my father's back to me.

"Yeah, it would beat having to run on my own steam. This is getting tiresome, running from one end of Elphame to the other. I'm not built for this."

Faolan chuckled. "Could you imagine a horse here? Not only would we terrify them, but they'd also be pretty useless in most cases."

"Not in my case."

"Fae can move faster than any horse. Plus, horses cannot creep through the forest. They'd have to carry us in the open. Would you want to be out in the open right now or any of the other times you've had to run?"

"I suppose not," I answered. "But right about now, I'd probably risk it."

"I've seen you on a horse in Whitwick. I doubt they'd be of any help to you here, regardless. Horses don't like you any more than they'd like me. In fact, I'd be carrying both you and your father, once you broke your neck."

"Point made." I smiled. "Don't you have something similar here in Elphame?"

"Do any of us look like we'd willingly carry you around on our backs?" I stared at him, carrying my father over his shoulder, and he grinned. "Point made. But no, there's nothing similar to a horse."

The journey to Tylwyth was uncomfortably calm as we moved through Solas' territory, skirting the edge of it as much as possible. There was no opposition, no Solas, no darkness, no army standing in our way...nothing. The quietness did nothing to ease my anxiety. If anything, it made my nervousness worse. Nothing in Elphame was this easy. Nothing was this calm. Elphame was the very definition of chaos. Death crawled across the earth as it flew in the sky. There wasn't ever a time you weren't hunted, either for power, for revenge or for food. But now, there was nothing, and that terrified me more than if I were to run smack into Solas' chest. Not because I was scared of him but because I knew I wouldn't be able to keep walking toward Winter Court. I wondered where he was and if Zephyr had told him about me crossing the Gate. He would have to have known. He saw everything. Was he waiting, or was he already pillaging Faolan's land?

Faolan pointed forward. "Almost there, Perdi. I want you to run."

"What about you, my dad?" I asked.

"We'll be right behind you," he answered. "If Solas comes, keep running. I'll bargain for your father."

"If he has you both, what kind of bargain is that?" I asked.

"I'll think of something. It wouldn't be the first time I've walked out of Solas' lands in one piece. Whatever comes of it, he won't kill your father. His dislike is for me, not you, not your family. I need you to go, Perdi."

"I doubt that very much, Faolan. If the Gate comes down, my family will die as quickly as the rest."

"Solas is many things, Perdi, but a traitor is not one of them. Throughout all of time, he has never broken his word. He would protect your father because he knows how important he is to you. I wouldn't doubt it if your father was the only one that would be left standing at the end."

"Why the sudden defense of him?" I asked.

"I'm not defending him. But the truth is the truth, regardless of what else is happening. Our dislike of each other doesn't water down who the other is simply because we wish it so."

Faolan breathed in the air as if tasting it and looked to the sky. Before I could argue, I felt it in my bones. I could smell their leathery wings...Sluagh. In the distance, hidden in the wind, they were coming.

Getting out of the Dark Courts was all that mattered now. I couldn't stop for anything, and I sure as hell wasn't going to slow down. My legs burned but didn't fail me as I put everything I had left into my run. I was faster than I once was—not Fae speed, but mortal no longer. My eyes stayed glued to my front, as Zephyr had taught me. I jumped over ditches and around stones that would have broken my bones had I tried to climb them. I didn't look back to see if Faolan were coming. I could feel him coming like a storm at my back.

"Run, little Crow," Solas' voice pushed at my back and carried for only my ears to hear. *"War is coming. My lands are no longer safe for Crows to wander."*

Once we crossed into Unseelie territory, I froze at the display of force running toward us. I tried to veer, but Faolan grabbed my arm to signal they weren't who we had to fear. He had his people waiting for us. They stormed to our sides and surrounded us the moment we stepped foot on Faolan's land. His army, what was left of it from the last war I had started, squeezed around us and moved us through the field to safety. I couldn't see much more than the back of vests and boots on the ground. The march rang in my chest like rocks tumbling down a mountainside.

"How often do you do this? Your men look mighty used to this walk." I asked Faolan, sandwiched between his guards.

"Maybe once or twice." He winked.

I heard one of his men bark a laugh.

"Right," I teased.

"Well, I did just spend this last year trying to rescue a little Crow out of a net without starting a war in the process."

"Thank you." I smiled but didn't feel it in my soul. I felt guilty—guilt for asking Faolan to put himself at risk. I wasn't built for these games, not like he was. Whatever Faolan was to me, friend or foe, putting his people at risk didn't sit well with me.

Once we were in the middle of Faolan's territory, the guards moved out and gave us space. We were free from surprise attack—or so they said—but I couldn't keep my eyes off the sky. Faolan passed my father to one of his men after having carried him the majority of the way, limp and sick, near death, in his arms.

"Where are you taking him?" I grabbed the guard's arm.

Faolan squeezed my hand. "He needs attention if he is to make it. Bringing a mortal into Elphame is deadly. He will come to no harm."

"I'll see you soon, Dad," I whispered and gave the guard a nod, but it took the guard pulling away with force for my hand to drop away.

I walked with Faolan and took in everything his land had to offer, from the beauty to the dread that crawled up my legs and told me to run in the other direction. I felt like walking with a nightmare clawing at my legs, promising me death should it reach my throat.

"What the hell is that?" I groaned and rubbed my chest. "It feels like how I'd imagine knowing the exact moment I was going to die."

Faolan nodded. "It keeps out the riffraff."

"Dear God, it's awful."

"It's meant to be. It'll go away in a few minutes." I put myself closer to Faolan. Whatever was out there, it would have to eat us both. But true to his word, the feeling melted away like peeling an orange, piece by piece, the farther we walked through the forest and beyond walls covered in vines.

Tylwyth was nothing like how I expected it to look. It wasn't as grand as other courts I had been in. It wasn't lush or opulent. It was a community. It reminded me of the Dark Court, the Court of Shadows, in how it was beyond words and simple, both at once. Tylwyth was tucked behind forests and mountains, massive chasms in the earth, and wards that made you think you were walking into the waiting mouth of a beast. I had felt that feeling before. The tickle on the back of my neck was both dread and safety. When I stepped off the path, the warning shot down my spine until I stepped back in the direction I was meant to walk.

"Faolan, is this your magick? This dread I feel?" I asked. "It's familiar."

"It's not magick, and I urge you never to go look for it. You'll not like what will find you long before you could ever find it. But I did use it to guide you when you came to Elphame, when you escaped the Golden Courts. I was trying to lead you to Unseelie territory, to me. Whenever you ran away from me, I'd guide you back onto a path to Tylwyth. Unfortunately, each time I got close, you bolted."

"You picked dread to guide me?" I laughed. "Why on earth would you pick something this horrible to send my way? No one in their right mind would follow it."

He blushed. "At the time, I thought it would work."

"When I left the Golden Court, where were you? Why didn't you help me? And maybe this time, try for the truth?"

"Yes, I was there. I fought against King Aelfdene's men while you escaped. I did what I could. Unfortunately, I was there alone, and there wasn't much I could do once you sprang Zephyr loose. I did what every other sane person did. I ran." He answered and shivered at what I suspect was not a fond memory of Zephyr. "I was there, Perdi…every single day."

"I remember seeing you, and those were not good days for me."

"Nor me," he answered. He opened his arms and stepped to the side. "Welcome to the Winter Court."

Tylwyth, closed off from the rest of Elphame, guarded better than the very gates of hell, opened into streets lined with shops and parks and a community square in the center. Trees and flowers and everything that didn't represent an Unseelie Court, painted the city and told me why it was worth protecting. It didn't look like a court or a kingdom. It looked like a home where everything held a slight sparkle, like freshly fallen snow. Icy hues painted the city, blacks and whites, with hints of blue and minty greens. It was as if the problems of Elphame hadn't touched the city, and no one had noticed. The sidewalks bustled with people, all of them going about their day as they had for hundreds of years, not bothered by what happened outside of their walls.

"Where's my father?" I finally asked, noticing Faolan and I stood alone at the top of the hill overlooking Tylwyth.

"At my home," he answered. "He's going to need rest. Pulling a mortal into Elphame, one who has not been marked for Taking, a full mortal at that, is hard on their system, if not deadly. It took you hours to overcome the Fae sickness the first time. But you are a halfling and a Darkmore. Elphame calls to your blood. Your father, though, at his age, without Fae blood in his line, will likely take days or weeks to overcome, with the help of our healers. He needs medications and rest, or he won't make it."

"At the Golden Court, there were mortals. How did they survive?" I asked.

"I don't think you want that answer." Faolan's face flushed. Anger, shame, disgust, passed over his face like reading a book. But I didn't relent. "Most who came looking for Elphame, if not all, had a little Fae in their lineage. But all, regardless of their bloodlines, were nursed back to health by Fae and presented to the court as gifts."

"You were right. I didn't need to know that. Nursed back, only to die," I answered with the same disgust on my face. "Did you ever take anyone from the mortal realm?"

"No." He shook his head. "I never took from the mortal world because I know what it's like to live in fear. I know what it's like to be controlled and have no choice."

"Will we be safe here?" I finally asked.

"Safer here than anywhere else in Elphame. The walls of Tylwyth have stood for as long as Fae have been here. No court and no king have braved our forests, defied what haunts our lands, stood against what keeps Tylwyth a place of sanctuary and safety."

"Have the Aos Si ever tried to enter your lands?" I asked and thought of Zephyr.

"No. But you must understand, Perdi, if they do come, they come with the blessing of the Gods and Goddesses. Not even our most deadly would dare to stand against a God. If the Aos Si come, there is nowhere to hide."

"They come with hell at their backs, not Gods or Goddesses," I countered. "Regardless, that's not very encouraging."

"It wasn't meant to be."

"Do you think they will come for me?"

Faolan shook his head. "Not for war. Not yet. If they come, they will send an emissary. They'll want to talk before they strike. It is their way. They'll try for peace before they use force, especially for this. We have done nothing for the Aos Si to wage war. I didn't take you from Solas, Perdi. You left freely. There is a difference. Solas, on the other hand? I doubt this is sitting well with him. The Aos Si may be the lapdogs to the Court of Shadows, but even they must follow protocol."

"What happens if someone were to try to take me?"

"War," he answered. "I know you don't want to hear this, but you're considered my property now. They can't come here and take you, just as I couldn't simply take you from the Golden Court or the Dark Court. I'd have risked all my lands, including Tylwyth. These people, my people, would have died for having taken you. Despite what you think, I know you, Perdi. You'd have not lived with a sacrifice this great, for your life."

I looked out over the city and could feel, right down to my soul, why he couldn't risk it, and I wouldn't have let him. "When I came to Elphame, I blamed you for it all."

"I carry the blame, Perdi."

"You shouldn't have lied to me, but nothing you could have done would have stopped this, what is happening now."

"If I would have Taken you before Aelfdene, you wouldn't have endured what you did. You would have simply hated me, but you wouldn't have suffered," he replied. "But I feared your hate more. I feared for the safety of my people more. And did not act as I should have."

"I'd have ended in the Golden Courts eventually. I'm a Wildling. We can talk about this in circles, Faolan, but we don't know what would have happened if other choices had been made. Would this place have fallen had you Taken me and gone against the Golden Court? Would I have died because of it? Would you have died? What about Nix? He wouldn't have found his family. This happened how it had to happen, how the fates decided it happen."

"Nix made it to the Hallows and found his sister. I've sent word that you and your father have made it here. He and Orrian have safe passage to come to you."

I smiled down to my toes. "Probably the best news I could have ever heard."

He offered me his hand. "Shall I show you around, or do you want to rest for a bit?"

"Rest, if you don't mind?" I was exhausted once he mentioned the option to rest.

He led me through the city streets slowly as I took it all in until we stopped in front of a house that looked no different from the rest of the homes. A simple two-story house that didn't stand out from any other home on the street. It wasn't the largest I had seen, but also not the smallest. Everything about it said average, no better, no worse.

"For some reason, I expected a castle or palatial estate," I teased.

"With the price of land around here? You've got to be kidding," he teased back. "This was my mother's home. She lived with my father but had a small home of her own for when things got...rough between her and my father. My father's house, I donated to Tylwyth. It houses the school, medical center, community center and training grounds for our army. It gets more use now than it ever did before when I had it. Now, I can stomach going into it. While it was mine, I thought of burning it to the ground several times. It wasn't a place of fond memories. Now, it's just a building and hasn't the same power over me."

We stepped into his cozy home, all wood and art and comfort. The living room, to the right, already held a roaring fire and enough books to keep me busy for years. A dining room and kitchen were to the left and two staircases were ahead. I stared at the set that would bring you to the basement, and I cringed with memories.

"Wine, canned goods, a workout room...but no dungeon," Faolan answered without me needing to ask what was down there. "You're free to look on your own, or I can show you. Or we can lock the door, and you can hold the key. There's nothing down there that can hurt you. But I'd warn you against too much Tylwyth wine. It's a doozy. And in all my years knowing you, wine is not something you can handle. A war? Yes. Wine? Nope."

I wasn't completely relieved, but it did take some of the fear away. I followed him up the stairs and looked in each room as we passed them. I don't know what I was looking for, but I had to open every door and leave them open. The survivalist inside me couldn't move beyond a closed door. I think he knew what I was doing and why and started to open the doors for me. He introduced each room and opened the closets to show no one was waiting to snatch me. He opened and closed each window to prove that no room was a trap. I could see it in his eyes. He, too, feared being trapped. I doubted anyone in Elphame enjoyed the thought of stepping into an unknown room.

"This is my room," he said and pushed the door open.

It was simple. A large bed, dresser, desk and nightstands. The sun beamed in and danced over tiny crystals that hung in the windows, leaving rainbows on the walls. The dark hardwood floor had a massive brown fur rug, but that was the only extravagance in the room. It looked lived in and smelled of Faolan. I leaned in and smiled at the stack of books he had taken from Whitwick many years ago. They looked well-read and opened more times with Faolan than they would have been with me.

"Where is my dad?" I asked.

He motioned to the room at the end of the hall. I poked my head in and saw my father under heaps of feather blankets and furs, and a wood fireplace blazed at the foot of the bed. At his bedside were bowls of herbs and pastes. A healer knelt beside my dad's bed, wafting incense over his sleeping body. Two guards sat around a table, their noses in books. They each looked up and smiled. When they started to stand at the sight of Faolan, he motioned with his hand for them to sit and continue reading. Once I saw my dad, relief flooded me, and I staggered. My legs were rubber, and every pain I had, every scratch and cut and bruise, tugged me into exhaustion. I felt like I had been dragged behind the scared horses I had wished for, from one end of Elphame to the other.

"Let's get you to bed." Faolan led me to the room beside his. It wasn't as simple as his was, but it didn't slap me in the face with indulgence. I was grateful for that.

He led me around and showed me the bathroom and the closet. Little bits of Whitwick, pieces from home that I had given him over the years, decorated the room. I glanced at my nightstand and froze. Sitting on top was the book I had been reading the day before I'd left the Dark Court. A letter was tucked inside. Faolan opened the wardrobe, already furnished with clothing, most of which was from my home with Solas. On the floor was the bag I had packed from Whitwick. "It isn't much, but we didn't have a lot of time to prepare. Whatever you need, just let me know, and I'll have it brought to you."

"How did my things get here?"

"Some things are best left unsaid. We may not always be the only ones to hear. We both know why you're here. Let's leave it at that." He lifted his finger to his lips. "Your things are here to make your stay away a little less painful. *He* said you'd be less likely to burn my house down if you had a piece of home with you."

I nodded and left it alone. I knew he was referring to Solas. "Everything I have ever given you is here, in this room. Why?"

He shrugged. "I started this room years ago when I knew there'd be no saving you from Elphame. I kept telling myself that it would be for you once I got the courage to tell you everything. But I think, truthfully, this was more for me, to always have a place to feel you when we weren't together. I built up this idea in my head but could never do what needed to be done." His cheeks reddened. "I think I had always known that I'd never find it in me to Take you. I wanted to, I told myself to but I didn't. Every time I had planned to tell you everything, I'd never find the words. I never wanted to steal away your future. And when you'd give me something that made you happy, I fought harder not to Take you from the places you loved most. I had always thought myself to be better than Solas, but he had the courage to do what I couldn't."

"And what's that?"

"Save you at great risk to himself and his people."

I wandered the room and touched the things I'd once held dear. I let my Malice roam through the room and come back without the need to run. Once I was satisfied I wasn't going to be stolen from right under his nose, I sat on the bed and wrestled with my boots. I felt like a soggy blanket was finally lifted off my shoulders. Weight, which I didn't even know I was carrying around, was gone. I had lived several lifetimes in a year, and each one had added baggage that weighed a ton. These last few weeks had cramped my shoulders with the weight of the world. I took a deep breath and groaned as I breathed out.

"It'll be okay." Faolan knelt at my feet and helped pull my boots off.

I nodded, although I disagreed. "No, Fao, it won't be."

"When that time comes, we *all* will face it together."

"I put you all in danger."

"The danger we don't speak of has always been there, with or without you. There is no corner of the world or being within it safe from her," he answered. "Lift your arms."

"I wish I had your stamina. I can barely keep my eyes open," I said around a yawn.

"Give yourself a break. You're just shy of two decades. A few more, and you'll be tip-top," he joked and struggled with my damp and dirty clothes. "I honestly pray you never get used to this. This is not living and not the life I ever wanted for you."

"It's not the life I thought I'd have, but it's the only one I do."

I felt like a sack of rocks that needed to be dragged around. I had nothing left and couldn't do much more than lift my arms and let him do the work. He carried me to the tub and held me as he filled it with warm, soapy water. The smell reminded me of cinnamon sticks and candy canes. He set me into it, and I flinched.

"Too hot?" he asked.

"No. Too many wounds," I answered. "Burns a little."

"I keep forgetting you're not full Fae yet and can't heal like the rest of us. I'll get some salve to speed the healing."

"I'm closer to being Fae than you think. I can feel it."

"As can I," he answered and left the room to get creams from the healer.

I fell asleep before he returned. I woke only for a few brief moments, when he lifted me out of the tub and when the first burn of the salve hit me. The pain wasn't enough to keep the sleep from yanking me back under, hard and fast. I had slept through worse pain before. This was nothing compared to my first night in Elphame. I was safe — or as safe as I could be for now — and let my body relax into that knowledge.

* * * *

The night drenched Elphame in complete darkness, taking away everything familiar. Waking up in a room I had never seen before today, I panicked. I reached under my pillow for the blade I had usually slept with and came back empty-handed. With my pulse thick in my throat, smells I wasn't accustomed to flooded my lungs. I swallowed my scream, and I called on the shadows.

"Perdi." They crawled up from the foot of the bed. "It's okay."

"Where am I?" I whispered.

"Tylwyth."

"Right." I groaned and breathed in the smell I now remembered to be of Christmas, pine and mint, and candy canes. The reality of where I was slinked back in. I lifted up my book and breathed it in. Lavender calmed my soul. I opened the book and pulled out the letter inside, penned by Solas.

Don't get too comfortable, little Crow.

Your little slice of hell expects you back within a couple of weeks.

I love you.

S.

P.S. Don't be afraid to set it all ablaze. You know how much I like your flames.

My smile faded quickly, replaced with homesickness. I rubbed the center of my chest. "This already hurts, and it's only been a day."

"It will hurt more when Zephyr comes. You will not enjoy what he has to say," the shadows offered.

I shuddered at the thought. I knew he'd have a few choice words for me. "This wouldn't be fun unless I was also running from a pissed-off Soul-Eater."

"You shouldn't have oathed one to protect you if you didn't want him knocking on your door as he pleases."

"That's true," I answered and thought on it for a moment. Why had I only bound Zephyr and not thought to ask Solas for protection before I left? If I could burn even one string Solene had around Solas, I would. "Where is Solas right now?"

"He's in the Sluagh caves with his grandmother, Elda," they replied.

I climbed out of bed and found my leathers had been washed and hung off the back of a chair. "Can you take me to him?"

"Zephyr will feel us. If he calls us home while we have you, we'll be dumping you wherever we get the call. Be ready to run, in case we dump you somewhere you don't want to be. He's that angry, Perdi."

I zipped up my jacket and hoped they wouldn't leave me to plummet to my death. The shadows wrapped around me and carried me through Winter Court. The moment we crossed into the Dark Courts, I felt the tension in my muscles relax. My lungs filled with lavender and mint, pushing out the smells of Faolan's territory.

"Zephyr is calling us home. He can feel us at the caves." I was slammed into the cliffs of the Sluagh. I yelped once and grabbed onto the rocky face while the shadows pulled away from me. "Climb, Perdi. The Sluagh are coming."

"What? You're leaving me here?" I groaned, but they were already gone.

I held on to the cliff and climbed. I wasn't even a beginner-level climber, but I learned pretty quickly. It was hold on and climb or be eaten by the monsters that ate whatever didn't have protection from their court. Thankfully, the rocks weren't smooth, with plenty of gouges for my grip made by claws. The thought of their talons made me climb a little quicker. I pulled myself onto the lip and belly crawled onto the flat rock entrance, then maneuvered on my hands and knees, until I was flush with the stone. I released a long shaking breath. My arms and legs felt like jelly, and my hands and knees burned from leaving skin on the wall of the Sluagh.

"Damn my soul," I wheezed. My lungs burned, matching my muscle's complaint.

"Little Crow." Solas stood over me, grinning.

I glanced up and smiled. "That's one hell of a climb."

"You climbed up here?" He laughed. "I find you in the oddest of places and predicaments."

I used the wall to brace myself as I stood. "The shadows got me halfway up before Zephyr called them home. There's a pack of Sluagh coming up behind me. Tell them not to eat me, please."

"They'll leave you alone. Are you here to see Elda?"

I shook my head and pushed myself from the wall, wrapping my arms around him. "I didn't get to hug you goodbye."

He pulled us into the tunnel, out of sight, and gripped me in his arms like he used to. "This already hurts. I knew it would be bad, but I didn't think it would feel this awful."

"We can do this, Solas. We've been through worse," I countered.

"This feels like the day I brought you here."

"Is that why you're here, with Elda? Am I disturbing you?"

"No. The house feels empty. It smells different without you there. So, I came here. It was come to the caves or go to Winter Court and ask you to come home, that I'd rather die than have you gone."

I sighed. "It feels worse than I thought it would, too. I thought, since it was for a good reason, it would be somehow easier…but it's not."

"Nothing is easy here, but it's made sharper when love is involved."

"I love you. I had to make sure you'd hear me say it before the real games began and there wouldn't be any room for love."

"It doesn't make this easier, but it does give me hope that you'll come home, and this will be just another nightmare we share." He breathed me in. "I hate the smell of winter on your skin."

"So do I," I replied.

"As much as I needed that, did you climb the cliffs to hug me?"

"Wouldn't that be romantic?" I replied with a smile. "No. I came looking for an oath."

"Did you, now?" A small laugh shook his body and made me smile.

"What oaths can you give me that will protect me? Knowing what I'll have to do at the end of this all, how can you help me?"

"Zephyr was right. You're much more conniving than I give you credit for," he replied. "I can give you what I've never oathed to another…the Sluagh. I can oath to send the Sluagh to your aid. Trust me when I tell you, you will need them."

"What would you like in return?"

"You're already doing enough. I oath myself to you, Perdi, I will send the Sluagh in your time of need and never against you."

His words slithered over my soul and locked into place. I pressed myself into his chest, not wanting to leave. "Have I missed anything interesting since I've been gone?"

He laughed. "No. Same as usual. Still warmongering. Is your father okay?"

I nodded. "How's Zeph?"

"Not good, lost, hurting. I'm sure you'll hear from him once he's calmed down. Have you heard from Nix?"

"Yes. He found his sister and her children in the Hallows," I answered.

"I know," he replied. "I told you, I see and hear everything. I felt it when Faolan approached with his army. I was there when you said goodbye. I'm sorry I couldn't comfort you. I was scared you'd tell me of your plans. I couldn't risk her hearing. It's only here, at the caves and in my dreams, where her ears can't reach."

"How are you doing? Are you okay?"

He huffed a laugh. "Don't worry about me. Worry about yourself. You're on your own out there. There is no protection for you in the Dark Courts anymore, and truthfully, you won't find any with Faolan, either. You, my little Crow, are a Court of One."

"I think I should get a throne and a crown," I teased. "Queen Perdita has a nice ring to it, no?"

"I'd kneel in front of your throne," he teased back, pulling me into his kiss. "Survive this, Perdi, and I'll give you the crown from my head."

"I accept that challenge," I replied. "I wasn't lying when I said I could take it. I'm not as worried about myself as I am about you." I gripped him a little tighter, trying to squeeze his broken pieces back together. "Now that I'm in Winter Court, where do I start? What do I do?"

"Faolan isn't as tightly bound as I am. He'll give you the answers you'll need. Let him lead you to them. He can show you what you need. Keep calm, focus, listen and run if you're out of options. Zephyr may be pissed off right now, but he'll come when I can't, and he won't care who will fall at his feet for him to get to you."

"I love you."

I pulled back from his hug and cupped his face. I kissed him as if it were the last one I'd ever have. He pressed my back into the stone wall and kissed me back, filling his soul with my taste. As terrifying as my first night away from the Dark Courts could have been, this moment took away the edge of it. From the first day I'd met him, he had tried to shave the edges off the world.

"And I love you, little Crow." He kissed me again. "I'll see you in my dreams, and that will be enough to keep me going until you're home again."

"Can you get me back to the Dark Court, so the shadows can take me back to Winter Court? I don't really want to climb back down the cliff and run the distance," I asked.

"I've done the climb. It's not fun." His laugh rolled into a sad sigh. "I'm glad you came, that I got to see you again, just like this, my little Crow."

"I had to see you once more. Without the games of court, before we cut each other to bits. Can you give me a few days to make sure my dad is okay before you storm Faolan's territory, demanding me back?"

"Who said I'd do such a horrible thing?"

I smiled. "Because everyone expects you to, and I know you enjoy terrifying Faolan."

"This is true. If your dad takes a turn for the worse, send word, and I'll get him here to the caves, to Elda. She's the only other who is trained in Fae sickness. It's how I kept so many of you Crows alive," he replied.

"Time to become monsters, Solas. Are you ready?"

"No. Although, I do enjoy the competition," he replied. He pulled me into his chest with a grin. "Pull your mask on, Perdi. Monsters don't love anything but death and war."

"I'm going to kill that bitch for this."

"I know." He smiled. "We're all counting on it."

His hazy darkness wrapped around us, and we blasted from the caves. I pushed my face into his chest and screamed at the plummet and rush of moving as quickly as the night sky. The shadows grabbed me from him before I could say another word and delivered me into my room in Tylwyth. They were gone before my feet were safely on the floor. I curled on my side, fully dressed, and refused to cry. Solene wouldn't get that from me tonight, but she could have all my rage and wishes for her death.

For all to see, I was now an enemy of the Dark Courts, the most fearsome territory in all of Elphame. Gone was my protection of the monsters feared by all. I should have been terrified but I wasn't. There were bigger monsters than the beasts that hunted in the night. I was one of them. Whoever wanted to come, I invited them with open arms. I was a Soul-Eater, and

I'd eat the fucking world before I went to my grave willingly.

We were playing for keeps, and no one took from the Finis without suffering for it.

No one plucked the feathers of a Crow and lived to tell about it.

And neither would Solene.

I died to become the last Crow.

I was willing to die again to remind Elphame they'd never get another.

And from my Court of One, I was willing to do a lot worse to save the man I loved more than my soul.

Want to see more from this author?
Here's a taster for you to enjoy!

A Cursed Crow: A Court of One
Lanne Garrett

Coming October 2023

Excerpt

We are all monsters here. Some have fangs and claws, while others have wings as dark as night and eat souls—innocent and evil alike. But there would never be a monster bigger than I had become, for I was willing, eager and had names to cross off my list before I was done. From my Court of One, I'd do wicked and vile things to save those who could not afford to be as awful as I could be.

I was told that this world ate warriors and bards alike. It drowned the babies of temperamental mothers and strangled those who flinched at their cries. Told that if I couldn't eat the monsters, I should stand back and wait for the scraps. But I had no desire to eat what was left after I burned this world with war. Monsters, after all, didn't love anything *but* war. That was the horrible truth of Elphame. Those who managed to survive the ugliness of this world were why Elphame was so ugly in the first place. And I'd learn that lesson in the same fashion as every other—on my knees, crawling through hell, tearing my soul apart and becoming comfortable with the monster within me.

From inside the frosted lands of the Winter Court, I was not the only vile creature that lurked, but I was the only one content with the darkness, wearing a mask crafted when I had first come into these cursed lands of the Fae. In the Golden Court, I'd learned how to wear that very mask. But from the war-torn fields of Elphame, I had realized I didn't need the façade. We were all hideous beasts here, and I blended in perfectly fine, with or without it. The only difference between them and me was our motivations.

Within the borders of my once-enemy, I was covered in the smell of winter. My mask hid my broken soul, which yearned for darker places. *Monsters can cry, can't they?* And that's exactly what I was...broken. I was holding on for dear life, willing my heart to keep beating. A shattered soul feels like a childhood home burning to the ground and being the only one to have survived the flames. It tasted of ash, salty tears and burns that never fully healed. Willingly, I left pieces of myself scattered throughout a land that made no move to ease a single moment. I scrubbed off parts of myself from one end of Elphame to the other. I gave little bits of myself to the winds of a land that tried as hard for my death as I had for my life. But there was no room for wishes of better things in Elphame—only nightmares made of things that crept in the dark and attacked when your back was turned. Because that is what it took to endure Elphame, to survive *her*, the Caller of Crows.

With each passing minute I spent away from home, this new winter world became scratchy against my skin. The guise I wore chaffed against every fiber of my being. It reminded me of the Golden Court when I'd had to become a creature to be feared. I hadn't thought I'd ever have to become that Crow again. But here I stood, shaving away at who I had died to become, to survive another day.

I stood in unwanted moments in a place that wasn't my home. And Tylwyth was very much *not* my home. It didn't matter how breathtaking it was. The beauty of it was stained with my wish to be somewhere darker and more feared. Nothing would ever be as soul-settling as the Dark Courts. No smell was as calming as breathing in the wind of home. More than anything else, nothing could wrap around my heart as tightly as Solas could. Everything else held a taint and an edge of laughter from the Gods. From within enemy territory, now an enemy to every other land, I was on my own and trying to find my way back home. Each day, I inched closer to terror, lost in a world I didn't know and had no protection against.

I had left my home to find the truth and found my new path covered in shards of glass and new memories to stain my mind. Leaving Solas was the most challenging part, even knowing what I'd have to do to get home. Since stepping into the Winter Court, running toward truths others would kill me to protect, I was torn between thrones—Fire and Ice, Dark and Winter, Truth and Lies, Life and Death, Blood and Bones. It was all or nothing. Final moves were left to play in a game I didn't know or understand. But this is what it took to survive in Elphame—become a monster or be eaten by one, kill or be killed.

I was taken from my home in Whitwick, died to keep mortals safe and found my new home in the land of Fae. And now, I was on the run once again—only this time, I didn't want to burn everything or everyone. I only had one name on my list to hunt, and I'd focus my rage on the one who deserved the touch of a Soul-Eater — Solene, the Caller of Crows, the Lady of Blood and Bones, the blooded sister of Solas.

With my father tucked safely in Tylwyth, I breathed the air stained by my lies a little easier. I hadn't gone too far from him since he had stepped out of Whitwick Gates and into the land that had stolen his daughter. He was still healing from Fae sickness. Stepping through the Gate without a drop of Fae blood felt like stepping into the middle of a war. Hell on earth climbed down your throat and made you wish you hadn't come. That my father was still alive was a surprise. On *my* first day here, I had hoped for death. And I remember that day, regrettably…crystal clear.

Nix and Orrian, back from the Hallows, found me in my father's bedroom, helping him put his shoes on. He was feeling better — not perfect, but better. The healer encouraged him to walk around and get used to Elphame and the magick his body naturally fought against. It would take weeks before his soul gave in to this new world and accepted the energy of Elphame. The thought that any of us had weeks of life left was amusing, but I kept that laughter to myself. My father had slept for twenty hours straight before he had called out my name in a panic. He looked how I had felt on my first day here, so long ago it seemed like someone else's life I remembered, where everything hurt in a frostbitten and fire-burned sort of way. The air around me had smelled of seared flesh, scorched with flame and left rotting in the sun. Some things never changed. Even used to Elphame, I was still tired, scared and sore.

Once he saw I was okay, he calmed down and was ready for the mend. He had said he had too much to do to lie in bed all day. I, on the other hand, could have used a week in bed without the perils of Elphame gnawing at my insides. But I had only ever indulged in that luxury when my soul was near ruin and my deathbed called me by my full name, like a parent scolding a child.

"I've missed you," I cried as soon as Nix was in my arms. He looked happy and rested, the Nix I remember meeting, the friend I had before my Taking. "Your sister... I've heard you found her?"

"I have, and I can't thank you enough, Perdi. I feel — I don't know — thankful, grateful, at peace, finally."

"You look it. You look like all the pieces of your soul are finally back where they belong." I hugged him a little tighter. "You didn't have to come back, Nix. There's only war here now. Gone will be your peace."

"My sister and every niece and nephew of mine are safe where they are. But you are my home now. Wherever you go, I will always be there." He lifted one of the tears off my cheek. "You are my home, wherever that may be. I will always come when you need me."

"So will I...for you," I answered. "Where's Orrian?"

"She's probably eating someone or something," he answered. It was only half a joke. "Now, what has happened to send you so far from home into Faolan's land?"

I shook my head and tilted my head to the door. I could smell Christmas carrying on the cool breeze that was Faolan. "I'll fill you in later."

"Nix, I see you've made it back," Faolan said as he stepped into the room.

"Almost didn't make it. Your forest isn't a walk in the park." Nix tried for a joke, then shuddered. "What the hell is out there?"

"Imagine if you hadn't had safe passage?" Faolan snickered. "And your little fairy is in the town center — *not* eating anyone, I hope."

"There are no guarantees with her," I answered.

Faolan searched my face for humor and looked to one of the guards in the room when he realized I wasn't joking. The guard moved quickly, no doubt to check on Orrian. I was pretty sure she wouldn't be eating the children, but I couldn't say for sure what she did when no one was looking. Even I was scared of her, and I considered her my friend.

"Sir, are you ready to see Tylwyth?" Faolan asked my father.

My father grinned while we got him dressed for Winter Court. Although he moved slow, he was the first out of the front door. Exploring a part of Elphame would be a dream come true for him. At a pace my father could walk, Faolan led us through the streets, pausing every so often to point out places he loved to visit. Each time we stopped, someone would step out of a shop and welcome us. My father was mortal, and I wasn't sure yet what I was, but no one seemed to care. They were as warm to us as they were their own king.

I couldn't help but notice how different it was in Tylwyth compared to the other places I had been unfortunate enough to know of and experience—how warm and kind they all were, regardless of who we were. My father tired after less than a half hour and was led back to the house for rest and more herbal teas, very much against his wishes. This was his first time in Elphame, and he wanted to see it all in one day. Nix returned with him to settle in and snoop around, as I knew he was dying to do. Tylwyth was a mystery to most Fae, and Nix was nosey. I stayed with Faolan, curious about where he'd grown up.

"Your home is beautiful." I finally broke the silence as we walked. "It's not what I would have imagined."

"We are not the symbol of the rest of Elphame. We have no desire to gain more lands or courts. From here, we watch as the rest of Elphame fights and squabbles over inches of land. We're content just as we are," Faolan replied. "Here, in Tylwyth, it's home — not war, infighting or courts. It's just home — nothing more, nothing less."

"I can see why you love it here." I smiled on the outside, but on the inside, I felt homesick.

"I recognize that smile, and it's as fake as ever. As much as I enjoy showing you where I'm from, I'm sorry you're missing your home and wish, more than anything, you were home right now. There's a reason we never took part in the Taking of a Crow. It's barbaric and cruel," Faolan said. "Before you, I never went to the mortal lands during the Taking. I went to Whitwick before you, though. I wanted to see your realm, not conquer it. I stayed hidden and didn't meddle or interact with your people until you."

"What do you mean, until me? Why me?" I asked.

"Aoife," he answered. "She told me about you and that you would interest those who wished the Gate remained open, those who wanted more of the mortal world than was ever allowed. She told me that you would close the Gate and end this madness. I suppose, at first, I was just curious. The mortal lands have always been a place of interest for the Fae. But I found myself going back over and over. I was no longer only interested in the mortal lands. I wanted to go back to see you. With you, I could pretend I wasn't who I am. I could simply be Fao, without the throne or the demands and responsibility that came with it."

"How could you pass through the Gate and not everyone else could without sounding every alarm?" I asked. "You came every day."

"I am not simply Fae. I am Daoine Uaisle, and my blood is Royal-born. My line is from the original Gentry, the original Fae. That alone gives me abilities others don't possess. It is how I got you home and you and your dad both back here in one piece," Faolan explained. "But I think it has more to do with my intentions. I never went to you with the purpose of harm. On days my temper was uneven, or court business had me feeling aggressive or ill-willed, the Gate wouldn't let me cross until I was calm."

"I saw you almost every day. I imagine calm was a skill you learned quickly."

"That skill was born out of necessity and had nothing to do with the Gate. Under my father's rule, you didn't survive the Winter Court without learning to swallow every emotion."

My skin crawled, thinking of his childhood, and I quickly changed the subject. "Solas and his father were from the original lines, weren't they?"

"Yes and no. Both were of the guard, part of the original Elphame Guardians. The Aos Si comes from that line. Solas and his father were not original Royals until they seized land and created their own court. They created their line. During the wars, my family was locked outside of the wall when we were fighting the rebels. We had no choice but to build our lives outside of the Court of Blood and Bones. We fought to protect this court, not for territory but for peace. We took in everyone we could and built Tylwyth to shelter them. Tylwyth is made of those from different lines. Very few of us come from my line through blood."

"His sister, Solene… She's still a Lady of the Court of Blood and Bones," I told him.

He squirmed a little at the mention of her name. But I think everyone did, not just him. "*My* cousin, Solene.

She's my cousin and more than just a lady of that court. She *is* that court. When her mother died, it all went to her. She comes from one of the original families, like Solas and me. The court began with two families, each creating a line—one of Royals and one of Guardians," he explained. "She is from the line of Seers, a Royal Seer at that, given who her mother was, while Solas was born into Guardianship, like his father. When a child is born here in Elphame of two different courts, there is a half-chance they'll have the powers of their mother or father. It depends on who is stronger. Solas and his sister were born into two different powers. Only the women of the court can become Seers. It skips males. As for Guardians, they are only male."

My mouth dropped. "Solas is your cousin? How am I only now just learning this?"

Faolan laughed. "All of us trace our lines to Blood and Bones, to one of the two founding families. We are related through blood. But we do not practice those relations as humans do."

"Weddings must be monstrous here." I joked.

"We don't have weddings here, not like the mortal realm. We don't have wives or husbands. We are oathed to each other for life. Consorts, we'll call them if we must give them a name. We are coupled, and we blood oath ourselves to them until the end of our life."

"Have you ever given your oath to another?" I asked and felt my cheeks heat. I didn't really have the right to ask him that question, but I couldn't help it. There was so much about him that I didn't know—and damn it if I wasn't curious now that the curtains had fallen. "Hundreds of years seems like a long time to be alone."

"No, not yet. Giving your oath is severe, Perdi, and not given lightly. No matter the circumstance, we cannot leave once we've given our oaths. Unlike in the mortal world, where you can leave your mate, we can't do that here. Here, that oath lasts for as long as your heart beats. Hundreds of years is a long time to be with someone you don't love or someone who treats you poorly." Faolan's mind was elsewhere. He grew up in a home with two people who didn't want each other, and it played out over his mother's flesh, day in and day out. "There are times when the choice is not yours. And when that happens, those are very long years to be tied to them if you can't stand their touch."

"Like an arranged marriage?" I asked.

"That isn't as common anymore, but it still happens. Usually, it is done between courts to strengthen their ties. In those cases, most are not contested. But an arrangement is not permitted anywhere in the Unseelie Courts. Neither Solas nor myself will allow it."

"Why not?" I asked.

"There is no tie I want to have bad enough to force two people into a lifetime together. We live too damn long to be saddled with someone we hate or that hates us."

"The idea that I'd be trapped with someone who hated me for all my days is scary." I thought of my time in the Golden Court, and my stomach flopped at the idea that I could have been stuck there on the arm of the dead King.

"When fate chooses for you, there isn't much you can do about it. You just try to make it work. But it is breathtaking when it is a good match, and there isn't much work to be done. You become one. It is everything we hope for, to be tied to someone we would die for, someone who will care for us in our final moments. Like mortals, we, too, crave companionship and love. It is everything one could ever want. But it is also terrifying. I'd suggest never coming between two who are oathed. It can be deadly, to no real fault of their own. The men, especially, can be overly territorial. But the ladies? I'd fear them even more. They won't just kill you. They'll torment you first."

"Fate chooses for you?" I asked and let the rest of his comments fall away, but not before wondering if Solas was on the verge of insanity with me gone.

He nodded. "There are times when two Fae are brought together, and the oaths slip into place without much thought or notice. You forget, and the words just spill from your mouth, like saying you love someone. That happens more often than an intentional coupling. And when it happens, no force on this earth can keep them apart."

"I don't think I like the sound of that." I laughed. "Imagine waking up and being married?"

"This is why most kings keep multiple partners or none at all. It is harder to grow attached to one when you have many. Imagine a king with armies at their disposal, lovestruck? He'd wage wars to get to her."

I could imagine. Solas was one of those men.

"Do you have many partners?" I blurted out and instantly felt my face redden. "I mean, that's fine. I just want to know if I will run into them in the hall or hear you all night."

Faolan laughed. "No. I have none. I'm not one for bed jumping. Before all of this, your Taking, there was only you — and none since your Taking."

I squirmed at his comment. "Is there some oath between us that I don't know about?"

"No. I could never allow myself to get that close. It's not because I didn't care, but I have thousands of people who need a king and my love more. Unfortunately, when you sit on a throne, your life is very much not yours to live. Your people must always come first. Every choice made is for them before all others."

"Sounds like a bleak life," I replied.

"It can be. Often, it's just a simpler way to live. It's the only life I've known, and as lonely as it can get, it's not one I'd willingly give up," he replied. "Inside these walls, I lead a relatively normal life by your standards. My inner circle is small, which is how I like it. I work, cook and clean, fish, spend time with my community and participate in building a better world for my people."

"You work? You mean, as a king?"

"No. I teach at the school—history and arts. Being a king is my duty. We all must work here. We can't build a future for the next generation unless we all work toward it. I cannot lead from the back. I can't do what is best for my people unless I am one of them. I must make the same sacrifices, or I cannot ask it of them." His passion was almost physical. As his heart beat for his people, I could feel it move the air around us. "I couldn't imagine not being part of my community. It would be such a lonely existence. I'd feel trapped."

"It is lonely. Trust me," I answered.

Faolan took me to a small café for lunch, where we sat at the front window for me to see his world through his eyes. There, we were approached by one of Faolan's people, a guard who watched over my father. He didn't bow or kneel. Instead, he pulled up a seat and flopped down like a casual friend. But that is how everyone was in Tylwyth…friends and neighbors. It reminded me of the Dark Court and how Zephyr was with Solas. There was no show of power until others were watching. The thought of Solas and Zephyr pulled at something in my core. I missed them. I felt homesick. I felt empty.

"It seems chance would have us meet again." His words rolled over my skin, cooling as they drifted by. "What a cruel mistress fate can be."

I stared at him a little longer, letting my Malice roll to the surface to taste the energy that rolled off him in waves of delicate snowflakes. I recognized him and fought not to squirm. "You were there the day Faolan came into the Court of Less."

He nodded. "The day you stole my king into your lands. Yes. I was very much there for that. Not the best first impression."

"Don't, Oisin." Faolan warned the man.

Oisin's face didn't flinch. Instead, he held out his hand to me. "I didn't get a chance to introduce myself on that fine day. I'm Oisin." He pronounced his name as 'O-Sheen'. His handshake was firm, and he didn't treat me as if I were breakable. I liked him more for that.

"Thank you for watching over my father." I tipped my head in appreciation. "It's nice to meet you again, Oisin. I'm Perdita, Perdi to my friends."

"And, are we friends, Perdita? What do you plan to take from me today?" he asked, glancing up through his lashes. The look wasn't as friendly as he tried to make it. It reminded me of Zephyr and his warning glances.

I would never be the tough or bad guy, not when sitting at a table of men who had hundreds of years to practice and pounds on me. I let the amusement drain from my face and stared back with a smile that held only the fire within my belly. Those flames never went out and burned only for those who dragged me into war and chaos.

"I'll leave that decision to you, Oisin. We can be friends, or you can always wonder what I'll do to you when you close your eyes or turn your back to me." I let my friendly smile return. "I'll never win a hand-to-hand fight with you, but it's not beneath me to kill you in your sleep, poison your drink or push you off a cliff. That's the thing about witches. You just never know what end we'll choose for you, but rest assured, it'll be painful — and this smile will be the last thing you see. You may be Fae, and I am just a mortal, but I'm pretty sick of this shit and would caution your next words. This may be your last chance before choking on your regret."

"Interesting," he answered.

"What's that?" I asked

"I had wondered how a little Crow could survive not only her Taking but the Golden Court, then the Dark Courts. But I think you've just answered those questions."

"We can be great friends, or I can start thinking of creative ways to tell Faolan of the tragic accident that claimed your life. Trust that I'll make it look like an accident."

"I think I like you." Oisin's smile widened. "Perdi it is."

"If you two are done grandstanding," Faolan interrupted. "Oisin, what can I do for you on this fine day? I thought you had the rest of the day off and were caving?"

"Caving?" Oisin rolled his eyes. "It's not caving when it stops to chase someone else."

"It?" I asked and felt the panic begin. "Chase?"

"Oisin here likes to drop into the caverns at the borders and outrun what is down there." Faolan's smile broadened. "It's what Nix was referring to when he crossed into Tylwyth. The dread you and they felt? Oisin likes to play with it."

"Dear God," I whispered. "Why would you chance it?"

"Live this long and see how you fill your time," he answered and chewed on a bread roll from the table. "I was down in the caverns, as I am on my time off, when the chase ended long before it should have. Someone had come to our border, and I'm not talking about that little gnome or the tiny-winged creature that bit me twice before I let them pass."

"She bit you?" I asked and tried not to laugh at him.

"She bit me, and he stabbed me. I tried to get out of their way. I knew they had safe passage, and I'm not stupid enough to get in the way of a gnome, let alone one accompanied by a fairy. But they were on me before I could step to the side." Oisin showed me his hands, which were bitten and clawed. Small slashes marred his flesh from Nix's blade. It made me grin. "Anyway, after I bravely fought them off—which was life and death, I'll have you know—I was doing my thing in the tunnels when the fun ended." Oisin pushed a letter to Faolan. "Zephyr came with a letter for you both."

"How brave of you." I teased, and he lifted his chin in pride.

"I'm surprised he waited this long. I was expecting him the first night," Faolan answered. "Thank you, Oisin."

He stood and looked from Faolan to me, then groaned. "I knew, from the first time Faolan went to the mortal lands, you would be nothing but trouble. I may have wondered how you could make it this far, but now I question if you're worth it."

Faolan cleared his throat. "Don't, Oisin."

"You have always allowed me a voice, Faolan," he countered.

"It's fine," I interrupted. "If he has something to say, I'd prefer him to say it now. I'd rather know if he'll let me die when he's supposed to be at my back. If that's the case, I'll make other plans, and he can stand behind someone else."

Oisin jerked back as if I had slapped him. "If I say I have your back, it would take my death to pull me away. My personal feelings about you have nothing to do with whether or not I do my duty."

"Yes, they do, and that's the bitter truth of our emotions. You will hesitate if you dislike me, do not trust me or even wish I had never stepped foot on these lands. A split second could mean my life. I'm not judging you. There are plenty I would let die while I watched. Hell, I would help hold several under water and drown them of life, myself. The facts are the facts, and how we feel drives how we react," I countered. "Take this very moment. I'm not fond of you. This leads me to question if I'd protect you over myself. We protect most what we love—and you, Oisin, I do not love any more than you love me."

"I would give my life for my king. If you belong to him…"

I gripped the table and stood on the heels of a horn that no one else could hear. My body shook with anger. It hummed with Elphame. "I belong to *no one*, Oisin. Let's get that straight. *No one* owns me—not him, Solas, you, or any other bloody Fae in this fucking realm. I belong to *me*. This is not up for debate, ever. I don't care what the rules say about who owns who in this bloody world. Don't *ever* repeat those words. This is your only warning…end of story."

Oisin stood his ground. It irritated me, but I could respect him for it. Faolan didn't remain a king because he surrounded himself with those who scared easily. Fools, perhaps, but not cowards.

"If you are here, you put us all at risk. If we are going to die for you, I am ensuring you are worth it." His very tone was winter…ice cold and bitter.

"Fair enough, but I'm not asking you to die for me. I would never expect that from you. I'm asking you to give me a chance to run," I replied and took my seat.

"Running is weak."

"Running is all I have. Unlike you, I will die from a head injury. One good punch, and I'm out cold. A simple cut could turn infectious, and I will die. However strong I think I am, my body is not. I'm not Fae. I have no choice but to run."

Oisin breathed me in and shivered. "You're more Fae than you care to admit."

"Got to hell." I snarled.

He smiled. "Keep that anger with you, Perdi. You'll need it when we meet with the darkness who stole you into the lands of slavery."

Faolan finally stood. "Oisin, are you done making a mess of my day?"

"I told you, Faolan. The first time you stepped through that Gate, I warned you of this day. Is it worth it?" Oisin asked.

"Love and peace are always worth it," Faolan answered. His words made me fidget with discomfort.

"It's the only worthy death," Oisin answered and patted his friend on the shoulder. "You, Perdi, I will see on the field. I hope you can run as fast as you think you can. No one can outrun the dark."

"It is not those who lurk in the dark we should fear. It's who hides in plain sight."

He tipped his head. "Ain't that the truth."

Oisin left as he had come—casually, laughing, the friend next door. But I knew, under his calm exterior, was a blizzard that rivaled the greatest of gales. The moment he was gone, I missed him. He reminded me of Zephyr, a storm that cared nothing for your feelings and tore your house out of the foundation as you begged for mercy, but he secretly grieved when he was the cause of your pain.

"Who the hell was that?" I asked.

"Oisin is my Commander. He heads my armies."

"I don't think he likes me," I answered.

"I think it went well, considering."

"Considering what? I'm human? I'm a Crow? I come from the Dark Courts, your enemies? I helped jail you? I could continue. The list is long."

"No. Oisin doesn't care about that. And, for the record, he told me I'd be imprisoned the day I came to offer you freedom from Solas. But, considering his sole purpose is to ensure I live a very long life, that my people are never forced into combat and that Tylwyth never feels the pains of war, it went well. His job is not to trust you, Perdi, for no other reason than that is his duty."

"I shouldn't be here. Oisin's right. I cast war and death with my shadow." I felt guilty. It had been a good idea to come until I got here and saw what my being here could do. When I considered him a tool I could use, I didn't think of everyone else who would suffer for it.

"Oisin will come around. Don't worry about him. He's an honorable man. He's a good one to have on your side."

"For you, maybe," I mumbled under my breath. "What's the letter say?"

Faolan snapped the black seal — its crack echoing in my ears — and unfolded the letter we both knew was coming. He didn't try to hide it from me or read it first. But I leaned away from it as if it could touch me, and I'd be gone before I could read the first sentence. "Solas requests an audience tonight. We can select the location."

"Why?" I asked, then raised my hand. "Never mind, why else? I'm gone, you have me, he wants me, the Gate, the power, the ego, war, death, horror. Did I miss anything?"

"No, that pretty much sums it up. Do you want to go?" He asked.

I shrugged. "If we don't play the game, things will only get worse."

"Likely. Whatever the reason for your being here" — Faolan glanced around the room and brought his finger to his lips. We wouldn't speak only about it, not in places where ears hung too closely to our lips — "Solas is honor bound to ask for your return. It is the way of Elphame. But more than that, his heart, love and ego would never allow him to stand by and watch. No Fae, dark or light, could swallow this pain. He'd be….pushed to come for you. He won't get to you, but it'll take many to stop him. In truth, my concern is not Solas. It is who he will send in his stead."

"Zephyr." I groaned. There'd be no hiding from him. He'd eat this world to get to me. "Let's see what he wants before he comes to your door with his demands."

About the Author

Lanne Garrett writes books. Considering where you're reading this, it makes perfect sense. She lives in Vancouver, here she spends her days getting lost in the beauty of reading and writing and can be found behind a mountain of books on any given Sunday.

Lanne loves to hear from readers. You can find her contact information, website details and author profile page at https://www.finch-books.com

FINCH
B O O K S

Sign up for our newsletter and find out about all our
romance book releases, eBook sales and promotions,
sneak peeks and FREE romance books!